FOLLOW ME DARKLY

A NOVEL

FOLLOW ME DARKLY

A NOVEL

#1 *NEW YORK TIMES* BESTSELLING AUTHOR

HELEN HARDT

Entangled Publishing, LLC
10940 S Parker Road
Suite 327
Parker, CO 80134
rights@entangledpublishing.com

Amara is an imprint of Entangled Publishing, LLC.

Visit our website at www.entangledpublishing.com.

Edited by Liz Pelletier
Cover design by Bree Archer
Cover images by heckmannoleg/GettyImages
iStock/Getty Images Plus
Interior design by Toni Kerr

ISBN 978-1-68281-499-4
Ebook ISBN 978-1-68281-500-7

Manufactured in the United States of America

First Edition September 2020

10 9 8 7 6 5 4 3 2

Also by Helen Hardt

WOLFES OF MANHATTAN

Rebel
Recluse

STEEL BROTHERS SAGA

Craving
Obsession
Possession
Melt
Burn
Surrender
Shattered
Twisted
Unraveled
Breathless
Ravenous
Insatiable
Fate
Legacy

For Dean, Eric, and Grant

Chapter One

Addison Ames hates coffee.

In fact, she says the smell of it gags her.

But here she stands, cinnamon mocha latte in hand, as I snap a photo with her smartphone. She extends her left arm because it has to look like a selfie. A perfect selfie, which is where I come in. A normal selfie is subject to silly things like an arm's length and faulty lighting, so we have to create the *illusion* that it's a selfie.

Bean There Done That, a new coffee joint hoping to give Starbucks a run for its money, just paid Addison a buttload to post a "selfie" with one of their hipster drinks. Apparently having their brew sipped by a Boston hotel heiress means something.

I just haven't figured out what.

Addison couldn't possibly spend her fortune in three lifetimes, yet she's getting paid to pose with a pouty fake smile and a latte.

I edit it quickly, making her look even more gorgeous than she is, and hand the phone to her.

She shakes her head. "No. I look fat in this one, and my hair's a mess."

Fat? Addison weighs all of a hundred pounds soaking wet. Still, I take the phone back. I hate not getting it right the first time—I'm a control freak by nature—but I'm used to her. She grabs a compact out of her purse, fiddles with her blond hair, and then resumes her pose.

I need this job. I'm lucky to have this job. I worked my butt off to get this job, calculating every move I made. How else would Skye Manning, Kansas farm girl and aspiring photographer, be hired as assistant to Addison Ames, hotel heiress and Instagram influencer extraordinaire? This was a business move on my part, and I'm not about to screw it up, no matter how much my employer grates on my nerves.

I shoot the photo again. It's nearly identical to the first. I edit and hand her the phone.

"Much better," she says. "Get this up right away. Use the copy the company sent us. They're already after me about not posting it earlier this week."

I nod, tag the location, and post the photo.

Hanging out at the new Bean There Done That coffee shop in downtown Boston. The cinnamon mocha latte is to die for! @beantheredonethat #sponsored #coffeeisdope #coffeeaddict #coffee #latte #beantheredonethat

Within five minutes, Addison has a thousand likes and a hundred comments.

Unbelievable.

Sometimes Addison writes her own copy. More often, I write it. This time, we go with Bean There's copy, since Addison has nothing good to say about coffee of any kind.

I disagree about coffee. I can't get enough of the stuff, and my mouth waters over the cinnamon mocha latte that will end up in the trash. Does she ever think of offering it to me?

Nope.

Addison Ames doesn't concern herself with the "help."

My phone dings constantly with new comments on Addison's latest post. I look down. Yeah, more of the same.

You rock, Addison! #luvyourface

Love me some cinnamon mocha latte!

Love your lip gloss. What's the brand?

Bean There is the greatest! #whoneedsstarbucks

You and I both love cinnamon mocha lattes!

Love you, @realaddisonames!

Until my jaw drops.

Nice try, @realaddisonames. Coffee makes you puke. I should know. #youreafake

Uh-oh.

Part of my job is to delete all negative comments as soon as they post, and I'm about to, until I notice the sender.

@bradenblackinc

Braden Black?

The billionaire? Can't be.

Except it is.

His profile pic is on the money. Gorgeous dark hair and blue eyes the color of the hottest flame. I know, because I've spent the last month drooling over his spread in *GQ*. It's Braden Black all right. He's fairly new to his money, not born into it like Addison, and definitely from a blue-collar background. How do they know each other?

Doesn't really matter. I quickly delete the offending comment and search through the rest. This part of my job is unending. Social media posts are forever, so a negative comment can pop up anytime. My only consolation is that Addison rarely checks her Instagram account. Those questions she sometimes answers? That's me, not her. She has a private Instagram for her large circle of rich friends, and she also uses other social media. Her public Instagram, though, is where she makes money.

I catch an Uber by myself back to her office. It's in one of Daddy's most posh hotels in the heart of Boston. Although Addison doesn't keep normal hours, I'm expected to. I don't mind. It's a job. A job is supposed to have normal hours. Of course, oftentimes she calls me outside those normal hours if she needs a "selfie." "No one takes a selfie like you do, Skye," she says with a smile.

I should be flattered. My skill as a photographer had a big part in landing me this position. So it's not exactly art. At least I'm doing what I love.

Sort of.

It's all part of the master plan.

A few minutes after I return, Addison walks through the office door.

"Hey, Addie," I say.

She's staring at her phone, rapidly typing, when—

"What the hell?" Her cheeks turn a fiery red.

"What is it?"

"This comment. Shit! Why didn't you delete it?"

"The one from Braden Black? I did."

"Uh…no, you didn't. Damn!" She throws the phone against the wall, where it clatters to the floor.

I quickly pull up her Instagram.

Crap.

It's still there.

I was sure I'd gotten rid of it. I must not have pressed Delete hard enough. That's not like me. My attention to detail is usually freakishly impeccable. Why did she pick today to actually look at the account?

This time I make certain it's gone and then read through the rest of the hordes of comments, looking for anything that might reflect badly on Addison or Bean There. Nothing else so far.

Addison picks up her phone. It's fine. She has the most shock-absorbent cover available. Good thing. She throws the phone a lot.

"Sorry about that," I say. "I saw it at Bean There and I thought I deleted it then."

She doesn't reply.

"Your followers love the photo," I say, trying to sound cheerful. "Bean There will be happy."

"Not if they think I hate coffee."

"It's gone now."

"No thanks to you."

She's being a bitch, but I can't fault her this time. I screwed up. I roll my shoulders, trying to dislodge the tension between them. Will she fire me over this? I inhale a deep breath and flip through her last couple of posts. Nothing I need to delete.

"He's such a douchebag," Addison says.

Not firing me after all. Good. I look up. "Who?"

"Who do you think? Braden Black."

"I didn't know you knew him."

"For about five minutes the summer after I graduated from high school," she says. "We had kind of a thing."

I stop my eyes from widening into circles. "Oh?"

"Yeah." She taps her foot on the marble floor. "In fact, contact him. He's not going to get away with this."

"Sure. I'm on it."

Braden Black is based here in Boston. Everyone in town knows the Black, Inc. building. I put a call through.

"Black, Inc."

"Good afternoon. This is Skye Manning from Addison Ames's office. I'm calling for Braden Black."

"Mr. Black is in a meeting. I'll have to take a message."

"Addison Ames. The number is—"

Addison still taps her foot, hovering above me. "Tell them to connect you to his voicemail."

I clear my throat. "Actually, I'd like to leave a voicemail, please."

"Mr. Black prefers a paper message."

"He prefers a paper message," I say to Addison.

"Oh, for God's sake. Give me the phone." She grabs it from me. "This is Addison Ames. Braden and I go way back. Connect me to his voicemail at once."

She continues tapping her Prada-clad foot.

"That's ridiculous. Give me his voicemail, or I'll have your job."

More tapping.

Addison huffs. "Fine. Tell him to call Addison Ames right away." She hands the phone back to me. "See? Douche."

"That wasn't him. That was a receptionist."

"Carrying out the douchebag's orders. Who the hell doesn't take voicemails?"

I have no answer for that, so I say nothing.

Addison stomps into her plush private office, shutting the door behind her. Thank God. Time to answer this afternoon's emails.

Mostly fan mail, and I have a canned response I copy and paste, adding just the name and any other personal details to make it sound like the response is actually from Addison.

Another offer from Susanne Cosmetics. Addison scoffed at their first offer, fifty grand for a photo with their new lip plumper that's guaranteed to get rid of those lines on the upper lip. They've upped it to one fifty. I forward that one to Her Highness. She'll probably turn it down.

I delete all the sales pitches and spam, and then I take another look at today's post, scanning for negative comments and those that require a response. I respond to two. Then I check the time. Five thirty. Nothing more to do today. I'll watch the post from home, but I'm now free to leave the office. I gather my purse and—

The office door opens.

And my jaw drops.

Chapter Two

"Good evening," a deep and husky voice says.

The deep and husky voice belongs to Braden Black.

Braden Black is standing in Addison's office, right in front of me. I gulp, stand, walk out from behind my desk… and unceremoniously drop my purse. Its contents spill over the marble floor.

Kill me now.

Front and center is a condom.

So I'm ready for anything. Good policy, right? Still, my cheeks warm. "I'm sorry. I was just leaving for the day." I kneel and begin to gather the items. Should I take the condom first? Or would that just draw attention to it?

My humiliation is complete when Braden Black kneels down across from me. "Let me help."

I meet his searing blue gaze, wishing I were invisible. "That's kind of you, but I've got it." I grab the condom along with a tube of lip gloss and shove them back into my purse. Then I gather the rest and rise.

He's standing again. He's nearly a foot taller than I am, with shoulders so broad, I could get lost in them. He seems to darken the room—not in a bad way, though.

I force out a laugh. "That was embarrassing. Would you believe I meant to do that so you'd know I'm not hiding a knife in my purse?"

"Do you really think whether you're hiding a knife—or anything else dangerous—would be my first thought when looking at you?"

His voice. Shivers crawl up my spine. "What woman doesn't want to appear a little dangerous?"

"You don't seem dangerous so much as someone who likes to be in charge."

"Doesn't everyone?"

His lips quiver. Just a touch, but I notice. How can I not notice every little thing about him? He fills up the room.

"I guess it depends on whether you're horizontal," he replies.

Warmth gushes through me. I must be red as a beet. And I thought dropping my purse was embarrassing? I'm hardly the type to be engaging in sexual banter with a billionaire. I'm intrigued, though. More than intrigued. Already my body is responding. To him or to his dark manner? I'm not sure.

I draw in a deep breath and clear my throat. "What can I help you with?"

"I'm Braden Black. I'm here to see Addison."

"She's in her office. Did you have an appointment?"

I know very well he doesn't have an appointment. I keep Addison's calendar. I have a sneaking suspicion I'm not fooling him by the sly half smile he gives me.

"No. She's an old friend."

"Of course. I'll tell her you're here."

"No need." He cocks his head toward her closed door.

"She in there?"

I nod. "Yeah."

He walks toward Addison's private office.

"You can't," I say.

"Sure I can. Watch me."

Before he knocks, however, the door opens.

"Skye, can you—" Addison's lips curve downward into an angry frown. "What the hell are *you* doing here?"

"Thought I'd come over to tell you if you ever bully my receptionist again, I'll make sure every one of your followers knows the truth about you."

"Truth about *me*? Are you kidding? I'm not the one with something to hide, Braden."

"You have a lot more to hide than a hatred of coffee," he says.

"And what about you? You want your business associates to know—"

"Enough!"

Braden Black's voice booms through the office, making me shiver. I swear the walls vibrate and shrink back against the darkness exuding from him.

I wait for Addison to say more, to mention what he's hiding. She doesn't. His command seems to stop her.

Oddly, I understand. I stop what I'm doing as well. Something about the ominous tone in his voice makes me want to obey without question.

Which isn't like me at all.

Finally, Addison says simply, "Stay off my Instagram."

"I'm not sure you should be telling me what to do," Braden says, "but I'll play it your way for now."

"Good." Addison stomps back into her office and slams the door.

He stands still for a moment and stares at her closed door,

running his fingers through his hair. What is he thinking? I have no idea…until he turns around and meets my gaze.

"She hasn't changed," he says.

Am I supposed to respond? "You mean she's slammed a door in your face before?"

"Many people have."

I smile. I can't help it. His tone is so nonchalant. Clearly he doesn't care who slams a door on him, and I like that. It speaks to me in a way, shows me how I want to be. "I suppose it's better than someone being nice to your face and then stabbing you in the back."

"I get my share of that, too," he says. "And I agree. It's always better to know where you stand." He stares at me then. Really stares, as if he's starving and I'm the special of the day.

I look down at my feet and then catch myself. Yeah, I was a klutz a minute ago, and he saw my condom. So what? It happens. At least that's what I want to think. I'm actually still kind of mortified, but I look back up and meet his gaze.

"I guess you know where you stand with Addie," I say. "Pretty much everyone does."

His lips bend ever so slightly upward. I suppress a shiver. The subtle smile is a flash of light in his ominous demeanor. It's suddenly chilly in the heated room.

"I couldn't help myself," he says. "She hates coffee."

I smile, forgetting for a second that this man just saw me pick up a condom. "I know. She threw out the latte after the shoot. Perfectly good and hot. I'd have happily drunk it."

"You're a coffee drinker, then?"

I nod. "Absolutely."

"Me too." He stares at me again, seeming to zero in on my mouth. "Care to go for a cup…"

This time I can't stop my eyes. They widen. Is Braden Black asking me out?

He looks toward my desk where my nameplate sits. "...Skye?"

Say something, Skye. For God's sake!

"It's almost six."

"Dinner, then?"

Every nerve in my body jumps. I mean really jumps.

Braden Black, the most eligible bachelor in Boston—hell, in the country—just asked me to dinner.

I look down at my wrinkled silk blouse and skinny jeans. I worked a ten-hour day, and exhaustion weighs on me. My mousy brown hair is falling out of its ponytail, and God himself only knows what my face looks like.

And Addison? What will Addison think? I eye her closed door.

"You don't need her permission," Braden says. His dangerous demeanor has returned.

My legs weaken and my cheeks grow hot with embarrassment. "I wasn't—"

"Sure you were. Your boss doesn't particularly like me, so you were wondering if going to dinner with me would somehow cost you your job."

I open my mouth to respond, but nothing comes out.

"Are you good at your job, Skye?"

Yeah, embarrassment again. "Well, I—"

"Let's attack this from a different angle. How long have you been working for Addison?"

"Almost a year."

"Then clearly you're good at your job, or she would have gotten rid of you long ago. Addison might be a pain in the ass, but she's smart. She won't let a good thing go." One corner of his mouth twitches slightly, as if he wants to smile but can't. Then, as if some type of magic pulls at him, he lets the smile out.

And I nearly melt into a puddle of goo right on the slick marble floor. His dimples show through several days of black stubble, and one of his eyes squints slightly. An adorable imperfection on an otherwise perfect visage.

"I'm not dressed appropriately," I say, forcing myself to meet his blue gaze.

"I didn't say we were going to a black-tie affair."

Gulp. What a boob I am. This isn't a date. It's probably a business thing. He wants information, or maybe even dirt, on Addison. They have some kind of history. Makes sense. Addison is way more his type than I can ever hope to be.

"I don't think—"

He interrupts me. "You look fine. It's dinnertime, and I'm hungry. I don't feel like eating alone for once. Don't make more of this than it is. Your job will be safe."

So definitely not a date. Of course it isn't. Braden Black can have any woman he wants. He certainly doesn't want a Kansas farm girl.

I open my mouth to decline when my stomach lets out a famished growl.

"You're obviously hungry," he says. "Let's go."

Without thinking, I walk toward the door of the office. "Okay. Where are we going?"

Apparently I've made my decision.

"I feel like oysters," he says.

I love oysters. I love all seafood. Actually, I love all food. "Sounds good," I say as he opens the door for me. "Wait," I add.

"What?"

"I don't even know you. I… I'll meet you there. What restaurant are you thinking?"

"Union Oyster House. You want me to get you a cab?"

Kismet. Union Oyster House is one of my favorites. This seems right. Or do I just want it to seem right? "Sure. I guess."

"Or you can drive with me. It's not far, and I personally guarantee your safety."

Am I being silly? Not really, but something inside me wants to trust him. He's Braden Black. Everyone knows him. Plus, I have my phone and it's fully charged.

I turn to him. "As long as you personally guarantee my safety."

"Absolutely."

I follow him to a black Mercedes parked in front of the hotel. A driver emerges and opens the door. The back seat is lush with cream-colored leather interior. Braden gets in next to me.

"Union Oyster House, Christopher," he says to the driver.

"Yes, sir." Christopher closes the car door and takes his place in the driver's seat.

I'm dressed fine for Union Oyster House. Plus, it won't break the bank. Not that Braden Black has to worry about money, but I plan to pay for my own meal.

I don't normally mind quiet, but the silence during the short drive deafens me. I have no idea what to say. I'm in a Mercedes with Braden Black. I'm sitting close enough to him that I can smell him. His scent is intoxicating—cloves and pine with just a touch of leather. I want to inhale it deep into my body so I never forget it.

Because I'll never be this close to Braden Black again. Never this close to human perfection—and his scent, like the rest of him, is perfect.

He relaxes. I can tell by how his body reacts. His knee touches mine, and I tense at the effect. I'm hot and cold at the same time, as if my body can't decide how it wants to respond to him. How am I ever going to get through an entire meal with this man? I'm ultra-aware of every part of him.

The car stops, and Christopher opens the door once more.

I take his gloved hand as he helps me out of the vehicle. Surreal.

"Thank you," I murmur.

"You're welcome, ma'am."

Ma'am? I've never been called ma'am before. I'm not sure I like it. Twenty-four is too young to be a ma'am.

"Thanks, Christopher," Braden says.

"You're welcome. I'll be here when you're done." Christopher waves.

Then I'm walking into Union Oyster House with Braden Black.

Braden fucking Black.

"Mr. Black," the maître d' says, "we're thrilled you're joining us tonight. Your usual table?"

"That'll be great. Thanks, Marco."

Marco personally leads us to a table. It's near the back where it's a little less noisy.

I sit when Marco pulls out a chair for me. "Thank you," I murmur again.

"Sometimes I like to sit at the bar," Braden says. "Those shuckers tell the most amazing stories."

I nod. I've sat at the bar a few times myself. It's fun. I almost wish we were sitting there tonight. I wouldn't have to make as much conversation.

I take the menu Marco hands me and stare at it. I know it by heart, but it gives me something to do.

"Skye."

"Yeah?" Still staring at the menu.

Braden lifts the menu out of my hand. "Look at me."

His deep voice speaks to me on a level I don't quite comprehend. I meet his gaze.

"I want to take you to bed tonight."

Chapter Three

I freeze.

Braden Black did *not* just tell me he wants to take me to bed.

Gentlemen don't talk like that, and I don't go to bed with every man who crosses my path. Or who buys me dinner.

I'm not sure what to say. Finally, "Excuse me?" comes out.

A gleam tugs at the corner of his eye. Is it playful? I'm not sure.

"I'm pretty sure I didn't stutter," he says, "and I'm also sure there's nothing wrong with your hearing."

I clear my throat. "I'm not going to bed with you, Mr. Black." Though my thighs are already quivering at the thought.

Seriously. They're quivering.

"Call me Braden."

His voice is low and sexy and sends a tickle straight between my legs—a tickle I'm used to in the company of a man I want but a tickle I know won't lead anywhere. "Are you always so blunt?"

"I find it useful in negotiations to lay most of my cards on the table outright."

I regard him. He's not smiling, and his demeanor has darkened.

"I guess I didn't realize this was a negotiation."

"Everything's a negotiation, Skye."

"This is dinner, not a negotiation."

"That's where you're wrong. Think about it. You have a reason for everything you do. You may not think it through, but your subconscious does. For example, you have a reason for accepting my dinner invitation."

Only I never actually accepted it. I just went. "I do? Other than being hungry?"

"You didn't have to accept my invitation to sate your hunger." He licks his bottom lip.

My thighs are quivering again. "What other reason would I have?"

"You tell me."

Way to put me on the spot. "I don't know. Maybe I want to be seen with you."

"That's a crock."

"How do you know?"

"Because you're working for Addison Ames. You work behind the scenes. You're not interested in being seen just for the sake of being seen. You're interested in furthering your career, and you're willing to put in the time."

Strange that he reads me so well. He's absolutely right. I clear my throat. "Maybe I want to— "

"Stop this game, Skye. There's only one reason you accepted, and we both know what it is." His eyes burn blue fire. "You want to go to bed with me."

He's not wrong, but I'm determined to stay calm. I will my voice not to crack. "You said you lay most of your cards on the table up-front. Most, not all."

"True. I usually keep an ace up my sleeve."

"What's that ace tonight?"

"I'd be a shitty negotiator if I gave that up so early," he says, lowering his eyelids slightly.

Sparks run down my spine and explode in my pussy. I draw in a deep breath. "I'm still not going to bed with you, Mr. Black."

"Braden," he says again. "And you are, Skye. You definitely—"

A server appears. "Hi, Mr. Black. I'm Cory, and I'll be taking care of you and your lady this evening. Would you like to begin with a cocktail?"

"Absolutely, Cory," Braden says. "Skye?"

A drink? A drink is the last thing I need at the moment. What would a woman eating dinner with Braden Black order?

On second thought, a drink might be just what I need. I'll keep it at one, but I desperately need something to help me to relax. "Vodka martini," I say. "Extra olives."

"Any particular vodka?"

"Grey Goose?" The only brand I can think of.

It must be okay, because Cory nods and then turns to Braden.

"Wild Turkey on the rocks."

Wild Turkey? Not one of the top-shelf brands that Addison orders? She likes the Pappy Van Winkle fifteen-year to the tune of about seventy-five dollars a shot.

Then I remember.

Braden Black is new to his money. He comes from a working-class family in South Boston. I love Wild Turkey. I grew up on it. My grandpa used to let me have a very small sip of his when we sat on the porch in the summer evenings. My mom put a stop to that eventually, but I'd already developed a taste for it. I should have ordered it, rather than the martini.

I like vodka martinis, but I honestly prefer bourbon to just about anything.

Unbelievable that I have something in common with the man across from me.

I'm still not going to bed with him.

Even though I want to.

I *really* want to.

Braden orders raw oysters. "Do you want anything else?" he says to me.

I shake my head. "I love raw oysters."

He smiles, and my heart skips a beat. So cliché, but I swear, it really skips a beat.

A few silent minutes later, our drinks arrive. Thank God. Now I have something to do with my hands.

Braden lifts his glass to his lips and tosses some liquid onto his tongue.

I imagine that tongue doing other things, and I squeeze my thighs together to ease the ache between them.

"Tell me," he says after swallowing, "a little about Skye Manning. You must be something to be working for Addison."

"I have a degree in photography and media from BU. She hired me for my photography skills."

"For her influencing?"

"Yeah."

"But those are selfies."

"Actually, they're not." I spill the beans about how we take fake selfies before I realize Addison might not want that information made public. Then I remember passersby see us all the time in public places when we take the photos.

A wide grin splits Braden's handsome face. "Sounds like classic Addie. Everything has to look perfect."

I agree, but no way am I saying that. I don't want to lose my job.

I gather courage and ask, "How do you know Addison?"

"She didn't tell you?"

She did, but this gives me the chance to find out his side of the story. Whatever their connection, it clearly didn't end well.

"Not really. I'd love to hear it from you."

"But you witnessed the interaction between us."

"Yeah. You weren't overly friendly."

"No."

Interesting. I've learned exactly nothing.

Cory arrives with the oysters. He rattles off the name and origin of each one, but none of it matters to me. I love them all, the brinier the better.

Braden takes out his phone and snaps a photo of the oysters that arrived. "Got to keep the followers happy."

Is he posting to Instagram? Braden Black? That surprises me, though it probably shouldn't. After all, he commented on Addie's post.

"How many followers do you have?" I ask.

"Not as many as Addison, but enough."

I can easily check, so I don't ask for any elaboration. "I never would have thought you were the social media type."

"I'm not, really, but people seem to want to know what I'm up to. Probably only because I'm richer than God, which still seems a little unreal to me. I'm definitely a self-made man. I wasn't born into money like Addison and her sister."

I've only met Addison's fraternal twin, Apple, once. She's the anti-Addison, into Zen, yoga, and the chakras, and wears only flowing Bohemian frocks.

"Anyway, I never really got out of the habit," Braden says. "You on Instagram?"

"Yeah. Of course."

"What's your handle?"

My cheeks warm. "@stormyskye15."

His lips twitch. "Stormy? Why not sunny or blue? Or even cloudy?"

"Because I like stormy skies. They're a lot more interesting than blue or sunny skies, don't you think?" When I was growing up, stormy skies were often the norm. I took shelter from more than one tornado when I was a kid. Talk about feeling out of control.

The corners of his eyes crinkle. "I suppose I never thought about it. What's interesting to you about them?"

My cheeks grow hotter. No one's ever asked me about my profile name before. "The colors. The gray that turns almost to green. The cumulonimbus clouds that stretch for miles but are fluffy on top."

"Cute," he says.

Cute? Before I can decide whether I'm touched or insulted, he continues.

"Why fifteen?"

"Because fourteen was taken."

He regards me for a moment, his expression seeming both puzzled and amused. "I'm tagging you."

"On a photo of oysters?"

"Sure. We're sharing them, so why not?"

My nerves jump. Being tagged with Braden Black is not something that was ever even a minuscule dot on the radar of my life. For a second, I worry that Addison will see the post, but then I remember she only follows ten people, and I'm not one of them. Is Braden? I doubt it, given she seems to detest him.

He puts his phone away and nods toward the oysters. "Ladies first."

Should I slurp or use the little fork? If I use the fork, will I look like a novice? I finally decide on the fork because that's how I always eat oysters. I never quite got the hang of slurping. I choose one of the smaller ones and squeeze a few drops of lemon juice on it. Then I scoop it expertly on the fork and into my mouth and take a sip of my martini. The martini was a good idea after all. It's much better with oysters than Wild Turkey.

Mmm. Delicious.

"Just lemon?" Braden says.

I swallow. "Yeah. It's perfect."

"I like a little cocktail sauce."

"Amateur," I say before I realize the word came out of my mouth.

He regards me, his eyes hypnotic. "We'll see who the amateur is by the time this night is over."

Chapter Four

My heart thumps wildly. The innuendo isn't lost on me.

Cory comes back to take our dinner orders. I flash back to an employment interview workshop in high school. "Order the fish of the day, broiled," the teacher said. "If you're nervous and you drop some on your clothing, it won't leave a stain."

Union Oyster House doesn't have a "fish of the day," so I decide on the pan-seared haddock with mashed potatoes and fresh vegetables. Nothing to get me in too much trouble there.

Braden orders fried oysters. He wasn't lying when he said he was in the mood for them.

"Do you enjoy your job, Skye?"

I'm about to answer when my phone dings. I quickly grab it out of my purse. It's blowing up with notifications.

"Congratulations," Braden says. "You're famous."

Because he tagged me in the post of the oysters, I'm being notified every time someone makes a comment.

"Turn off notifications," he says, "or it'll drive you bananas."

I follow his advice and then tuck the phone back in my

purse. Wow. A few people know I'm Addison's assistant, but this is ridiculous.

"You going to answer my question?"

"Sure. What question?"

"Do you enjoy your job?"

"Yes and no."

"Meaning...?"

"I get to take pictures, which is what I love to do, but I'm not exactly photographing anything significant."

"Addie trying on scarves isn't going to make it into *National Geographic*," he says. "You're right about that."

I warm a little. Is he making fun of me? Plus, how did he know that having a photo in *National Geographic* is my dream? Ever since I saw that gorgeous photo of the Afghani girl with the searing green eyes in a book of magazine photographs, I've wanted to capture something that profound.

"I'm making good contacts."

"That's true. Maybe you can become the official photographer for Bean There Done That. Getting those sprinkles of nutmeg just right on cappuccinos."

Yeah, he's making fun of me. Addie was right. He's kind of a douche. A gorgeous douche, but still a douche. "Did you really ask me to dinner to diss my job?"

"That wasn't my intention," he says, his blue eyes on fire. "I asked you to dinner because I really want to fuck you."

Again with the thighs quivering. I'm wet already. I can feel it.

"How am I supposed to respond to that?" I ask, willing my voice not to shake. I'm not completely successful.

"I wouldn't be where I am today if I didn't go after what I want," he says, his voice slightly lower and raspier.

I get that. I do. I'm pretty enough and I have good boobs, but this man can have *anyone*. He's way out of my league. So why does Braden Black want *me*? I desperately want to ask that question, and I'm desperately afraid at the same time that if I do, he'll realize his ridiculous mistake and send me home.

I compromise and say nothing while my cheeks warm and my heart flutters.

He raises one eyebrow. "You can tell me you'd like to fuck me, too."

I resist the urge to squirm in my chair. Does he really want me to say that? Even weirder, I actually *want* to say it.

This will be a fuck. Just a fuck. I've had "just a fuck" before. I can live with that. Braden Black probably has some extra-smooth moves, plus there's something about him that seems to call to me, though I have no idea what.

"Because you do," he says. "Don't try to deny it, Skye. I see it in your eyes." He slurps an oyster and licks a dab of cocktail sauce from the corner of his mouth.

I bite my lip. "If I were to agree to this… Where?"

"My place."

"I don't even know you."

His right eye crinkles a little, and for a moment I think he's going to smile, but he doesn't. "Sometimes it's better that way."

I cock my head slightly. I have no idea what he means, and I wait for him to explain. But no explanation comes. He simply loads cocktail sauce onto another oyster, slurps it, and again licks the dab of red from the corner of his mouth.

How would that tongue feel between my legs? I take a slow drink of my martini. I may need another.

Instead, though, Braden orders a bottle of some kind of French white to go with our dinner. Good thing I like wine. My boyfriend in college used to order for me all the time, and it pissed me off.

When Braden does it? It kind of turns me on.

What is happening to me? I squirm again against that incessant tickle between my legs.

My martini is gone, and the wine arrives, followed by our meals. My haddock looks plain, which is what I was going for. I take a bite. Tasty. Maybe not mouthwateringly delicious, but tasty.

I should make conversation. I could ask Braden how he made his billions, but I already know that story. Everyone does. He and his younger brother, Ben, worked for their father's small construction company in South Boston. Braden made some modifications to a pair of safety goggles, which turned out to be state of the art. He patented the design, and he and Ben started Black, Inc. when Braden was twenty-five years old. Now, at thirty-five, he and Ben are billionaires, and most construction workers in the world use his goggles. But he's gone far beyond goggles. His investments in real estate, luxury assets, public and private holdings, foreign currency, precious metals—you name it—have made Black, Inc. a household name.

Braden is the CEO, while Ben handles marketing and their father, Bobby Black, is chairman of the board.

Not bad for a guy who never went to college.

Yeah, we all know the story. He'll probably think I'm ridiculous if I ask about it.

"Do you have any pets?" I ask after swallowing a bite of broccoli. I have no idea where that question came from, but it's too late now. The words have left my mouth.

"A dog."

I widen my eyes. "Oh?" I'm not sure why I'm surprised, but I am. I love dogs, but Braden doesn't seem to be the dog type.

"Yeah. A rescue pup. She's adorable."

I smile and lift my eyebrows. "You rescued a dog?"

"Is that so hard to believe?"

Is it? I'm not sure. "Well…no."

His eyes soften and he pulls out his phone and hands it to me. "She's great. Part border collie and part Australian cattle dog with some other stuff thrown in. I did one of those doggie DNA kits on her."

And just like that, Braden Black is even more attractive to me.

"She's beautiful." I give his phone back.

"How about you? Any dogs?"

I shake my head. "I love them, but my apartment complex doesn't allow them."

"Then move."

"It's not that easy when you don't have millions sitting around collecting dust like you do."

I freeze, my fork halfway to my plate. Did I really say that? I probably just ended our dinner date.

"I'm sorry," I say. "That wasn't called for."

He shakes his head. "No worries. I'm used to it. But, Skye, I'm not any different from the next person."

"Except that the next person can't buy whatever he wants."

"I can't, either."

"Exactly what do you want that you can't buy?"

"You," he says. "In my bed."

Chapter Five

Nice. He knows he can't buy a woman like me. His words are the first sign all night that he's not the douchebag Addie says he is. Well, that and the fact that he rescued a dog.

"No," I say. "I'm not for sale."

"That's why you'll come willingly." He lowers his gaze to my mouth.

He's right. I'll go willingly. As soon as he said he wanted me in his bed, I knew I'd do it. Something about Braden calls to me. I doubt I'm alone. He probably has this effect on every woman he comes across. Does he bed all of them? He isn't known as a womanizer. He had a pretty public relationship with a lesser-known model named Aretha Doyle for a while, but that ended more than a year ago.

Probably he just wants a fuck, and I'm the lucky squeeze du jour.

He's still staring at my mouth. I grab my napkin and wipe away whatever piece of offending food he may be gawking at, and then I gather all my courage. Two can play this game. Braden Black wants me in his bed? I'll show him who has control.

"Let's go," I say.

He eyes my plate. "You didn't finish your dinner."

"I'm suddenly not hungry. You want to fuck me? Let's go fuck."

His eyelids lower slightly. "Works for me." He motions to Cory. "We're ready for the check."

Braden's lush downtown penthouse is decorated all in black and forest green. A black lacquer grand piano sits in one corner. A pretty black, brown, and white dog scurries out from under the piano, running to greet him. She's even more gorgeous than in the photo he showed me.

"Hey, Sasha." He pets her head.

"She's beautiful." I kneel down to scratch her behind the ears. "Hi there, Sasha. You're so pretty."

Sasha licks my face for a few seconds but then grows bored with me and heads somewhere else in the penthouse.

I nod toward the piano. "Do you play?"

"No."

"Then why do you have a piano?"

"I hire a pianist for my parties," he says. "Guests love it. Do you play?"

I shake my head. "We didn't have a piano. My dad plays the guitar, though."

He leads me to the piano, where a guitar also sits. "I do, too. Just dabble really. But I love playing classical guitar and then of course some folk songs. All acoustic stuff."

I'd ask him to play something if I weren't shaking from the top of my head all the way down to my toes. Rather, keeping myself from shaking.

I'm standing in Braden Black's home.

Yeah, I came to a virtual stranger's home—a home with so much security, no one could find me here. A home where he can do anything he wants to me, and I have no way to stop him.

Anything he wants.

So much for me staying in control.

The thought makes me shudder, and again a jolt arrows between my legs.

Yeah, he has security, but he hasn't done anything to make me feel unsafe so far tonight. I can always leave. I don't have to do this.

Except I want to do this more than I want my next breath.

I want to go to Braden Black's bed.

I want him to fuck me until I can't walk.

As if reading my mind, he closes the distance between us and gazes down at me, zeroing in on my mouth again. He trails a finger over my upper lip and then my lower. "I've wanted to kiss those full pink lips since I saw you at Addie's office. You have the sexiest mouth I've ever seen."

I have a sexy mouth? Before I can contemplate further, he crushes his mouth to mine.

My lips are already parted, and he thrusts his tongue between them.

This isn't a normal first kiss.

No. This is a kiss of untamed desire, a kiss of two people who want each other desperately.

A kiss that drugs me, takes away my will.

A tiny groan, more a vibration than a sound, echoes from his throat and into me, fueling my desire. My hands, seemingly of their own accord, drift up his arms to his neck and I entwine my fingers in his dark-brown hair. He wears it long for a businessman, and it feels like silk against my fingers.

He growls into my mouth and roughly tugs on my ponytail,

his tongue still tangling with mine. We kiss and we kiss and we kiss, until—

"Bedroom," he gasps, breaking the kiss. "God, I want to fuck you so bad. I need to get inside that tight little body of yours."

Tight little body? That's Addison, not me, but I don't care at the moment. He wants me, and I want him. I've lost capacity for rational thought. I don't care that I know next to nothing about him except what everyone else knows. At the moment, I don't care if he's a serial killer.

All I know is I want him. I yearn for him more than I've ever yearned for anything.

I'm out of control. Completely.

And that's why I know I can't do this, no matter how much my body is aching for his touch.

Not now. Not until I'm myself again.

Skye Manning doesn't lose control. Not ever.

What will I say to him? What will he say to me? He'll probably call me a cocktease, and he'll be right.

I'm playing *Push Me Pull You* with myself, my body going one way, my mind going another.

He takes my hand and yanks me down a hallway toward a closed door at the end.

His bedroom.

Braden Black's bedroom.

If I go in, it'll be all over. I'll go to bed with him. I'll give up the discipline I so desperately covet in my life.

He touches the brushed brass doorknob, ready to turn it.

I bite my lip, nearly drawing blood. "No."

His sapphire eyes are on fire, and they're shooting flaming darts at me. "Excuse me?"

I clear my throat. "No. I can't do this. We barely know each other."

He stares at me, but his eyes seem different somehow, like he's looking not at me but through me. Unease sweeps over my flesh. I'm still turned on, still hotter than ever, but now something icy exists between us, and though we're only inches away from each other, the distance seems like miles.

I expect him to argue with me. To tell me I've already agreed. To pressure me to change my mind.

He says nothing. Instead, he takes my hand and leads me back to the living area. Sasha prances around us, and Braden leans down to give her a pet on the head.

"I'm sor—"

"Not a problem, Skye," he says, tapping into his phone.

Not a problem? After he said he had to have me? Loved my sexy mouth? My tight body?

This was truly just a fuck to him?

Of course it was. Braden Black can have anyone he wants. He'll have someone up here to replace me at a moment's notice. He's probably calling one of his standbys. Maybe a tall blond supermodel type with legs a mile long. She'll take my place tonight because I gave up the chance for the night of a lifetime—all for control.

And control is something I can't ever afford to give up.

I'm a fool.

I changed my mind.

The words hover on my lips. I open my mouth—

Braden clears his throat into the phone. "Christopher? Ms. Manning needs a ride home."

Chapter Six

"I can't believe you." My best friend, Tessa Logan, echoes my own thoughts at breakfast the next morning. "You'll never get this chance again. Plus, he might have been the one who could help you with your little problem."

I roll my eyes. I don't want to think about my "little problem" at the moment. I try to never think about it. It's not a huge deal, anyway. Why should I miss what I've never had?

"I'm not that easy," I say.

"So what? This is Braden Black, hottie extraordinaire. Not to mention billionaire. When Braden Black wants you, you do it."

"I just felt so—"

"Out of your element?" she finishes for me, tilting her head so her brown-black hair grazes her shoulders.

Tessa knows me better than anyone and is the only person outside of family who understands why I have a need to be in charge all the time.

"Well…yeah."

"Skye, let me tell you something. I get your history, but

you need to let go, babe. You're missing out on adventures because of your ridiculous need to be in control. I've never even seen you drunk."

Yeah. And no one ever would. I got over that when I was sixteen. I shared a bottle of Southern Comfort with a high school friend and puked all the next day. Never again. I allow myself two drinks if I'm driving—only one if I'm not eating—and no more than four if I'm not. If I get tipsy with the third, I don't take it to four. I know my limits, and I stick to them.

"Sorry, Tess. You'll never get me drunk. Tipsy, but not drunk, and don't even bring up drugs."

"Who said anything about drugs?" She shakes her head. "You know I don't indulge. You don't want to get drunk? Fine. You can let your hair down in other ways. Let's get you laid."

Classic Tessa. Sex is just sex to her. She can separate the act from the emotion. She's lucky that way.

"I don't go to bed with just anyone. I think I proved that last night."

She shakes her head again. "That's my point. Get laid. Have a one nighter. Yeah, you missed out on what was probably the one nighter of a lifetime, but Braden Black isn't the only guy in the city."

He's the only guy I want.

I don't say the words out loud, but they're cemented in my mind. I blew it. I totally blew it.

In truth, I've never wanted a man the way I wanted Braden Black last night. My body responded to his every word, move, touch, in a way it never had before. I thought I could handle Braden Black.

But I couldn't. Not when he kissed me, touched me, led me to his bedroom.

I was ready to let him take me in every way possible, do anything he wanted to me. I didn't care.

And that frightened me more than anything ever had.

"As much as I'd love to search the streets for someone to take me to bed"—*not*—"I have to get to work. We're shooting a selfie at that new pretzel stand this morning."

"You're not getting away this easily," she says. "Tonight. We're going out."

"I don't go out—"

"On work nights. Yeah, I know. God, Skye. Sometimes I wonder why I hang out with you at all." Tessa rolls her brown eyes and smiles.

"Because you adore me," I say, smiling back.

Tessa and I met in college at Boston University. We were on the same floor freshman year and got paired together for a team-building exercise during orientation.

We had nothing in common.

She's a Boston city girl. I'm a rural girl from Kansas.

She studied accounting and sees everything in black and white. I studied photography and see everything in shades and layers.

She's tanned and beautiful with a great body. I'm fair and reasonably pretty. Yeah, I'll give myself a fairly good body, too, compliments of walking, yoga, and the occasional Jazzercise class.

But we clicked and are still friends today. I'd do anything for her. Except something ridiculous, like getting drunk for no reason or having a one nighter with a stranger just to get Braden Black off my mind.

I have my limits.

"I do adore you." She smiles. "You're not getting out of this, though. This weekend, prepare for some off-the-charts fun."

• • •

The shoot went off without a hitch, and Addison promptly threw her pretzel in the trash. She hates carbs almost as much as she hates coffee. Actually, she loves carbs, but she can't maintain her waifish figure if she indulges too often. I saw her put away a whole pizza once, though. I'm pretty sure she barfed afterward.

"I'm taking the rest of the day off," she tells me. "Be sure to stay at the office until six thirty because I'm expecting some important calls."

"Okay, have a good day."

I head back to the office. I walk through the ornate hotel lobby—complete with crystal chandelier—to the conference wing where Addie's office is. We keep it locked up when we're out on shoots.

Someone's standing outside the door and leaning against the wall. He's wearing a navy-blue suit and reading the *New York Times.* I can't see his face, but already my body reacts.

It's him.

It's Braden Black.

Chapter Seven

I check my watch. It's noon. Lunchtime. Addie and I left around nine thirty to do the shoot. How long has Braden Black been standing there?

Don't get too excited. He's probably here to see Addie.

I clear my throat.

He lowers his paper. His expression is noncommittal. Is he happy to see me? Surprised? Angered? I can't tell.

His full, firm lips twitch slightly, and I flash back to the memory of them sliding over mine, of his tongue diving into my mouth for a deep, raw kiss the likes of which I'll never experience again.

"May I help you?" I ask.

"Sure. You can open the door."

I quickly retrieve the key from my purse and unlock the office. "Addie's not here."

"Good," he says.

Okay, then. I open the door, walk in, and set my purse on my desk. I take out my phone quickly and check the comments on today's post. Everything's in order so far. I'll respond to a few later. After he's gone.

My heart is racing. Really racing. When I turn around, away from the desk, Braden Black will be there, standing tall, his glorious body filling out his blue suit in all the right ways. My blood pulses through my veins, heating to boiling.

"Skye," he says, his voice dark.

I turn. "Why are you here?"

"For this."

He grabs me and kisses me. Hard. I gasp, and he thrusts his tongue into my mouth, exploring at first but then taking. Another raw kiss, and my pussy is already pooling with desire. My nipples tighten and harden, and I push my breasts into him, move my hips without thinking.

He groans into my mouth, the hum like a bass clef crescendo on a piano. Is this truly why he came here? To kiss me again?

He tastes of morning coffee and peppermint, different from the wine-laced kiss we shared last night. Fireworks explode inside me, and soon my thoughts turn to mush, obliterated by Braden's lips.

Only feeling remains—pure, raw emotion that coils through me and leaves me like a coyote trying to keep from springing on its prey too soon.

Control. Maintain control.

Fuck control.

I grab his head and thread my fingers through his silken hair. I pull him toward me and explore him as he explores me, our tongues locked in a sword fight, our lips sliding against each other. Nothing matters. Nothing except this amazing kiss.

Until he breaks away, sweat dotting his brow.

His full lips are sexy and swollen, and they glisten from our kiss. His hair is mussed from my fingers, and yes…his cock is bulging against the blue wool of his trousers.

"Dinner tonight," he says huskily. "I'll pick you up here at seven. And this time, Skye, you're coming to my bed. Get used to the idea. It's going to happen."

He turns and walks out the door, leaving my legs wobbling.

Sitting next to Braden in the back seat of his car, I clear my throat. "Where are we eating tonight?"

"My place."

My body turns to melted butter. "Oh? You cook?"

"I have a personal chef. She's taking care of everything."

I nod. Of course he does.

Everything's okay. I've been to his place. I'm safe there. I don't have to do anything I don't want to do. Which doesn't really matter anyway. I *do* want to go to bed with him. Hell, I wanted to last night. I never dreamed I'd get another chance with Braden Black. Seriously, he can have whoever he wants.

So why does he want me?

Is it the thrill of the chase? Does he only want me because I got away the first time?

Probably.

Does it matter?

You need to let your hair down, phantom Tessa whispers in my head.

I know one thing. I've been given another chance for the night of a lifetime, and this time I'm not going to blow it.

My skin tingles—with excitement or fear, I'm uncertain. *Get ready to give in, Skye.*

We arrive and take the elevator to his place. Sasha greets us at the door.

"Hey, sweet girl," Braden says, petting her. "Annika will

take you out, okay?"

"Is Annika the chef?" I ask.

"No. She's my housekeeper. She's probably upstairs."

There's an upstairs? Braden taps something into his phone. Within a few minutes, a gray-haired woman enters the room—where did she come from?—leashes Sasha, and walks her out, never saying a word.

A sweet yet pungent fragrance punctuates the air—tomato and basil. We must be having Italian. Great. I love Italian. Except at the moment I'm feeling like anything that goes into my mouth will come right back up.

"Make yourself comfortable," Braden says.

I stop myself from laughing. Comfortable? Here? Does he know how impossible his request is? We hardly know each other. We've shared one meal and two kisses. That's it. Besides, for a girl who grew up in a modest farmhouse and now lives in a tiny downtown Boston studio, this glitz will never be comfortable.

I almost wish we could just go to bed and get it over with, spare us the strain of a dinner together.

"Wine?" he asks. "Or something stronger?"

"Wine is good."

"Red?"

"Sure."

"How about a Chianti Classico? It'll go well with dinner." He pulls a bottle from an ornate wrought-iron rack.

I was right. We're having Italian. "What's for dinner?"

"Penne arrabiata and veal Marsala. You like Italian?" He opens the bottle, pours two glasses, and hands me one.

I take a sip. "Yes. Love it."

"Good."

He hasn't smiled since he picked me up at the office. Last night, he smiled a few times. He seems darker tonight, and though his demeanor should frighten me, it doesn't.

I'm all in now.

His kisses invade my mind, negating all other thoughts and keeping my brain fuzzy. I'm hyperaware of him next to me, and an invisible energy pulses between us. If I touch his arm, I fully expect a shock to spark through me.

"Marilyn set out some antipasti for us. Follow me."

He leads me to the kitchen. All marble and hardwood, of course, with a giant island surrounded by barstools. The antipasti—olives, melon, salami, prosciutto, and small blocks of white cheese—rests on a silver platter. A cruet of extra-virgin olive oil and another plate holding short wooden skewers sit adjacent.

"Please." Braden waves his hand over the platter. "After you."

"No, go ahead," I say. "I'd like to enjoy the wine for a few minutes."

"Of course." He takes a skewer, loads it up with the antipasti, and then drizzles olive oil over it. He holds a napkin to catch the drips. He pulls the green olive off with his teeth.

And I imagine those teeth around my nipple.

Oh my God.

At least now I know how to eat the antipasti. Of course if I eat…

"Please," he says again after swallowing.

I nod. I'll choke it down somehow. I grab a skewer and push a piece of cheese onto it. Then an olive, a piece of folded prosciutto, and cantaloupe. I move it toward my mouth.

"You forgot the best part, Skye."

I lift my brows.

"The olive oil."

Actually, I left the olive oil out on purpose. The "preparing for an interview" workshop pops into my head again. I don't want olive oil dripping on my blouse.

"I'm watching my fat intake," I lie.

"It's only a bit. Here." He takes the skewer from me and drizzles the light-green liquid onto the food. "Try it."

I pull the chunk of cantaloupe off with my teeth.

He inhales sharply.

The olive oil is peppery and slightly bitter against the sweet melon, and the effect is delicious. Braden was right. I pull the next piece, the prosciutto, off my skewer.

He inhales again. "Your mouth. Watching you eat is better than porn."

I widen my eyes and meet his gaze. His eyes are like blue lightning.

This is turning him on. I'm eating, and he's getting turned on.

It's not completely out of the blue. I thought about my nipple when he bit into his olive. But he's Braden Black. I'm just...*me.*

I set the skewer down on a napkin and take another sip of wine, wishing it were bourbon. I don't know a lot about wine, but Wild Turkey, I get. I grew up with the woodsy scent and the notes of caramel and cinnamon. It burns a little going down, part of its charm.

"You don't like the wine?" he says.

"No, it's fine."

"You made a face."

"I did? I didn't mean to."

"You winced a little."

"Did I?"

"Yeah, what were you thinking?"

I hesitate, unsure if I should tell him the truth. "Just thinking I'd rather be drinking Wild Turkey."

Finally his lips turn upward and he laughs like he's happy.

"Why didn't you ask for it, then?"

"I don't know. You offered wine."

"Ask for what you want here, Skye. Trust me, I plan on asking for what *I* want and then taking it."

He picks up my wineglass and leaves the kitchen while his words spark embers in my body. In a few minutes, he returns with a lowball glass of the distinctive amber liquid.

"I'm a Wild Turkey fan myself," he says.

"I know. You ordered it last night."

"But you didn't. Why?"

"I like a vodka martini with oysters." Definitely not a half-truth, though I always prefer Wild Turkey.

"Good call, but this goes with everything." He hands me the glass. "I added one ice cube. Hope you like it that way."

"Yeah, I do. I think watering it down just a touch brings out the flavor."

"A Wild Turkey connoisseur, huh?"

"I'm from Kansas, so—"

"You're not from here?"

I take a sip of bourbon and smile. "You didn't notice my lack of accent?"

"Yeah, but I just figured you were from somewhere else on the East Coast. Not the Midwest."

"Why?"

He shrugs. "You look like a city girl."

"Kansas has cities."

"True, but not like the East Coast."

"Also true," I say. "I come from a farm anyway."

"A farm?" He lifts his eyebrows. "A real, honest-to-goodness farm?"

"Uh…yeah. Does that surprise you?"

"A little. Do you milk cows and everything?"

I roll my eyes. "I didn't grow up on a dairy farm, Braden.

I grew up on a corn farm. You know, knee-high by the Fourth of July?"

"That's interesting."

Interesting? Really? Corn is the most uninteresting thing on the planet, to my way of thinking.

"Why did you leave?"

I can't help a short laugh. "Because I've taken about all the photos of corn I want to take in my career."

"Right, photography. Makes sense." He gazes at me, his eyes twinkling but never leaving mine, as he takes the last sip of his wine. "Ready for dinner?"

I've only had two small sips of my Wild Turkey. Not near enough to relax me. If I'm going to do this—leave my control at the door—I can't depend on booze. I have to do it myself.

"Sure, let's eat." I take another small sip, resisting the urge to shoot it, ice cube or not. I set the glass down and lick the tangy spiciness from my lips.

His gaze burns into me.

"Fuck dinner," he growls.

Chapter Eight

He grabs my hand and leads me to his bedroom.

Yes, the bedroom door. I've seen it before. It looms before me like the entrance to a fortress hiding jewels and treasures. My body is a warm mass of boiling honey, my heart a stampeding herd.

This is it.

This is going to happen.

I'm doing this. I'm not chickening out. I want this. I want *him*.

He pulls me toward his body and pushes his erection into my belly. "Feel that?" he whispers, tugging on my earlobe with his teeth. "Feel what you do to me. You won't leave me wanting tonight, Skye. I'm going to fuck you."

He lets me go and opens the door to his bedroom.

And it's a sight to behold.

While the living room was black lacquer everywhere, the bedroom is masculine mahogany with navy-blue and ivory accents. As thrilling as his decor is, though, I'm drawn to the window that encompasses an entire wall overlooking the

Boston Harbor.

I walk forward, as if in a trance. The glass is so clear that I feel like I could fall off the edge.

"One-way glass," Braden says. "We can see out, but no one can see in."

I'm only half listening. I'm much more interested in watching the yachts sailing into the marina. "Is one of those yours?" I ask.

"The *Galatea*, yeah. Ben's got her out tonight."

"Ben your brother?"

"Only Ben I know. He's more into the boat thing than I am."

"How can you *not* be into the boat thing? They're so beautiful."

"They're a damned lot of work."

"But don't you— "

He tugs on my ponytail. "Do you really want to talk about boats right now?"

I turn, and now I finally appreciate the rest of the bedroom. His bed is king size. Honestly, it looks larger than a king to me. The headboard is magnificent—mahogany rungs with odd little metal pieces artistically placed just so. I've never seen anything like it before. The navy-blue comforter covering the bed is a shiny fabric, probably silk. The bed is on the main wall facing the large picture window. On one adjacent wall is a highboy dresser and chest, the mahogany matching the bed frame perfectly. Next to the highboy is an old-fashioned mahogany wardrobe, which is odd, because right next to it is a huge walk-in closet. The door is ajar, so I can see right into it. Why would he need an antique wardrobe?

On the opposite wall sit two wingback chairs in navy with gold flecks. The bed is flanked by two mahogany end tables with lamps on each.

"This is amazing," I say.

"It's a nice place to come home to at night."

"I'll say. If this were mine, I'm not sure I'd ever get out of bed."

A soft growl emerges, seeming to come from his chest as he takes off his suit jacket. "I like the sound of that."

I hold back a quiver.

I'm already wet between my legs. Have been since he picked me up at Addie's office. Everything about Braden is sex on a stick—his silky dark hair, his searing blue eyes, the baritone timbre of his voice, his masculine hands, the way his suit hugs his body.

Yeah, I've seen his body.

The *GQ* spread included a shot of him on the beach. Yum. I'm about find out how much he was Photoshopped.

Not much, I hope.

Actually, it doesn't matter. I'm doing him no matter what. I made that decision in the restaurant last night, even if I postponed it twenty-four hours.

Or did he make the decision for me?

I erase that thought from my mind. I need to think I'm the one who decided, to save at least some semblance of being in charge.

I'm going to fuck Braden Black.

"Take off your clothes," he says, "slowly."

My face heats. Am I actually going to do this? If the pounding of my heart is any indication, the answer is a very resounding yes. I unbutton my blouse. No problem. I can still stay in control. Though I don't want to disobey him. I want to obey him without question, which scares the hell out of me.

One button. Two buttons. Three—

Until he yanks the shirttail out from my jeans and finishes the job by ripping the two halves apart. Buttons fly, one pinging the wardrobe door but most of them falling quietly onto the plush ivory carpeting.

"Couldn't wait," he says huskily.

My nipples harden and press against the lace of my bra. Braden flicks one over the fabric, and my knees buckle.

"Take it off," he growls. "I want to see those tits."

Again, I obey without question. I unclasp the bra slowly, ease my arms out, and let it fall to the floor at my feet. My ample Cs fall gently against my chest.

Braden's eyelids lower, and the soft growl comes from his chest again. He loosens his tie and removes it, tossing it on the floor. Then he unbuttons the first two buttons of his crisp white shirt. Black chest hair peeks out. The perfect amount, like I saw in the *GQ* photos. Braden Black doesn't manscape, and for some reason that's a huge turn-on.

He reaches toward me, and I shiver as he cups my breasts.

"Beautiful," he murmurs and thumbs both my nipples.

I sigh softly.

"Do you like your nipples sucked? Or pinched?"

"All of the above," I say.

"Oh, baby. We're going to get along just fine." He twists my nipples just hard enough to make me groan. "You like that?"

I close my eyes. "Mm-hmm."

"Say yes, Skye. Always say yes. I need to hear the word."

Why? I wonder briefly before I say, "Yes. I like that, Braden."

"Your voice is sexy. I love the way you say my name. Say it again."

"Braden."

"Again."

"Braden."

"Now, tell me what we're going to do here tonight."

"You're going to fuck me, Braden."

"Yes, I'm going to fuck you."

My body turns to gelatin. I'm standing in front of Braden Black, my sandals and jeans still on, my breasts exposed, my nipples hard and ready.

"You say you like your nipples pinched."

"Yes," I say on a soft sigh.

"What else do you like?"

"Whatever you want to do to me." The words fall off my tongue with no thought or effort.

I can't deny the truth of them.

I'm here.

He's here.

And he can do whatever he wants to me.

"Take off the rest of your clothes, Skye."

"Are you going to take yours off?"

"Does it matter?"

I open my mouth to respond, but he stops me with a gesture.

"Undress."

I swallow, my heart thundering, and I kick off my sandals and then unsnap and unzip my jeans. I slowly lower them over my hips and peel them off my legs until I'm standing only in my panties.

"Keep going," he says.

I wiggle out of the panties and kick them a few feet away, next to Braden's tie. I haven't shaved my vulva in a few days. Will he be turned off by the ugly brown stubble?

"Very nice," he says, licking his lips.

Apparently not turned off. Good.

"I can smell you," he says. "You're ripe. Wet. Aren't you?"

I bite my lower lip. "Mm-hmm."

"What did I tell you?" he says sternly. "About using the word?"

"Yes. Yes, I'm wet."

"Who are you wet for, Skye?"

I clear my throat. "For you. I'm wet for you, Braden."

He grabs me then and crushes our mouths together. My tongue wanders out to meet his in another raw kiss. Raw and beautiful. His full lips slide against mine as he plunders my mouth, and I want him to do the same to my body.

My belly flutters and nerves skitter across my skin. My pussy throbs in time with my rapid heartbeat.

Braden moves one hand seductively over my shoulder to my chest, cupping a breast and pinching a nipple. I inhale sharply, breaking our kiss just slightly for air. Then his hand travels downward, over my belly, to—

"Oh!"

He touches my clit gently...and then not so gently as he slides his fingers through my folds.

This time, he breaks the kiss. "So wet," he growls in my ear. "I'm going to drive my cock into you, Skye. I'm going to drive so far into you that you'll be sore tomorrow. Every time you move, you'll think of me inside you, taking you, fucking you. You'll know I was here."

Chapter Nine

Before I can respond, I inhale sharply when he slides a finger into me.

"God, you're so tight. I can't wait to fuck you."

I can't wait, either, though his finger in my pussy feels pretty damned great. He has beautiful hands, long, thick fingers. Perfect for what he's doing.

And he's a master at it.

Maybe this time... Just maybe...

But I don't want to think about that at the moment. I want to enjoy the pleasure, not stress out about what might not happen.

He continues to finger fuck me, adding another while working my clit with his thumb. My legs wobble, but he steadies me, keeping me in the perfect position for the delicious things he's doing to me.

"Feel good, baby?"

"God, yes," I sigh. "So good."

He nips my earlobe with his teeth. "By the end of this night," he whispers, "I promise this will be the least of what you remember."

No. Not possible. I'll never forget his fingers and how they find just the right spot to make me hotter and wetter than I've ever been.

Until he pushes me down on the bed, moves to spread my legs, and closes his eyes.

"I need to taste you."

His tongue, soft against my own, is rougher against my clit, the perfect texture to make me squirm beneath him. I ache at the loss of his fingers, but as he tongues my folds, sliding from my clit to my perineum and back, I revel in the new, though less intense, pleasure.

Why not go slowly? Why not experience each touch in its own right?

He laps at me, licking the wetness from my inner thighs and then shoving his tongue into my heat. He seems to know instinctively when to go back to my clit and get me going again and again. I'm riding a roller coaster of pleasure—up and down and up and down, fast and slow and fast and slow and fast and slow…

Just when I think I'm about to explode, he brings me down again.

Can it happen? Can it really happen?

"God, you taste good," he says against my thigh, his breath like a warm breeze.

I open my eyes. Something hangs above me on the ceiling over his bed, but I don't dwell on it. I raise my head and look between my legs. "Are you ever going to undress?"

"In time," he says again. "But if you ask again, I won't."

His voice is low, with more than an edge of dominance. I'm not sure how he's going to fuck me with his clothes on, but I won't ask again.

I close my eyes, ready for more of his mouth on me when—

"Oh!"

He flips me over like a pancake, so I'm facedown on the bed, my legs hanging off. He pins me in position. "Don't you dare move."

The clanking of his belt and then the zing of his zipper…

The tear of a wrapper… Curious, I turn to look at him.

He pushes me back down harshly. "I said don't fucking move!" Then a low groan as he plunges deep into me. "Fuck, yeah."

I haven't seen his dick, but he must be huge by the way he fills me. I burn as he tunnels into me, and it's a good burn. A *really* good burn.

His stubbled cheek scratches my jawline when he leans down, trapping me under him. "Don't move, Skye. I'll stop if you do. Do you understand?"

"Yes," I whimper.

He sucks my earlobe between his teeth. "You're so damned tight. Fuck, you feel good."

He rises slightly, planting his hands on my shoulders—not hard enough to hurt but hard enough that I truly can't move. I'm trapped, at his mercy. Completely under his spell.

My heart speeds up, anxiety setting in.

Get back in control. Get back in control.

But I can't. I'm immobile.

And God, I'm totally loving it.

I'm not gagged. I can tell him to stop.

But I don't.

Let your hair down, Skye.

Let go, let go, let go…

I close my eyes and surrender to the rapturous feelings taking over my body. Electricity sizzles around us, and I swear I can see it in my mind's eye, feel it in my core.

Braden plunges in and out of me, slowly at first and then

increasing his speed. The cotton of his shirt brushes my lower back as he pushes, pushes, pushes, and with each push, my clit abrades against the comforter, giving me jolt after jolt of magnetizing pleasure. His dick slides in and out, hitting spots inside me I never knew existed—spots that increase my pleasure, increase the energy swirling in my clit.

I grasp the comforter in my fists, still immobile, biting my bottom lip so hard I fear I draw blood.

Something's different. I've been excited before, turned on before, but this is new, as if I'm running naked through a forest at dusk, reaching, reaching, reaching for a mysterious black bird that holds a secret I need. It flies closer and closer but then flaps away, always just a foot out of my grasp.

God, I've never felt this way.

"I'm going to come." Braden thrusts and thrusts and thrusts. "Come with me, baby. Come with me."

His words are a command—a command I can't obey, except—

"Oh my God!" An intense and tingly heat begins in my core. My pussy shatters, warmth coursing through it, and I swear electricity surges through my veins and sizzles outward all the way to my fingers and toes. The roller coaster finally reaches the pinnacle and plunges me into nirvana. I pulse in time with him, each stroke, as he finishes inside me.

My whole body becomes one with Braden, with the bed, and with myself.

This.

This is what I've been missing.

This is what I've come so close to but never experienced—this intensity, this dreamy high.

What would Braden say if he knew this was my first orgasm ever?

Chapter Ten

I don't have much time to ponder the complete wonder of what just happened. Braden pulls out, and I turn over to see what's going on. My mind is luxuriating in the kaleidoscopic whirlwind of the climax when Braden finally rips off his own clothes.

And I gasp.

GQ didn't do him justice.

The man is a fucking god.

His eyes are ablaze with blue fire as he looks down at me. His cock, though he just came, is nearly erect again sans condom. He must have disposed of it when he undressed.

"Move to the head of the bed," he says. "Lie on your back and grab two of the rungs of the headboard."

I stare at him—his glistening lips, his perfect chest with scattered black hair, his hard washboard abs, his black nest of curls encircling his huge cock.

"Now, Skye."

I'm still intoxicated from the climax, but I hastily scoot backward as he demands, rest my head on one of his fluffy pillows, and grab the headboard.

"I'm not going to bind you," he says.

Bind me? He was thinking of *binding* me? Oh, hell no! I let go of the headboard and meet his gaze, my own on fire.

"Grab the rungs," he says calmly but darkly.

"No, I won't. You can't tie me up."

"I think I just said I wasn't going to."

A strange sliver of disappointment edges through me. I shake it off.

"I—"

"Grab the rungs, Skye. Now."

His voice. What is it about his voice that makes me want to obey him? To never question him? My God, if he asks me to do something illegal, I may just do it. That's how hypnotizing his husky timbre is.

I grab the rungs.

"Good." He scoots on the bed so he's straddling me, his cock dangling at my mouth. "Get me hard again. Use that sexy mouth of yours."

He wants a blow job. Of course. I never knew a man who didn't want a blow job. That I can do. Braden is bigger than any man I've been with, but I'm pretty sure I can pull this off.

He pushes his cock between my lips slowly, letting me go at my own pace. When he hits the back of my throat, he's only a little over halfway in. I let go of one rung to use my hand—

"Don't let go!" he says through clenched teeth.

I want to tell him I can make it better for him if he'll let me use my hand, but I can't because my mouth is full of cock. I quickly re-grab the rung.

He still moves in and out of my mouth slowly. His erection has returned in full force, and I'm excited to get it inside me again, to do an instant replay of the most amazing several minutes of my life.

Tessa was right. An orgasm can't be described.

"I enjoy sex," I once told her. "Maybe I'm climaxing and I don't realize it."

"No," she replied. "You'll know when it happens."

How had I ever doubted her?

Now that I've experienced the thing that has always eluded me, I want more. A lot more.

Braden finally removes his cock from my mouth and eases down my body. "Your tits are perfect," he says, and then he sucks one between his lips while lightly pinching the other.

Goose bumps erupt on my flesh. My nipples feel as if they've never been touched before, as if Braden Black is the first man to ever tantalize them.

He sucks, nibbles, bites.

I squirm beneath him, circling my hips, searching for something to rub against my clit to relieve the pressure building in it again. My breasts are swollen and achy, and each tug on my nipples rushes straight to my pussy.

Braden sucks and bites, his stubble abrading my sensitive skin. How I long to run my fingers through his thick hair, smooth back the wet strands sticking to his forehead.

But I can't let go. I can't. I'm not bound, but I can't.

I'm bound by Braden's will, Braden's strength. I don't know what to think, but I know something in me…

Something in me likes it.

Something in me wants more.

I don't like being contained. My fingers itch and tingle. They want to move, embed themselves in the silk of Braden's locks.

I wiggle a finger. Yeah, I can still move them.

But I don't.

No matter how much I want to. I don't.

"You're beautiful," he says after releasing my nipple. He moves down my body, raining soft kisses on my belly and my vulva. "I want to eat you again, but damn, I need to get inside that hot pussy. Fuck." He moves from the bed and returns with a condom.

"Let me do that," I say.

He meets my gaze, his teeth clenched. "Don't you fucking move."

"Braden, I want to—"

"I said don't move!"

I inhale sharply and look up, a sliver of fear edging through me. The thing above me finally comes into focus.

It's some sort of contraption with pulleys and a harness.

I'm both frightened out of my mind and turned on beyond belief.

"I'm going to fuck you again, Skye, and this time, I'm going deep."

He hadn't gone deep last time? I swore I felt him pushing against my cervix. But he means business. He maneuvers my legs over his shoulders, opening me.

Then he thrusts in.

Damn! I bite my lip to keep from shouting. Yes, he's deeper this time. So deep. So good. I'm loose from the first time, and I'm wet as all get out, and still he burns through me as if his dick is made of fire.

"That's good," he grits out. "Sweet pussy. Sweet Skye."

His shoulders are hard, bronze, and beautiful. My fingers ache to glide over them, down his back, and grab his perfectly shaped ass so I can push him farther and farther into me.

But I don't let go of the rungs. I don't let go.

It's probably too much to ask for another climax. After all, one was a true surprise and a true gift. Another won't—

"God, Braden!" I grasp the rungs with white knuckles as he pounds into me, grazing my clit with his pubic hair, his balls slapping against my ass.

My world spins as I continue moaning and screaming.

"That's it, baby. Come. Come all over me. Come for me. Only me."

His words become his voice, a simple vibration that takes me soaring over the harbor. Still he fucks me, harder and harder. The tingling intensity builds again, and I jump off the peak of the highest mountaintop.

"Fuck. Skye. Yes!"

He roars as he thrusts so deeply, I swear he's touching the tip of my head. I pulse around him as he comes, our climaxes in perfect tandem.

Wow. Just wow. No drug can match this.

I meet his gaze, yearning to touch his face glistening with perspiration. Yearning for him to lower his lips to mine and kiss me—the perfect ending to the perfect fuck.

Instead, he rolls off me onto his back, one arm across his eyes.

And I wait.

Shouldn't he say something? Should *I* say something? Finally, he moves off the bed, stands, and throws the condom in the trash. Then he bends down, picks up his pants, and takes his phone out of his pocket. Now will he say something?

When he doesn't, I do. "Going to Instagram this, too?"

It sounded funny in my head, but now I just think it's immature.

Still he says nothing. He's tapping into his phone.

When he finally speaks, I wish he hadn't.

"I just called Christopher. He'll drive you home."

His cold words release my invisible bindings.

I let go of the headboard.

Chapter Eleven

"It was humiliating," I tell Tessa the next day at lunch. "The best sex of my life, and then it was just...*over*. He told me his driver would take me home, and then he left the room, saying he had an important message he had to respond to. It was awful."

"At least you finally had an orgasm." She takes a sip of iced tea. "Did I tell you? Or did I *tell* you?"

I can't help a smile. The first real smile since last night. "You were right. I don't get it, though. I tried everything. Every vibrator out there. Every technique...and nothing. Until Braden Black."

"Girl, just looking at Braden Black might be enough to send me over the edge."

Tessa was multi-orgasmic, or so she said. After the two I experienced last night—the way my body quivered and quaked—I'm pretty sure multiple climaxes would lead to a quick—but very satisfying—death. I can't fault her observation, though. Braden Black is the most gorgeous man on the planet, and he was right when he said I wouldn't forget where he'd been. Not just my pussy, but my glutes and thighs are sore. Muscles I never knew I had hurt like hell today.

"There's something about him, though," I say. "Something I can't quite put my finger on."

"What do you mean?"

"A darkness. Almost like an invisible cloud hovering over him. I know it doesn't make any sense, but I can't explain it any better. I can't see it, but I know it's there." I purposefully don't mention the other enigma about him—that I want to obey him without question. It's not like me at all.

"You're probably imagining things. Maybe because his name is Black. And, you know, black is dark." She giggles.

"That's ridiculous."

"Yeah, probably," she agrees.

"I'm sure I'll never see him again, so I'll never figure out what the darkness is." I let out a short scoff to try to hide the sadness I feel. "Funny. I hardly know him, but I feel a loss."

"That's because he made you come." She smirks.

"What if I can't ever come again?"

"You know how it feels now, so you can duplicate it. Try it at home with your toys. It's bound to happen."

I laugh softly. "I'll try."

"Atta girl. You'll be over Braden Black in no time."

"Maybe. I don't know. Something about him really got to me."

"Try to just remember it for what it was. A night of really good sex that gave you the first of many orgasms you'll have in your long life. Really, you should thank him."

"Maybe send him some flowers?" I say facetiously.

Tessa finishes her iced tea and signals the server for our check. "Maybe one of those erotic cakes."

I can't help it. I let out a guffaw. Send Braden Black an erotic cake? That's just damned funny, and not something

I'd ever do.

"Seriously. You can have them make a marzipan pussy and then write something like, 'Thank you for coming.' Great double entendre." She laughs hysterically.

Tessa is my best friend ever and I adore her, but sometimes she thinks she's funnier than she actually is. Okay, this *is* pretty funny, but no way in hell would I ever send anyone a marzipan pussy.

"Shouldn't it actually be 'thank *me* for coming'?" I say. "I'm the one who had her first orgasm."

"Yeah, but that sounds ridiculous."

"Like it all doesn't sound ridiculous. *You're* ridiculous." I laugh and grab the check when it comes. "My turn. You paid last time."

"I have to run anyway. Meeting at two, and I'm hopelessly unprepared." She stands and a huge grin splits her face. "Think about that cake."

I roll my eyes, grab a credit card from my wallet, and lay it over the check.

Then finish my diet soda and play with the remains of lettuce left on my plate.

And I think about last night.

How Braden made me feel. How he made me want to give up control. If any other man demanded I hold on to a headboard, I'd laugh in his face.

What is it about Braden?

I sigh. Doesn't matter. I'll never see him again. Still, what exactly did he do to make me explode the way I did? Everything was amazing, but what specific thing? I need to know, because I sure as hell want to come again, whether it's with him, another guy, or myself. I don't care.

Except I'd really like it to be with him.

I have a few minutes before I need to be back at the office, so I walk around the city a bit and find myself in front of my favorite bakery—a bakery that also makes erotic cakes. I go in on a whim.

"May I help you?" a young woman asks.

"Yeah." Please let my voice not crack. "I need a baguette, please."

Chicken.

She bags one for me. "Anything else?"

"No, thank you."

I pay for the baguette and walk to the door.

And wonder what Braden is doing at this same moment.

Back at the office, Addison is making the final arrangements with Susanne Cosmetics. They finally upped their offer to two hundred grand, so this afternoon, we're shooting the lip plumper post. Apparently that's the amount necessary for Addie to pimp a product that's supposed to get rid of lip lines. Turning twenty-nine has sent her into a tailspin.

I've set up a mini studio in the office, where I can adjust the lighting as needed. We'll shoot today's post there.

I'm getting the space ready when Addie storms in.

"Change of plans. They want the shot at the Susanne counter at Macy's."

"Crap. Really?"

"Yeah. I tried to talk them out of it."

"Department stores are the worst."

"I know," she says. "The lighting's atrocious, but that's what I have you for. You can work your magic."

I warm slightly. That's what passes for a compliment from Addison Ames. I'll take what I can get. She appreciates me—I know that. She just doesn't show it very well most of the time.

"Sure. You want to go now?"

"Yeah. We'll close up, and then you can take the rest of the day off."

I keep myself from laughing. It's nearly three thirty. The shoot will take at least an hour, and then I'll be monitoring it for the next hour for negative comments. So much for getting "the rest" of the day off.

In her way, though, she thinks she's doing me a favor. It's the diva's way.

Macy's is only a block away, so we walk, which means Addie will fuss with her hair for fifteen minutes or so before we begin.

The Susanne Cosmetics counter isn't busy. Only one or two customers are looking at products. That will change after today. Tons of women will want the new Burgundy Orchid shade of Susanne lip plumper. I hope they have enough in stock to accommodate the thousands who will want their lips to look like they just finished a grape Popsicle.

"May I help you?" a salesperson asks us.

"I'm Addison Ames," Addie says. "We're here to do a selfie with the new lip plumper."

"I'm not aware of that."

"Call corporate. They'll confirm it. This is my assistant, Skye."

"Yes, nice to meet you. I'll have to verify all of this with the store."

"With all due respect"—Addie glances at the employee's name tag—"Blanche, we don't need permission from the store to take a selfie. This is a public place."

"Still, I—"

"She's right," I say. "We do this all the time."

Blanche sighs. "I don't want to get in any trouble."

"You won't. We brought our own plumper and everything." Addie gazes in one of the mirrors. "God, my hair is ghastly. Where's the restroom, Blanche?"

"The south corner."

"Thanks. I'll only be a minute, Skye."

I nod. Yeah. Make that fifteen minutes at least. I walk around the cosmetics counter to find the best area to shoot the photo. Then I pull out my phone to check comments on the pretzel post and maybe get through some email while I wait.

I pull up Instagram. Hmm, I have a notification. I click.

And my heart stampedes.

I have a new request to follow me.

@bradenblackinc

Chapter Twelve

My Instagram is private, which is why Braden has to make a request. I actually deleted quite a few requests earlier today from people I didn't recognize. They probably wanted to follow me only because I was tagged in Braden's oyster post the other night.

To accept or not to accept?

That is the question.

He literally kicked me out of his bedroom last night.

Okay, not literally. But I'm not that far off.

He said he got an important message on his phone he had to deal with—apparently billionaires have to deal with important stuff late at night—and went into his office, while I dressed as quickly as I could. I left the room to find Christopher already in the living area petting Sasha.

"Ready to go, Ms. Manning?"

I nodded and knelt down to give Sasha a scratch behind her ears. "Yeah. Thanks."

What transpired next was a repeat of the previous night. I followed Christopher into the elevator, and he pressed the button. The car was waiting in the garage level. Christopher opened the door for me, and I got in.

He drove me home.

All of this took place in a span of about a half hour.

It seemed like a year.

When I finally got home, I went to bed in my clothes without washing my face, something I never do, only to wake up this morning with racoon mascara eyes, a huge reminder of the previous evening.

And now Braden wants to follow me on Instagram.

Why? I rarely post. Instagram is my job, and I don't take my work home. I don't have much of a private life. This afternoon, Tessa posted us at lunch. That's her thing. Apparently she thinks her followers want to know everything she eats. Maybe they do. I have no idea. Taking a photo of a BLT with avocado isn't exactly art.

Of course, neither is a photo of Addie wearing lip plumper.

Addie returns, hair coiffed and purple lips freshly plumped, delaying my decision whether to accept Braden's request. Good. It's too much to ponder at the moment.

"Ugh," Addie whispers to me. "Is it just me, or is this shade horrendous?"

"Not just you," I whisper back. Then, in a normal voice, "I've scouted out the lighting in here. I think the selfie will look best at the other end of the counter. Plus, there's less in the background to detract from your image."

"Sounds good."

We set up the photo with Addie puckering her lips and holding the tube of plumper in one hand, her other arm outstretched in the "selfie" pose. I take several, choose the best, and do some quick edits. I hand the phone to her.

"Skye, there has to be a filter to make this shade look a little less...purple Kool-Aid."

"I figured we shouldn't use it. Fair advertising and all."

She hands the phone back to me. "Sorry. Use a filter. I can't be seen like this."

"But—"

"The filter, Skye. I'll deal with the fallout from Susanne, if there is any. My bet is there won't be. They'll be super psyched about the mega increase in sales."

"You're the boss." I make the necessary adjustments and hand the phone back to Addie.

"Looks great. Post it."

"What about copy?"

"Susanne didn't send any?"

I shake my head. "Nope."

She sighs. "God. You write something. I just can't find the words to say how much I love this awful shade." She pulls a tissue from the box sitting on the counter and wipes furiously at her lips.

"I'll come up with something." It won't be the first time I've had to get creative.

Absolutely in love with @susannecosmetics new Burgundy Orchid lip plumper! Grab yours before they sell out! #sponsored #bigkisses #kissme #lipgloss #lips #kiss

Not my best, but it'll do the job. I post the photo.

So luscious! Ordering mine now, @realaddisonames.

Gorgeous!

What a great color on you!

Their lip plumper is the best. Love this new shade!

I hold back an eye roll as I scan for anything negative. I delete a few questionable comments.

Then I look back at Braden's request to follow me.

What the heck? He won't find much on my Instagram.

I quickly hit Confirm.

Maybe he'll see I'm living my best life without him.

Although my last two pics were of the interesting way a shadow played across a city sidewalk and a lonely fire hydrant in the heat.

I need to up my Insta game.

Chapter Thirteen

Two vibrators, a dildo, and a set of Ben Wa balls sit on my bed—all products of my earlier attempts to achieve the elusive orgasm.

I dug them out of my drawer when I got home from work. Am I going to take Tessa's advice and try to re-create what Braden did to me?

Apparently I am.

I laugh aloud. I didn't achieve anything previously when I used these toys. What makes me think I can now?

Because now you know what you're after.

Maybe. Now that I've experienced a real climax and am familiar with the magnificence of it, I may be able to do it again.

I reached both orgasms while Braden was penetrating me, but that alone hadn't gotten me off. It was the clitoral stimulation paired with Braden's delicious cock. I eye the blue dildo. Yeah, it's pretty big, but not quite as big as Braden.

Next to the dildo sits a pink vibrator with a built-in clitoral stimulator. Problem is the dildo part of the vibrator isn't even close to Braden's size.

The other vibrator, in clear, is just a dildo with batteries, no clit stimulator.

Then the Ben Wa balls. They look like large silver marbles, and honestly, I'm not sure what they're supposed to do. I know they go in the vagina, but that's about it. I could call Tessa and ask…but no. Just no.

I toss the balls and the clear vibrator back in the drawer. My best chances are the plain dildo and the hot-pink vibrator with clit action.

I've done this before, and I always felt really weird. At least now I know what I'm supposed to be feeling.

I undress quickly and slide beneath my covers with the dildo and vibrator. I decide to go with the vibrator first, since it has the clitoral stimulator.

Problem number one—I'm not even slightly wet.

No hot kisses and finger fucking to get me in the mood. Even a little sexual banter over dinner would help. I was wet just sitting next to Braden in his car.

I need something to turn me on. Pay-per-view porn? It's worth a shot. I grab the remote from the nightstand and flip on the television, quickly finding a porn network. $15.99? To watch people fuck? I'm desperate, so I click Rent Now.

Problem number two—porn has never done much for me.

Still, I watch the fake boobs and monster dicks and try like hell to feel enough to get myself ready so the vibrator won't hurt going in.

Finally, I'm able to ease the vibrator into my pussy. I flip the switch at the end and…

Nothing.

Not that I expect it to be instantaneous, but at the moment I just feel tight and full.

I gaze at the TV, flicking my other hand over one breast

and giving the nipple a pinch. I feel a little, but not enough to get going.

Maybe the porn isn't a good idea. Maybe I need to close my eyes and remember my time with Braden.

Except that will make me sad.

I try anyway. I turn off the TV and the light, close my eyes, and cup my breasts, letting my fingers wander and tease my nipples. They harden under my touch. Nice. Finally, my pussy starts to respond. Just a tiny tickle, not the gushing madness that Braden caused, but I'll take what I can get.

Slowly I move the vibrating dildo in and out of my pussy. When that doesn't get me going, I hold it inside me, letting the little flagella on the clit stimulator do their job. All the while, I'm thinking of Braden's firm lips on mine, his long, thick fingers inside me.

I imagine him flipping me over and thrusting into me.

I turn onto my hands and knees and work my pussy and clit with the vibrator.

My skin warms, a nice flush. A beginning.

But that's all it is. A beginning.

Not even close to the middle, and what I'm really searching for is the end result.

The peak.

The pinnacle.

The roller coaster finally reaching its highest point and then plunging me down in a heady euphoria.

Shit.

I get up and clean the vibrator. Then I shove it and the dildo back in my drawer.

This was a gigantic waste of time.

I'll never climax again.

And the fact that I've now experienced it—with Braden Black, no less—makes the loss all the more profound.

• • •

The next few days of work fly by with few issues. Susanne Cosmetics calls on Friday to tell us how happy they are with the post and its result. Addie was right this time. They didn't care about the filter to make their purple plumper look a little more human. They're only interested in results. In fact, they have a new offer for their skin-tightening serum. Addie won't be happy about that.

A few followers complained that the color was different from Addie's "selfie." I privately messaged them to remind them about Susanne's money-back guarantee, and then I deleted the comments.

Easy enough week.

Except that four days ago, that fateful Tuesday evening, I drank Wild Turkey with Braden Black and ended up in his bed.

I shake my head to clear it. Best not to dwell on something I have no power over. But damn, I hate not having control.

I definitely have no control over Braden Black.

Addie exits her office. "I'm out of here, Skye. Have a great weekend."

"You too," I say. "I'll be in touch if anything comes up with the posts."

"Great," she says and swiftly leaves. The door swings shut behind her.

I power everything down for the weekend, reveling in my freedom. I still need to watch the current posts, but Addie doesn't have any shoots this weekend.

"I'm free as a bird," I say out loud, smiling.

"Good to know," a low voice says.

I jerk my gaze upward.

Braden is standing in the doorway.

My whole body tightens, as if someone wrapped me in clear cellophane. "How did you get in here?"

"Same way I get anywhere. I walked through the door."

"Sorry. Addie's already gone for the day."

"Why would you think I came to see Addie? You witnessed our last encounter."

I open my mouth, but nothing emerges. I shut it quickly. What am I supposed to say?

"I came to see *you*, Skye."

I cross my arms. "You could have called."

"Why? And miss that look of adorable perplexity on your pretty face? Besides, you never gave me your cell phone number."

"You know where I work."

"Maybe I didn't want to put you in the awkward position of taking a phone call at work."

"So you showed *up* at my work instead?"

"I figured it's nearly quitting time."

"What if Addie had been here?"

"Then Addie would have been here."

"But you… She…"

He takes a step toward me. "Do you really think I give a damn if Addison Ames crosses my path? She doesn't scare me, Skye. In fact, she's probably first on the list of everything that *doesn't* scare me."

"Oh?" I say. "What *does* scare you, Braden?"

He regards me, his eyes dark and dangerous. "Nothing."

Chapter Fourteen

I inhale, trying to ease my jittering nerves. Already my body reacts to his presence. I want to walk toward him, grab his strong hand, cup his stubbly cheek with the other.

Just touch him.

All I need is to touch him.

That small thing would satisfy me in this moment.

And that's *first* on the list of things that scares the hell out of me.

"Why are you here to see me, then? Can I help you with something?" My voice is so soft it's almost a whisper.

He closes the distance between us. "You can come back to my bed."

I move backward, stumbling slightly. Braden steadies me with his hand, and his touch burns through me like his hands are hot coals.

God, yes. Just a touch.

I knew it would be like this.

I ease away from him until the backs of my thighs hit my desk.

"You going to answer me?"

"With all due respect, you didn't exactly ask a question," I say, forcing myself not to stammer.

"True. You did. You asked if you could help me with anything, and I answered. Still, I think my response is worthy of a reply."

I inhale deeply, willing my pulse to chill. I'm not successful, but I can act as though I am. "You're not even offering me dinner this time?"

"We didn't exactly get to dinner the last time."

My cheeks are so warm, they must be crimson. I clear my throat. "A girl still has to eat."

"Then dinner it is. What's your pleasure?"

I stare at him. Really? He's going to buy me dinner so I'll sleep with him? Exactly what does that make me? I know the answer, and I don't like it.

"You told me I was something your money couldn't buy, but now you think dinner will buy me?"

He grabs both my shoulders. He gazes into my eyes, his own burning hot. "I haven't been able to stop thinking about you, Skye. I want you in my bed. What's it going to take?"

"I—I can't be bought." Though I'm thinking, at this moment, maybe I can be. And that scares the hell out of me.

"I'm not trying to buy you. I *am* trying to bed you."

I resist the urge to bite my lower lip. "You just want sex, then? Not a date?"

He gives a half-hearted shrug. "We can go out on dates if you want. If that's what it takes for you to feel comfortable coming back to my bed. But it will be simply dating. I can't give you any more than that."

"Why not?" I ask boldly, not at all sure that I'm ready for an answer.

"Because I can't."

I narrow my eyes. "Nice try. But I'm looking for a reason, Braden. I'm twenty-four years old. I'm young, and maybe a purely sexual relationship would be fun. A day will come, though, when it won't be enough for me."

"If that day isn't here yet, why not come back to my bed?"

"I have my reasons."

"Care to enlighten me?"

Because you fucked me and then kicked me out of your bed like the douchebag you are. The words catch in my throat. Why should it matter that he kicked me out? Maybe I'd do the same if we were at my place.

Except I wouldn't. That's not me. I'm not cruel.

I wet my lips. "I'm not interested in being your fuck buddy."

Not the real reason, and part of me—that aching part between my legs—is *very* interested in being his fuck buddy. Another part of me—that intelligent part between my ears—is decidedly *not* interested.

"What will it take to get you back into my bed, then? I told you we could date."

"Tell me why it can't lead anywhere."

He shrugs once more. "I can't give you a reason."

"You mean you won't."

"Stickler for semantics, are you?"

I nod.

"Then you're correct. I won't."

I've trapped myself now. I'm curious, but if he continues to refuse to give me his reason, I have to tell him no.

Huge problem with that: I don't want to tell him no. Or at least I don't want to tell his dick no. Not until he apologizes for being such a douche that first night.

My body is already throbbing in anticipation of being in Braden's bed again, under him, his beautiful body tantalizing mine and bringing me to the ultimate finish.

I can't say yes, though. I just can't. It's…*wrong*.

Even though it feels so right.

What to say, then?

"I… I'll…think about it."

He crushes me to his body, his erection apparent. He presses it into my belly. "This isn't a game, Skye."

"I never said it was."

"There's nothing to think about."

"There's a *lot* to think about. I'm not someone's toy, Braden. I have some self-respect, you know."

"Of course you do. Do you honestly think I'd want to bed a woman who has no self-respect?"

Okay. Didn't see that one coming. Certainly not after the way he invited me to leave his bed. I actually steady myself, as if he were trying to knock me over.

"Honestly," I say, "I don't know what to think."

"Think about this." He cups both my cheeks and smashes his lips to mine.

I open without thinking, letting my tongue wander out to meet his. The kiss drugs me. Every part of my body responds, and the blood in my veins turns to boiling lava.

I care about nothing but this kiss—this kiss and how it makes me feel.

Already I'm feeling more than I did in bed with toys and porn. All I need is Braden's touch, and I'm halfway to climax.

Am I willing to give this up when he so obviously wants me?

I can have him in bed. I can have orgasms galore.

The only price is…no future. No relationship.

I'm young. I have time. Kids? Yeah, I want kids, but I don't need them yet. Can't afford them yet anyway.

Self-respect?

Does going back to him after the way he unceremoniously kicked me out of bed last time negate my self-respect?

No. Not if it's my choice. At the moment, my mind is muddled. I can't think straight. All I want is Braden's hands on my body, his lips exploring mine, his cock inside me again, bringing me to the precipice…

I deepen the kiss, groaning into his mouth, pushing my breasts into his chest. My nipples are so hard I almost think he can feel them poking him. I rise on my toes and rub my clit against his bulge. I surrender to his kiss, to everything about him—

He pulls away, breaking the kiss with a loud *smack*.

I fall back against the desk, gripping the edge to keep from stumbling.

"I want you. You do something to me, something I don't quite understand but want to." His blue gaze sears into mine. "Don't think too long."

Then he walks out the door.

Chapter Fifteen

"A no-brainer," Tessa says on the phone as I'm waiting for my meal at the Wendy's drive-through.

Yeah, I'm having a single with cheese and fries, when I could be eating with Braden tonight and then fucking him again.

Only to be unceremoniously kicked out when we were done, no doubt.

"Not a no-brainer." I grab my credit card from the cashier, take the food, and set it carefully on the floor of my car. "He freaking kicked me out of his place last time."

"You're more upset because you weren't the one to make the decision."

"That's not true."

"That's totally true, Skye. With Braden Black, you're not in charge, and that irritates you."

Except that it doesn't.

It *should* irritate me. I can't help it that I like to be in command of every situation. *Almost* every situation, apparently. Braden Black's behavior doesn't irritate me. It drives me absolutely wild.

He hasn't left my thoughts since Tuesday night. Even though he was a douche for kicking me out of his place, he's been on my mind twenty-four-seven. I wake up at night sweating, knowing I was dreaming about him.

"Just go for it," Tessa continues. "Who cares how long it lasts or that it won't lead to anything? You'll get a couple months of hot sex."

And more orgasms.

"It might be too late," I say.

"He's letting you think about it."

"Yeah, but he could still change his mind."

"Then you blew it." Tess is nothing if not blunt.

"I might have." I sigh. "I'm home. I'm going to pour myself a glass of water, eat this gourmet burger and fries, and try not to think about the evening I could be having."

"He'll be back," she says. "See you tomorrow at yoga."

Tessa and I practice yoga together Saturday mornings at the gym. She's working toward her instructor's certificate, and I just try not to look too clumsy. My downward dog still sucks.

"Yeah, see you." I end the call, park my car, and head up to my tiny apartment, where I spend the evening alone.

Yoga class is especially difficult the next morning. Tessa, of course, breezes through, but I know I'll feel this workout tomorrow in my thighs and ass, which only reminds me of my last intense workout. With Braden.

"Coffee?" Tess says after we change back into our street clothes.

"Always."

We head to the Bean There Done That where I photographed Addison on Monday.

"Is the cinnamon mocha latte any good?" Tessa asks as we get in line.

"I have no idea. I haven't tried it."

"You didn't taste Addison's when you shot the photo?"

"She didn't offer me any."

"Why not? You told me she hates coffee."

I let out a soft huff. "That doesn't mean she offered it to me."

"Really? Self-centered diva." Tessa scoffs.

"Pretty much," I say. "She can be nice sometimes. I think she's been so privileged all her life that she doesn't think about others."

"Yeah. Like I said, self-centered diva."

I laugh. "Semantics. You're right."

"May I help you?" the barista asks once we get to the head of the line.

We order black coffee, though Tessa will add a little cream to hers. A rich coffee drink doesn't seem right after a workout.

"Hey," the barista says, "Skye, isn't it? You were in here with Addison Ames?"

"Yeah, nice to see you"—I eye her name tag—"Trish."

"I love Addison's posts. I went out and got that new lip plumper yesterday."

"Do you like the color?" I ask.

"I love anything Addison recommends!" Trish gushes and shoves our coffees across the counter. "On the house today. I'm so glad you came back in. Why isn't Addison with you?"

Because she hates coffee.

And it's the weekend.

And we're not besties.

"She's busy," I say cheerfully. "This is my friend Tessa."

"So nice to meet you," Trish gushes again. "Please tell Addison I bought the lip plumper."

"Absolutely," I say.

Tessa and I take our coffees to a vacant table in the corner.

"What are you up to tonight?" she asks.

"I have great plans," I say sarcastically.

"Yeah? Did *he* call you?"

I take a sip of coffee, nearly burning my tongue. "Braden? Are you kidding? My great plans are to curl up in bed with a good book. I got a new romance novel."

"Why read about sex when you could be doing it? Call him, Skye."

"What are *you* doing tonight?" I ask.

"Nice pivot. If you're not going to call Braden and have more mind-numbing sex, you and I are going out."

"Tess, you know I hate clubbing. It's loud and obnoxious. Everyone's drunk, and all the men are looking for sex."

She takes a sip of her coffee, swallows, and then smiles. "Exactly."

Chapter Sixteen

Tessa and I make plans to meet for an early dinner and then go to Icon in the theatre district. While I'm getting dressed, my phone buzzes. Addison. Always great with the timing. What does she need from me on a Saturday night?

"Hey, Addie," I say into the phone, sounding a lot nicer than I feel at the moment.

"Skye, I need a huge favor."

Of course she does. "What do you need?"

"I'm supposed to go to this charity event tonight for Mothers Driving Drunk or something."

"You mean Mothers *Against* Drunk Driving?"

"Yeah, that's it. It's at the hotel, but I can't make it, so I need you to go, take a photo, and post it."

I consider asking why she can't make it but change my mind. She probably got a zit or something and can't be seen in public. "Tessa and I have plans."

"Don't worry. Take her with. I have two tickets. I'll email them to you now."

"Wait, wait, wait. How am I supposed to take a selfie of

you if you're not there?"

"Use your imagination. You weren't going to be there anyway, so I wouldn't be doing a selfie. Take a photo of the silent auction items or something and say how much I adore this charity. Whatever. This is what I pay you for, Skye. Besides, it's black-tie, a gourmet dinner, and open bar. You'll have a great time."

Except I have nothing to wear. "Addie, I—"

"Thanks. You're the best."

All right, then. I quickly call Tessa, who's thrilled, of course. She has clothes for every occasion.

"I'll bring you a hot little black number that will look great on you," she says. "Do you have some black strappy sandals?"

"I have silver strappy sandals."

"Perfect. You'll need a silver or white-gold necklace and earrings, then."

"Okay. I've got that covered."

"Awesome. See you soon."

Tessa wasn't kidding. The dress *is* a hot little black number, emphasis on the little. It hugs me tight, showing curves I never knew I had. Admittedly, though, it looks great paired with the silver shoes and accessories. She even brought me a silver evening bag to borrow.

I allow myself one Wild Turkey before dinner and drink it while I scout the silent auction items and photograph several. I post the Paris trip to Addie's account, gushing about how much she loves French food and culture and really wants to win this awesome package. I tag her family's hotel and throw in *#helpingothers #paris #MADD #silentauction*. Done.

She texts me a thumbs-up soon after, so my work here is done. Time to go.

"Are you kidding?" Tessa says. "We can't leave now."

"I thought you wanted to go clubbing." Not that clubbing is my scene, either, but I feel like a fish out of water here.

"It's free dinner, first of all," she says. "And free drinks. Plus, the dance floor is already set up. We can do our clubbing right here tonight. I already see several young men I'd like to get to know better."

None of the young men are Braden, so I don't share her enthusiasm. But I relent. She's right. Why not take advantage of our bounty? We find Addison's table and take our seats, politely exchanging hellos with our tablemates, who are all much older than we are. Since we have nothing in common with them, we talk mostly to each other during our dinner of roast duck breast with cherry and walnut sauce, potato puree, and green beans with *fines herbes*. I forego wine with dinner. Tessa wants to stay for dancing. I'm saving my Wild Turkeys to get me through that fiasco.

After dessert—chocolate mousse cake—is served and the auction winners are announced, the lights dim, a disco ball descends, and neon illuminates the dance floor. A live band takes the stage.

"Selfie!" Tessa yells.

The new lighting makes our complexions glow. I'm not a huge fan of the night life, but this is a nice little perk. Everyone looks gorgeous now. I pull out my phone and take a quick photo of us.

I smile. We do look hot. I post to Instagram, tagging Tessa and our location. My few followers may as well think I have a life. It's all a mirage, but they don't need to know that.

We amble to the bar and order drinks. I'm not driving, so I allow myself two more for the evening. I order another

Wild Turkey while Tessa, lover of all froufrou drinks, chooses a banana daiquiri.

We turn away from the bar to face the dance floor.

"Now what?" I say.

"We drink, of course. Maybe do some dancing. Lighten up, Skye. It's not like this is your first time at a club."

"We're not at a club," I remind her. "We're at the Ames Hotel for a charity event. A black-tie charity event."

Tessa shakes her head. "Semantics, dahling." She looks gorgeous, her black hair and tan skin perfect with the red dress she's wearing. Her mother is Mexican, and the band is playing a lot of Latin music, which Tessa loves.

Someone else notices her already. A handsome dark-haired man approaches us, zeroing in on her.

"Care to dance?" he asks.

"Sure." Her face lights up into a dazzling smile. "Watch my drink, Skye."

I nod.

This is my usual job at clubs and, apparently, charity events—watching Tessa's drink while she dances the night away. I can't leave the table or someone might take her drink. Fun time. I sip my bourbon, take out my phone again, and delete several questionable comments from Addie's post. Then I look at my own post. I look good tonight. My hair is curled and falls around my shoulders in loose waves. Tessa's black dress hugs my body, showing off my boobs. My brown eyes seem to sparkle in this fabulous lighting. I'm not gorgeous in the same way Tessa is, but I'm pretty, and I have a damned good body. As usual, Tessa's getting more attention. She always does, and I'm happy for her, but why aren't men flocking to me, too? Probably because, as Tessa's told me many times, my attitude is akin to having "I'm the boss" tattooed on my forehead.

While I'm staring at the post, I get a like from Tessa's sister, Eva. One so far. If I were Addison, I'd have about a thousand by now.

I put the phone away and take another sip of my drink. To my astonishment, it's gone. I need to pace myself a little better. I take a quick sip of Tessa's daiquiri. Ugh! Way too sweet. I turn toward the bar and motion to the bartender. "Another Wild Turkey, please."

I'll drink it slowly. Very slowly. But I need to have something to do. I can't just stand here staring blankly at the dance floor. I have to do something with my hands. Hence, the drink.

He delivers the drink, and I take a sip. Then another.

Tessa finally returns, wiping her brow. "Garrett can really move!" She picks up her daiquiri and downs quite a bit of it. It's probably mostly sugar and juice anyway.

"Ready to go?" I say.

She laughs. "Good one, Skye."

Yeah, I'm not kidding.

"Finish your drink," she says. "We need to get out there. This music is great."

"But I—"

"No excuses, babe. Just down it."

I down it like a shot. Not my usual MO, but I can handle two drinks after a big dinner. No big deal. We head to the dance floor. I'm not the world's best dancer, but I can hold my own. I'm feeling pretty confident at the moment, having two Wild Turkeys under my belt.

Garrett and a friend join us, and we dance as a foursome through the next four numbers.

"Sorry, I need a break," I say.

"Need a drink?" Garrett's friend asks.

Before I can tell him no, he grabs my hand and leads me

to the bar.

"I need a Guinness Draft and…" He lifts his eyebrows at me.

"Wild Turkey, right?" the bartender says.

"I don't—"

"Right," the friend says, throwing some bills in the tip jar.

So I'm on my third drink after dinner. Not a big deal. "What's your name?" I ask my companion.

"What?"

Exactly why I don't like the night life. The band is loud, and I can't hear myself think. "What's your name?" I ask again, louder.

"Peter. You?"

"Skye."

"Nice to meet you." He hands me my drink.

Peter is brown-haired with hazel eyes. He's very handsome in an almost pretty way, muscled, but a slighter build than Braden.

And why am I thinking about Braden? I have a good-looking guy who seems nice right in front of me, and he just got me a drink.

Screw Braden. I take a sip of my third Wild Turkey, still determined to go slowly.

"What do you do, Peter?"

"What?"

This is getting old. "What do you do?" Louder.

"I'm an architect. I work for my father, also an architect. You?"

"I work for Addison Ames."

"The heiress?"

"Yeah. I'm her personal assistant, but I'm really a photographer at heart. That's what I want to do full-time eventually."

"What?"

I repeat myself. Loudly.

"Cool," he says.

Okay, we've effectively run out of things to talk about.

"You want to dance again?" I ask.

"Sure." He grabs my hand and then appears to change his mind. "I'm sweating. You want to get some fresh air first?"

I'm about to respond when someone else answers.

"No, she does *not*."

Chapter Seventeen

Braden fucking Black.

He's here. At this event. Wearing a black tux and looking like he stepped right off the runway and into *GQ*.

All the other men here are wearing tuxedos, but I feel like I never saw a tux in my life until this moment.

Braden Black in a tux is something to behold. Something unique and one of a kind, like the *Mona Lisa* or Beethoven's Fifth Symphony.

"What are you doing here?" I demand.

"Keeping you from getting yourself into trouble."

I want to be angry with him. I am, in fact. Except all I can think of is how amazing he looks standing next to Peter. Peter's a nice-looking guy, but no contest.

Peter goes rigid next to me. Is that a spark of recognition in his eye? "Nice meeting you, Skye," he says, turning.

"Wait! Aren't we going to dance?"

"Another time." He disappears onto the dance floor.

"Come with me." Braden pulls me out of the ballroom, through the hallway, to the hotel lobby. My heels clack on the marble floor as I run to keep up with his long strides.

"What are you doing?"

"Keeping you from sneaking into someone else's bed."

"Seriously?" I huff.

"You've been drinking."

"You don't know anything about me. I'm not drunk. I never get drunk. And I can sleep with whomever I want. How did you find me anyway?"

He pulls his phone out of his pocket. "Instagram."

Right. My selfie with Tessa, and Braden now is following me because I confirmed his request.

"I'm going back in," I say.

"Not without me."

"Do you even have a ticket to this event?"

"Do you think I need a ticket?"

I shake my head. Pointless question. He probably made a six-figure donation at the door. "Fine, come along, then. I can't leave Tessa in there alone."

"Tessa's a big girl. She can take care of herself."

"Interesting take. Tessa's my age, Braden, and you obviously don't think *I* can take care of myself."

"Not true. I didn't show up because you can't take care of yourself. I showed up to keep you out of someone else's bed."

I shake my head, even though my body responds to his attempt to control me. "You're unbelievable. What makes you think I'd end up in someone's bed?"

"Look at you. You're beautiful with a killer body. Damn, that dress…"

I tap my foot and scoff. "Please…"

"Do you really not see yourself the way I see you?" He cups my cheek. "Your hair is the color of roasted chestnuts, your eyes the warmest brown I've ever seen. Your skin is like the richest cream, and God, Skye, your mouth…" He inhales.

"Your lips are pink and plump and heart-shaped, and fuck, I can't leave them alone. I've never seen a mouth like yours. The way your lips are always slightly parted drives me wild."

His description catches me off guard. Does he truly see me like that? I'm attractive, yes, but he makes me sound like something truly special. Electricity darts between my legs. I want to melt into him, but I hold my ground.

"You're acting like I was in there gyrating for ten-dollar bills in my panties. It's a hotel charity event for MADD, Braden, not a strip club."

"That dress—"

"Isn't even mine. It's my friend's."

"It can't look anywhere near as good on her as it does on you." His voice cracks a little.

Wow. Braden's voice cracks. Actually cracks. What can he be thinking? Maybe that he shouldn't have kicked me out of his bed? That's what he *should* be thinking.

I swallow. "I need to go back in."

"Why? Dancing? You want to go dancing? *I'll* take you dancing. Be sure to wear that amazing dress."

"I told you, it's not—"

"Your dress," he finishes for me. "It should be. It was made for you."

My nipples tighten and push against my bra while heat pulses through me. I want to be angry at Braden. Really.

"What are you doing here anyway?" he asks.

"Addie gave me the tickets."

"Of course," he says. "Addie. I should have seen her fingerprints all over this."

"So what? I got the tickets, and I wanted to go out with my friend."

"Like I said, I'll take you dancing."

"I don't want to go dancing," I say.

"What do you want, then?"

To go to your place. Back to your bed. Back to the most heavenly experience of my life.

Control.

"I want to go back inside. My friend will be worried."

"If I take you back inside, the men will be all over you."

"Braden, one guy was paying attention to me. *One*. And you scared him off."

"He's not good enough for you."

"You don't even know him."

"Neither do you."

"Of course I do. He's an architect." My knowledge ends there, but Braden doesn't need to know that.

"You're wrong, Skye. I *do* know him. That's Peter Reardon, and his father is Beau Reardon of Reardon Brothers Architecture. His friend is Garrett Ramirez, also an architect with the company. Beau is trying to get the contract on my new building."

I wrench my arm out of his grasp—it takes all my mental strength because I really want him touching me. "What are you saying? That the two of them are paying attention to us because of *you*?"

"I'm not saying that at all."

"Sounds like it from where I'm standing."

"Not at all. They didn't know you were with me before—but now they do. They're playboys. I guarantee you they both have two things on their minds tonight. That contract—which probably means a huge bonus from Daddy—and getting laid. I'll let you guess which one is foremost in their minds on a Saturday night."

"Interesting. What do you have on *your* mind tonight, Braden?"

His lips turn slightly upward, but his gaze remains shadowy.

"Not a contract."

I stifle a tremble. I'm wet. So wet. I can feel it almost pooling in my panties. But I hold my ground. "I'm going back in."

"Fine. I'm going with you."

"Suit yourself."

Braden follows me back to the ballroom. I strut in and head for our table.

Tessa runs toward me, nearly knocking over a server and her tray full of drinks. "Skye, are you all right? Peter said—" Her eyes morph to circles when she realizes who's standing behind me. "It *is* you."

I clear my throat. "I'm fine."

Tessa regains her composure and lifts her lips in a dazzling smile. "Aren't you going to introduce me?"

Braden holds out his hand. "Braden Black."

"Braden, this is Tessa Logan, my best friend."

"It's an honor, Mr. Black." Tessa flutters her ridiculously long eyelashes as she shakes his hand.

Tessa's a huge flirt. She'll never go after a guy I'm interested in, but her flirting has a mind of its own. She can't turn it off.

"Call me Braden. Any friend of Skye's." He turns to me as if he's not at all affected by Tessa's beauty or by the beauty of all the other women at the event. "Drink?"

"I've had enough, thanks."

"You?" He nods to Tessa.

"I'd love another banana daiquiri," she says coyly.

"Done. I'll be back." He heads to the bar.

"Okay, let me have it," I say to Tessa.

"Have what?"

"The grand inquisition."

"What's wrong with you? He's fabulous. He's even better-looking in person than in professional photos. You're one lucky woman, Skye."

"I can't believe he showed up here."

"Maybe he's just late," she says.

I shake my head. "He saw my Instagram post."

Her eyes widen back into circles. "No way. He saw that post and came here because *you're* here? That's great!"

"Is it? It's not a little… I don't know. Creepy? Like in a stalkerish way?"

She laughs. "He can stalk me anytime."

"For God's sake, I'm serious, Tess."

"So am I. Until he boils a rabbit in your kitchen, I say go for it."

"You're disgusting."

"You know I'm kidding. Besides, he doesn't strike me as the stalker type. Plus, the tabloids follow his every move. If he had stalker tendencies, we'd know by now."

Braden pushes through the crowd carrying three drinks and not spilling a drop.

"One banana daiquiri." He hands the canary-yellow drink to Tessa.

"Thanks so much." A grin splits her face.

"I took the liberty of getting you Wild Turkey in case you changed your mind." He hands me a glass.

"I didn't."

"Great. Then two for me. Follow me. I've got a much better table."

"I'm sure being Braden Black has its perks," I say dryly.

Braden lowers his head and softly blows my hair out of the way, his hot breath making me shiver. "Being *with* Braden Black also has its perks."

Chapter Eighteen

Tessa takes a long sip of her banana daquiri and then heads back to the dance floor, much to my chagrin. I both do and don't want to be alone with Braden. This *Push Me Pull You* game is getting exhausting.

Braden takes a drink and then slides his tongue across his bottom lip. Does he have any idea how sexy that is? How much it makes me want him?

"Did you notice how Peter Reardon made a quick getaway when I showed up?"

"Yeah. I'd have to be blind to have missed it."

"You said I thought he was hanging around you because of me," Braden said, "but that's not what I thought, and that's not why."

"Oh?"

"He was pursuing you because you're sexy as hell, Skye."

I gulped, warming.

"He made a quick getaway because when he saw me stake my claim—"

I cross my legs slowly. "Excuse me? Stake your claim?"

"You think that was a bad choice of words?"

"I do. I'm not something you can plant your flag on. I'm a person, Braden."

"A very intriguing person," he says. "At any rate, when he saw that I was interested—are those words better?"

I nod.

"He put the contract ahead of bedding you. Which is fine by me."

It's fine by me as well, but I'm not about to admit that to Braden. I have no interest in Peter Reardon. He seems nice enough and he's attractive, but only one man holds my interest at the moment—the man sitting next to me.

"I see," I say, trying to sound nonchalant.

"Sure you don't want a drink?" He nods to the second Wild Turkey sitting on the table.

"I'm good. Thanks." Though another drink would relax me. I long for relaxation, but I long just as much for control.

Control wins.

This time.

Tessa comes back to the table and sits down. Though she still looks great, perspiration is emerging at her brow line. "This band is fantastic, but I need a break. Care to accompany me to the little girls' room, Skye?"

"Yeah. Sure." I stand and grab the silver clutch. "Excuse me for a minute," I say to Braden.

"I'll be here." His lips quiver slightly, as if he wants to smile but is holding back. I'm not sure what that means. I'm not sure about anything pertaining to Braden Black, most of all my ambivalent feelings.

Several guests clamor up to him as Tessa and I turn to leave the ballroom. Everyone wants to shake his hand, it seems.

When we get to the restroom, Tessa grabs a few paper

towels and blots her forehead. Then she freshens her makeup. "How are things going?" she asks.

"I have no idea."

"He's obviously into you."

"I suppose."

"You suppose?" She laughs. "You are something, Skye."

I rub soap on my hands and stick them under the faucet. The warm water coats them. "What does it all mean, though? For some reason, something about me appeals to him and he wants to have sex with me." I reach past Tessa for a paper towel.

"And that's a problem because…?" She throws her lipstick into her purse.

"He kicked me out of his place, Tess. He left to take a call, and then his driver took me home. It was humiliating." I gaze at my reflection. My Susanne lip stain is holding up nicely.

"So tell him not to do that to you again."

I raise my eyebrows. Is it really that simple?

"Have some fun, Skye. If this is just sex, accept that. Enjoy it until it's over. You're young. There's plenty of time to find the love of your life. It doesn't have to be Braden Black."

But I want it to be.

The thought spears into my head on its own, jerking me by surprise. I erase it quickly. "No, it doesn't have to be him," I say.

"If he wants you back in his bed, establish some rules. No more kicking you out."

"What if he says no?"

"What if he says yes?"

"What if he says something else?"

"What else is there to say? Either yes or no." Classic Tessa. Always looking at things in a binary way. Everything is black or white, no middle ground.

"You're saying I need to establish some rules?"

"Yeah, why not? You love rules, Skye."

"I don't love rules."

She bursts into laughter. "You have rules for everything. You know what I think of your drinking rules."

"Hey, my drinking rules keep me from getting completely inebriated and doing something dangerous."

"There you go. So establish rules with Braden. Tell him if he wants you, he can't kick you out and refuse to talk to you after sex. Seems reasonable to me."

Seems more than reasonable to me as well. But will it be reasonable to Braden?

So much I don't know about this man who rocked my world. Who *continues* to rock my world. My body isn't my own when I'm around him. It responds to him in a way I've never experienced. I can act nonchalant, keep my voice dry and noncommittal, but none of that negates the physical response I have to Braden whenever he's near.

Even when he's not near. Just thinking about him here in the women's restroom has my pussy tingling and aching.

I really want another orgasm.

I really want hundreds of them.

Tessa fusses with her hair a bit and then turns to me. "Ready?"

I haven't touched myself up at all. "In a minute." I quickly powder my nose and dot on some clear lip gloss. "Okay."

As we reenter the ballroom, an attractive black-haired man asks Tessa to dance. She presses her evening bag into my hand and heads to the dance floor.

I head back to Braden's table.

And gasp.

A beautiful blonde is sitting next to him.

Chapter Nineteen

I paste on a smile. "I'm back."

God, I sound so saccharine.

Braden stands. "Skye, meet Laurie Simms."

I hold out my hand, willing it not to shake, and glue on the smile once more. "Skye Manning."

She takes my hand and gives it a strong shake. "Braden was just telling me about you. You work for Addison Ames?"

"I do."

"She's a doll. Please have a seat."

Except she's sitting in the seat I vacated only minutes ago. Braden holds out the chair on his other side. I suppose I can't expect him to be rude and make the other woman move, though I secretly wish he would. Who is Laurie Simms anyway?

I sit. The extra bourbon is within reach.

Yeah, I take it. This seems like a four-drink kind of night.

"Addie and I go way back," Laurie says. "I used to work for her father."

"Oh?" I say. "What do you do?"

"I'm an attorney." She slides a card over to me.

Nice promo. Slick. Though I have no need of an attorney, and I'm sure I can't afford her anyway.

"I interned with Brock Ames when I was in law school. He got me set up with my current firm."

I didn't recall asking, but good to know.

"So how do you two know each other?" I ask sweetly.

"We don't, actually," Braden says.

"Oh?"

"Shameless self-promotion." Laurie smiles. "Of course I recognized Braden and had to come introduce myself."

"As I said, Ms. Simms, I'm happy with my current representation."

She stands. "Can't blame a girl for trying. Nice to meet you, Skye."

"You too." I smile again. This time it's genuine.

Laurie is blond and beautiful and also very nice. I berate myself for questioning her motives. She's not after Braden. She's after his business.

"Thanks," Braden says.

"For what?"

"For getting back here. Seemed like you were gone forever. When I'm alone, people pounce. Laurie is the umpteenth person who came up to me while you were gone."

"Were the others beautiful females as well?"

He smiles. "Does it matter?"

How am I supposed to answer that? *Yes, it matters, because I'm experiencing petty jealousy that nauseates me.* Or *no, it doesn't matter*, which is a big damned lie.

"I suppose not." Back to trying to sound nonchalant.

"One was Peter Reardon. Apparently he was waiting outside the ballroom, and when he saw you and Tessa leave, he came back in and sought me out. He apologized for dancing with you."

"Oh, for God's sake. That's ridiculous. He had a perfect right to dance with me. I enjoyed his company."

"I'm sure he enjoyed yours as well. He just didn't know you were with me."

"I *wasn't* with you."

"You are now, and I aim to keep it that way."

His words both anger me and make me hot.

"Have you thought any more about coming back to my bed?" he asks.

Those words just make me hot.

"I don't want to talk about that here," I say.

"Why?"

"Why? Because we're nearly screaming at each other to be heard above the band."

"Let's go out to the lobby, then."

"I can't. I have to watch Tessa's bag."

"Tessa's bag will be fine. If it's not, I'll replace everything in it." He stands. "Come on."

"She'd never forgive—"

"For God's sake." He reaches for my hand and tugs me along behind him.

We walk along the outer edge of the ballroom to the entrance and then through the hallway into the lobby.

"Why did you come here, Braden?"

"I already told you. To keep you from getting into someone else's bed."

I tilt my chin upward. "Why is that any of your concern?"

"Because I want you in *my* bed, Skye. Haven't I made that clear? And I'm not very good at sharing."

"What about what *I* want? Has that occurred to you?"

"You seemed to have a good time in bed with me."

Oh, yes, I did. The problem occurred when it was over.

"You're not denying it," he says.

"No, I'm not. The actual act itself was...acceptable."

He lets out a boisterous laugh—the first time I've truly heard him laugh—and I mean really lets it out. His whole face lights up, and God, he's handsome.

He finally curbs his laughter. "Acceptable? You're something else, Skye."

I cross my arms, trying not to frown. "Making fun of me again?"

"No, I'm not, actually. You are a challenge, Skye Manning, and I never back down from a challenge."

Okay. Not sure what to say to that, so I say nothing. Just stand my ground, hoping I can keep up this charade of being in control.

Because I'm *not* in control. Braden strips me of it.

"The act itself was acceptable," he says. "Are you saying something else about our time together *wasn't* acceptable?"

"Yes, that's exactly what I'm saying."

He smiles. "Don't leave me in suspense."

Now or never, Skye. Time to fess up. I want this man. I want to go back to his bed, but not if kicking me out afterward is his habit.

I clear my throat. "Fine. I didn't like how it ended."

"I seem to recall it ended with both of us climaxing. What was wrong with that?"

"That's part of the act. The act was acceptable, as I've told you. I'm talking about after the act."

"I believe you left."

"That's not how I'd phrase it. You didn't say a word to me other than to tell me Christopher would take me home. You left me alone to get dressed— "

"Did you want help dressing?"

I uncross my arms and extend my fingers, trying to ease the tension that's overtaking me. "Would you let me finish?

God." I pull my hair off my neck. It's so hot in this lobby. Except the temperature in the lobby is fine—it's Braden who's supplying the heat.

"Fine. Go ahead."

"You kicked me out, Braden. It was…"

"It was what?"

"Humiliating, all right? It was fucking humiliating. I felt… disposable."

"I don't regulate how you feel, Skye. *You* do."

I shake my head, anger rising in my gut. That's the whole problem. I *don't* have any power with Braden.

And I don't like it at all.

Except that I do. And I really hate that I do.

I glare at him.

"I don't consider you disposable, so why do *you*?"

I curl my hands into fists. Seriously, fists. I really want to punch his superior nose. Another way I'm not in control. So much for releasing the tension.

"I *don't* consider myself disposable, which is why, Braden, if you want me in your bed so badly, you can't treat me as if I am. You can't just kick me out when you're done."

"We were both done."

"Maybe *you* were," I say. "Personally, I had several more orgasms left in me."

What a fucking lie. The only two orgasms I've ever had took place that night, but he doesn't know that, and I'm not about to clue him in.

He seems to struggle with what to say next before finally running a hand through his hair, mussing it up and looking extremely sexy. "I don't normally let anyone spend the night at my place."

Why? What made you this way? Will I ever be able to get close to you other than sexually?

The words hover on my tongue, but I can't ask the questions. Instead, "Then don't. I won't go back to bed with you if you're going to make me leave afterward. Simple as that."

He sighs, rubbing his forehead as if in resignation. "Fine. If that's what it takes to get you back in my bed, you can stay until morning. Does that suffice?"

No. It doesn't suffice. I don't even know what would suffice. "I don't have to stay. I just would like the option."

He cocks his head, pausing a few seconds before responding. "I'm beginning to see what you really want," he says. "It's not so much that you want to stay, it's that you want to be the one to decide, isn't it?"

How do he and Tessa seem to know me better than I know myself?

As much as I want him—even standing here in a hotel lobby with guests bustling around late in the evening—I can't agree to what he's asking, even if he lets me spend the night. I don't want to be his fuck buddy.

I want more than that.

"I can't go back to your bed, Braden."

"You can."

"No, I can't. It just doesn't feel…"

Braden moves his warm body into my space. "You want to say it doesn't feel *right*, Skye. But you're not that good an actress. It's a lie, and you know it."

He's right. Even though I want more than he's willing to give me, everything about being with him feels *right*.

My knees turn to jelly as heat surges through my body like fiery pinballs ricocheting everywhere at once and then landing right between my thighs. He's close to me, so close I could lean into him and easily regain my balance.

"Come home with me," he whispers, "and you can leave whenever you want."

Chapter Twenty

"I... I have to tell Tessa."

He takes my hand and leads me back to the ballroom. Tessa is sitting at our table when we get there.

"What have you two been up to?" she asks. "We just—"

"We're leaving," Braden says. "Can I give you a lift home?"

"I think I'll stay, actually. Garrett and I are hitting it off. Peter's a mess, though."

"What's wrong?"

"He's terrified of *you*," she says to Braden, smiling. "Though you don't seem all that scary to me."

There she goes flirting again. Braden *is* pretty scary, though not in the way Tessa means.

"He just wants a contract with my company," he says, "and he thinks I won't give it to him because he was dancing with Skye."

"Oh. Is that true?"

"No. I'm not giving it to him anyway. The decision has already been made."

"Does he know?" she asks.

"He will." Braden turns to me. "Ready?"

"Yeah, sure. See you, Tess."

"I'll call you tomorrow," she says.

Within a few minutes, I'm sitting in the back of Braden's car again with Christopher at the wheel. I inhale. Braden's ridiculously masculine scent is now my favorite cologne in the world. I yawn inadvertently.

"Tired?" he asks.

"No, I'm okay." Though I am a little tired, probably from the Wild Turkey. Not drunk but sleepy.

"Good. You need to be awake for what I have in mind tonight."

I suppress a quiver. I'm already wet. So ready.

We're quiet the remainder of the trip. Braden leaves me alone…until we get safely to his place.

We're not even through the door when—

"Fuck," he growls and pins me against the wall beside the entryway, the door still hanging open. "I've wanted to kiss you all night. That sexy mouth of yours…and this dress. I ought to rip it off you so no other man can see you in it."

I tremble. "It's Tessa's."

"Don't care. I'll buy her a new one."

"But I like—"

"Still don't care." He crushes his mouth to mine, grabs one of the straps of my dress, and pulls sharply as he thrusts his tongue between my lips.

The low screech of the ripping fabric. *No, not Tessa's dress!*

But that's the last thought of Tessa's dress. That's the last thought for a while as pure emotion bubbles through me, taking away all logic and rationale. All I want is this kiss, this raw meeting of our mouths, our lips, our tongues.

I melt into the kiss as he deepens it. Braden's kisses are not average kisses. Nothing about Braden is average. His sheer will and ambition take over with everything he does, including kissing and fucking.

I can't wait to get to the fucking again.

For now, though, I surrender to his lips, teeth, and tongue, let my hunger take over as our mouths slide together in a haunting rhythm that matches the cadence of my rapidly beating heart. His mouth is rough and merciless, and as he devours me, he rips the other strap and pushes it over my shoulder. My dress is banded around my waist, my strapless black bra in full view.

He slides his hands up my sides and cups my breasts, and then he pulls back, our mouths parting with a *pop*.

He gazes at me, focusing on my lips. "I wish you could see your mouth right now, Skye. Your lipstick is smeared, and your lips are swollen and glistening and parted in that slight way that's all you." He drops his gaze. "And these tits. Spectacular."

I'm panting at his words, my panties melting from the heat. "Bra," I say.

"Yeah, fucking sexy. Made for your tits."

"Bra. Don't rip it." The bra is mine, and it wasn't cheap. Finding a strapless bra to adequately support my Cs wasn't easy.

But please rip it.

He follows my thought instead of my spoken plea and rips it off me anyway, freeing my breasts. "I'll buy you a hundred bras, Skye. A new one for every time I fuck you, just so I can rip it off."

My nipples are tight and hard, so ready for his touch. But he doesn't touch them. Can't he see them reaching for him? Instead, he's still cupping the rosy flesh of my breasts, still gazing at them.

"Please," I say when I can no longer take the ache.

"Please what?"

"My nipples. Touch them."

His lips turn up into a surly smile. "You want me to touch your nipples, Skye?"

"Yes, God. Please."

He brushes his lips against the top of my throat. "How do you want me to touch them, baby?"

"I don't care. Just touch them. Please."

"What if I don't? What will you do?"

What? What *can* I do? Nothing. I can do nothing if he doesn't touch my nipples. What kind of mind game is he playing with me? Perhaps he's simply teasing me, and I'm so not in the mood for teasing. I meet his fiery blue gaze. "I… I'll leave."

He moves backward, releasing my breasts. "Go ahead. You're not obligated to stay here."

Seriously? He gets me all hot and bothered and then wants me to leave? I'm ready to call him out on this little mind fuck until I drop my gaze to his crotch. His tux trousers are tented. Big-time.

He doesn't want me to leave.

Two can play this game.

I clear my throat. "Fine. But I'll need a…shirt or something." An overcoat would be better.

He shoots darts at me with his eyes.

Do I repeat myself? He knows I can't leave here without something covering the top of me, and my bra and dress are in tatters. I open my mouth to speak, but he pushes me back against the wall, his hands gripping my shoulders. He moves toward me slowly until our lips are only millimeters apart. He's playing again. I know because his lips are trembling. He's using all his will to keep from kissing me. I'm not completely sure, but that's my take.

I close the distance and press my lips to his.

He pulls back, still gripping my shoulders. "I thought you wanted to leave."

"I thought you *wanted* me to leave."

"When did I say that?" he queries. "You're the one who brought it up. What kind of a game do you think I'm playing, Skye?"

"I…don't know."

"That's because I'm not playing a game. You may think this is a cat-and-mouse thing, but it's not. I enjoy making you want me."

"Braden, you know I want you, but if you ever tell me to leave again, this whole thing is over."

"Is it?"

I gulp. How much will I give up to remain in charge? How fucking much?

"I'm afraid so."

His bulge is still apparent. He won't let me go. He won't.

He releases me, walks through the entryway to a large door, and opens it. He pulls something out and walks back, handing it to me. It's a blue cardigan.

"Go ahead, Skye. Leave."

Chapter Twenty-One

If you ever tell me to leave again, this whole thing is over.

Leave.

This is a strange and frightening game I've walked into. I don't want to leave, but that's not the most frightening part.

The truth is that I *can't* leave. Can't force my arm to extend and take the sweater. Can't force my feet to move the few feet to the door.

I can't.

Braden's power over me is that strong, that omnipotent.

And that's the most dangerous part of this.

But I said it would be over if he told me to leave. I fucking said it, and if I don't do it, I'm nothing but a weak-willed mouse.

Think, Skye, think. How do you get out of this?

I wait. I wait for him to tell me again to take the sweater and leave. He doesn't. He simply stands three feet away from me, the sweater dangling from his hand.

Stalemate.

I have two choices. I can take the sweater and leave, or

I can stay, effectively giving up control over this situation.

My body wants one and my mind wants the other.

Frankly, my body's argument is a lot stronger.

I open my mouth to say I'm staying when Braden finally closes the distance between us, dropping the sweater and again gripping my shoulders. He's not hurting me, but his grasp is firm and I can tell he means business.

"No more games, Skye," he whispers darkly. "Give in to me tonight, and I promise you more pleasure than you've ever known."

His words enter my mind slowly in a deep drawl. Again and again they weave into me, searing my brain with their power. My body is hot and bothered, thighs quivering, pussy pulsing.

Give up control. Give up control.

"No more games," I whisper.

He kisses me. Hard.

Harder and deeper than ever. His own ache and hunger feed into me, and something in me blossoms. He breaks the kiss and then scrapes his teeth over my jawline and down my bare shoulder. My nipples are still hard and wanting, and this time he takes one between his lips and gently kisses it. Just that tiny contact sends me reeling.

He strengthens his hold on me, which is good, because my legs have turned to mush. My whole body aches with the throbbing in my clit. The soft friction and wet slide of his tongue around my nipple sends electricity shooting to my core. He's being too gentle. He's teasing me, driving me wild with desire.

So much for his "no more games."

Or maybe this isn't a game. Maybe it's part of his plan—his plan to give me pleasure I've never known.

I have some sexual experience. I've been with three

different men, one during college and the other two in the last three years. Even though an orgasm eluded me, I've been told I'm good in bed.

Braden, though, makes me feel like I'm being touched for the first time, kissed for the first time, licked for the first time. Like I've never experienced any of this before, and I want it all. I want it all *now*.

He teases my other nipple with his fingers while he sucks at the first. I gasp and thread my fingers through his unruly hair as his head bobs against my breast. He finally releases the first nipple, glides his lips over to the second, and clamps his mouth around it. No teasing this time. He full-on sucks it.

A low moan emerges in my throat, and I pull at his hair. He groans in response.

"Is your pussy wet for me?" he says against my flesh.

"God, yes."

"I can smell how much you want me."

He releases my nipple and slides his hands down my abdomen, pushing the dress off me to the floor. I stand only in my black panties. He lowers his head and inhales.

I always thought panty sniffers were kind of gross, but when Braden sniffs me while my panties are still on, it's incredibly hot.

He inhales again and then slides my panties over my hips. They land within the circle of the dress.

I'm naked.

Naked and horny and completely at his mercy.

That should frighten me. Indeed it does, but it also thrills me. Utterly electrifies me.

This is what giving up control feels like, and I've only just begun.

He trails his tongue over the top of my vulva, which is freshly shaven and smooth this time. He spreads my thighs and flicks his tongue over my clit. I inhale sharply and he tilts his head, meeting my gaze.

"Bedroom," he rasps. Then he stands and pulls me—naked while he's still fully clothed in his tux—to the gorgeous room where I first experienced euphoria.

Where I can't wait to experience euphoria again.

The view entrances me once more, though I don't have much time to enjoy it. Braden leaves me standing by the bed and walks to his highboy. He opens a drawer and pulls something out.

Before I have time to think, he ties the item around my head, blindfolding me. The fabric is cool against my eyes. Silk, most likely.

I open my mouth to—

Then I close it. What can I say? I gave in for tonight. No, I didn't expect to be blindfolded. What else does he plan to do to me?

Shadowy images play in my head, both scary and erotic, as I recall the strange thing hanging above his bed.

"Don't speak," he says. "Just enjoy."

"Enjoy what?"

"I told you not to speak." His voice is ominous and commanding.

I won't speak again.

"Because I've taken your sight," Braden says, "your other senses will be enhanced. You won't see what I do to you, but you'll smell it, taste it, hear it."

"What if—"

"Skye," he says gently, "if you speak again, I'll punish you."

Punish me? Like hit me? Oh, hell no. I rip the blindfold off my eyes. "I didn't sign up to be beaten."

"Who said anything about being beaten? What kind of man do you think I am?"

"You said you'd punish me. What other kind of punishment is there?"

He meets my gaze, his eyes heavy-lidded and smoldering. "You're about to find out."

Chapter Twenty-Two

I shudder as chills sweep over my body. My nipples and areolas tighten at the coldness, but my pussy remains warm and wet. My body is a mass of mixed signals and dichotomous temperatures.

It's thrilling.

I don't want to be punished.

But God, I do.

How frightening that someone who so values control wants punishment? That I *want* punishment.

"Are… Are you going to hurt me?"

"Only if you want me to." He slips the blindfold onto my eyes once more. "Keep it on this time."

"But are you—"

"Punishment doesn't have to hurt, Skye. At least not physically."

"So you're still going to…?"

"Punish you? Oh yes."

Shivers rack my body, and still my core is hot as a sunny day. "How—"

"No more talking," he commands. "You're used to being in control, Skye, so I'm trying to be lenient. But I have my limits."

I open my mouth—

"Do you want to be gagged?"

I shake my head vehemently.

A warm breeze wafts over my ear. It's Braden's breath. He nips my earlobe. "The first thing I noticed about you was your sexy mouth. The second thing was your amazing rack. But the third thing, Skye, was what truly drew me to you. Do you know what it is?"

I shake my head.

"When you dropped your purse, you wouldn't accept my help. You had to maintain a semblance of control in the situation. Then there was the condom."

I bite my lip.

"Yes, I saw it. Another way you keep your life in control."

"Because I don't want to get pregnant?"

"It's more than that, and you know it. If a situation arises where you want to have sex, you're ready. You don't have to rush to the pharmacy for protection."

"A lot of women carry condoms around."

"Less than you might think. Some depend on other methods, or they run to the pharmacy as needed. Some are concerned only about pregnancy and not diseases."

"And you know this because…"

"I've been with a lot of women."

Well, I asked for that one.

"I had a feeling about you. About your need for control. Then, after our first dinner and my attempt to seduce you, I knew for sure."

My mouth twitches, but I don't respond.

"I recognized it in you. I recognize it in people because it's part of who I am as well."

I nod. His words don't surprise me. At least not the part about who he is. What's odd is that he wants someone with the same tendencies.

"I wouldn't be where I am today without knowing how to exercise control in every situation."

I nod again. This not-talking thing is becoming more bearable. Is he still going to punish me? I both love and hate the idea.

"That includes controlling *you*, Skye. Right now, I control your pleasure. I have leverage over you. Do you understand?"

I don't respond. Is this a game to him? Seduce someone who's used to being in charge and take that away from her? I'm not sure how I feel about that. All I know is I still want him. I want him more than ever.

"I asked if you understand."

I'm not sure I do, but I nod once more anyway. I've come this far, and I'm not leaving without an orgasm.

He pushes me down onto the bed. "Lie down."

I obey. What else can I do?

He spreads my legs and draws in a breath. The swift intake of air *whoosh*es in my ears. He's right. My sense of hearing is heightened.

"Your scent intoxicates me, Skye," he whispers, his breath a cool breeze against my thighs. "I can sit here between your legs forever and never get tired of it." He inhales again, this time holding his breath longer until he exhales, again cooling my flesh.

A soft sigh emerges in my throat. Can I sigh? Does that constitute talking? I hold it back, going rigid.

"Relax, baby. No need to tighten up right now." He inhales once more. "As much as I adore your smell, you taste even better."

His tongue begins at my perineum and slides up over my

slit to my clit. I gasp sharply. He glides over my clit, swirling around, and then he closes his lips around it and sucks ever so slightly. He's lighting my fuse with his slow and deliberate movements, and he's driving me wild.

I let a sigh escape this time, and a moan follows. Who cares if it goes against his no-talking rule? I need to release the tension somehow. I controlled the last sigh, but he asked me to give up control. Part of that is making the noises my body needs.

He doesn't berate me for releasing the sounds. In fact, he seems spurred on, and he increases the speed of his tongue. I grip the comforter in both my hands and arch my back, undulating my hips as I chase his tongue. He's deliberately ignoring my clit now. He shoves his tongue into my pussy and then licks and pulls on my labia. God, it feels so good, but I need… I want…

Yes! A short lick on my throbbing clit. The fuse is lit once more. *Keep going, Braden. Please keep going.*

But he strays again, going back to eating my pussy. "You're so wet," he says against my flesh. "God, you drive me wild, Skye. You're so responsive to everything I do."

Yes. Yes, I am. Please. Please. Please let me come.

As if in answer to my thoughts, he slides his tongue up my pussy and grabs hold of my clit once more, this time nipping harder. Once. Twice. Then three times. The fuse is burning. Almost there.

He thrusts two fingers into my heat, and—

He releases my clit.

His fingers penetrate me, fill me, and the ache of the emptiness begins to wane, but the fuse has burned out. He released my clit too soon.

Damn!

I bite my lip to keep from demanding what I want.

And then it dawns on me.

He knows exactly what I want. My body speaks volumes louder than my mouth ever can.

He *knows*.

He fucking knows.

He's doing this to me on purpose.

This is fucked up. If I knew my own body better, maybe I could force an orgasm. But I don't orgasm on demand. I never have. As much power as I exercise over my own life, I could never attain climax by myself or with someone else.

Not until Braden Black.

And now he's holding it over me, dangling it like a carrot in front of a rabbit's mouth.

He pushes my thighs forward and lowers his tongue, sliding it over my asshole. I tense. No one has done that before, and it feels… It feels…

"Oh!"

He's jabbing his tongue into my ass gently, but it feels like a probe.

Smack!

His hand on my ass. I jerk against the sting of his slap to my ass cheek.

"That's for talking." Then he slides his tongue back over my asshole and up my pussy again.

My clit is throbbing in time with my rapid heartbeat. Before I can think, I let my hand wander to my vulva. If I can just touch my clit, just one little flick…

Braden grabs my wrist. "No, you don't. That clit is mine tonight. No one touches it but me."

"But I have to come."

The blindfold slides off my eyes, and he meets my gaze. His chin and lips are wet from my juices, and he's chuckling. He's fucking chuckling!

"I told you I'd punish you for talking."

"The smack?" I say.

"No, that was for pleasure."

Pleasure? It hurt, but only minimally. Now my cheek is warm where his hand was. Warm and tingly…and yes, it feels nice.

I never imagined.

What's the punishment, then?

His lips form a suction against my clit once more, and his fingers are ramming in and out of my pussy. I shudder on the bed, my hips moving frantically against Braden's lips and tongue. His delicious fingers massage the inside of me in a deliberate way that drives me nearly to the edge. My God, my God, my God…

The fuse is lit again, and it's burning, burning, burning…

Until he pulls away from my clit and removes his fingers from my pussy.

He moves forward, the texture of his shirt abrading my nipples. They're so hard. Every part of me is wound tighter than a bowstring.

He presses his lips to one nipple and then the other before he kisses my lips chastely. I taste myself on him. The citrusy tang of my juices.

"Do you understand now, Skye?"

"Understand what?"

"That punishment doesn't have to physically hurt."

Chapter Twenty-Three

Tension is coiled through me. I'm covered in slick perspiration, and my clit is throbbing in time with my heart.

That orgasm… The one I wanted so badly…

"I was right," I say when I can finally relax enough to speak. "You knew what you were doing the whole time."

"Of course I did."

"You freak."

"What's freakish about denying you a climax?"

"Most men love it when their partner comes," I say.

"I've never in my life been 'most men.'" His eyes are heavy-lidded. "That's not to say I don't enjoy it when you come. I do, actually. I enjoy it a lot."

"Then why—"

"You *know* why."

Because I didn't keep my mouth shut. He promised he'd punish me if I spoke again. My body is so hot and needy, I almost wish he'd flogged me rather than deny me an orgasm.

I don't actually want to be flogged.

But God, I want to come.

I want to come so badly.

Please, Braden. Let me come. Tell me what I have to do to come.

The words hover in the back of my throat, never quite making it to my tongue.

"You're still resisting, Skye," Braden says. "If you weren't so determined to be in control, you could have come three times by now."

"Why?" I ask.

"I've already answered that. You know why."

I shake my head. "No. I mean, why do you need me to give *you* control?"

"I don't need it."

My eyes pop into circles. "You *don't*?"

"That's what you asked. You asked why I need it, and the truth is, I don't."

I shake my head. "I don't understand."

"I don't need it. I *want* it."

"Why, then? Why do you want it?"

His face darkens, and God, all I want is to take him in my arms and tell him I'll do whatever he wants, just to keep that sad look off his face. But is it sadness in his eyes? Yes, but it's also something else. Something I can't read.

"Does there have to be a reason?" he finally says.

"Yeah, there does," I say. "How am I supposed to understand if there isn't a reason?"

"Still trying to stay in control, aren't you?"

I sit up, my cheeks warming. "Just because I want answers—"

"Means you're not giving up control."

"You said if I gave up control, you'd show me pleasure like I've never known. Then you deny me a climax. That's not showing me pleasure, Braden."

"True, but there's still an element missing to that agreement."

"What's that?"

He trails a finger over my cheek, almost a loving gesture. "You haven't given up control."

My cheek tingles from his touch. "But you want me in your bed, Braden. You've said that from the beginning."

"I don't deny it."

"Why not take me as I am?"

"Because you and I will both like it better my way."

"What makes you so certain?" I ask, sounding a lot more sure of myself than I am.

He slides his finger over my lower lip. "I see it in your eyes. You're a beautiful woman, Skye, but you're the most beautiful when you let go and surrender to your body."

His words ignite the embers burning deep within me. I zero in on his still-clothed crotch. His bulge is more apparent than ever. This must be affecting him, too.

"You want me," I say.

"Of course I do. I'm not made of clay. I'm a man, baby, and any man who lays eyes on you wants you."

I warm, and damn, my pussy is still so ready for his touch, his tongue, his cock.

How is he able to keep those desires at bay and tease me? Is it because he's older? He's thirty-five to my twenty-four, clearly much more experienced than I am. Or is it something else?

His expression remains stoic. He smiles so rarely, laughs even less. Does anyone truly know Braden Black?

I clear my throat. "Is my punishment over?"

"That's up to you."

"Meaning…?"

"Meaning…are you ready to give up control?"

Am I? I thought I was, but then I couldn't obey him when he told me not to talk.

"Before you answer," he says, "know this. I want to fuck you. I want you more than I've wanted anyone in a long time. I think I've made that abundantly clear."

I nod. I'm dying to ask why he's punishing me, then, because in punishing me, he's also punishing himself.

"I *will* fuck you tonight," he says. "The only question is whether you get a climax."

"But if you fuck me—"

He quiets me with a touch of his fingers to my lips. "Trust me. I can still fuck you and keep you from coming."

He doesn't know how right he is.

I finally get to come, only it's with a man who wants to rule my climaxes. So not fair.

"Do you want to come tonight, baby?"

I nod.

"Tell me. Tell me you want to come."

"I want to come tonight, Braden."

His eyes grow slightly cold. "Then don't disobey me again."

Why is this so important to him? He hasn't asked for control over any other aspect of my life. In fact, he made it clear earlier this evening that he didn't track me down because I couldn't take care of myself. No. He tracked me down to keep me out of someone else's bed.

He's domineering but not a dominant. He's controlling but not a master. Just who is Braden Black?

Why is he like this?

I may never know, and if I'm going to continue to sleep with him, I need to be comfortable with that.

And I need to give up control. Not just in words but in action.

Am I ready?

Am I truly ready?

I clear my throat. "Tell me what you want, Braden."

"I want to fuck you into next week."

I smile. "You're in luck. I've got all next week open."

Chapter Twenty-Four

Braden grabs the black blindfold and ties it over my eyes again. "No talking, Skye. Understand?"

"I have a question first."

"For God's sake. What kind of question could you possibly have? No talking means no talking."

I let out an exasperated sigh. "It's a valid one, Braden. Can I sigh and moan? Groan?"

"Sexual sounds are permissible."

"Okay. But you got me last time for saying 'oh.' Isn't that a sexual sound?"

"No. 'Oh' is a word. 'Oh God' are words. 'Yes, Braden, yes' are words."

I keep a smile from spreading across my face. "But those words are indicating that I'm enjoying myself."

"So what?"

"So…don't you want to know I'm enjoying myself?"

"I know you're enjoying yourself by how your body responds to me. The words are superfluous."

I scoff. "Seriously?"

He chuckles. I can't see his face, but I imagine his smirk. "You become more of a challenge every second, Skye Manning. You're my Everest, and I'm determined to conquer you. Now, be quiet."

I press my lips together and make a locking motion with my hand. I'm feeling sarcastic, but my action probably doesn't convey that to Braden. Just as well. I'm not up for more punishment. I want a climax.

He gently pushes me until the backs of my legs hit the bed. "Lie down."

I obey. My body is still tense and ready, needy and wanting. Braden is moving around. His clothes rustle. What is he doing?

I have no idea, and suddenly I'm thrilled. I don't know what's in store for me. It could be anything.

Anything.

The wait is excruciating. Every second, my body becomes tenser with yearning, and my mind comes up with something else he could do to tantalize me.

Seconds pass.

They turn into minutes.

I squirm, but I don't speak. I'm determined to get that orgasm.

I gasp when something flutters over one nipple. It's not his finger or his lips. Something cool circles my areola. Is it… ice? No. Not cold enough, plus no melting trickles of water. He traces the swell of my breast with the object and moves to the other nipple, tantalizing it as he did the last.

Prickles erupt on my flesh. The coolness dances around now, going from nipple to nipple and then trailing down my abdomen, making my belly flutter. He stops at my belly button, circling it. My clit is throbbing, so ready to feel the cool hardness of whatever object he's teasing me with.

Braden lingers at my belly button, though. "So beautiful,

Skye. You should have this pierced."

I open my mouth to say "hell no" but stop just in time.

I will *not* talk.

I *will* have that orgasm.

When he finally tires of my belly button and trails downward to my vulva, I let out an excited moan. Still he teases, though, gliding the coolness over my pubic bone and down the sides of my opening. The coolness is heaven against my hot labia, *but my clit, Braden. My clit…*

The object makes a path over my inner thighs down to my knees and then back up.

You're such a fucking tease, Braden Black!

But I stay mum. He can't keep me from climaxing forever.

Can he?

No. Can't go there. The coolness trails up my wet slit.

"Mmm. Nice and wet," he says. "How much do you want me, Skye?"

I open my mouth and then slam it shut. He's not going to get me with his games.

"Good girl." He slides the cool object over my clit.

I moan and circle my hips. The jolt to my clit glides through me like an icy carnival ride. I arch my back and undulate, reaching for more, more, more…

But he moves the object back up my vulva to my breasts and then to my lips. He pokes it into my mouth. "Taste yourself. See how delicious you are."

I swirl my tongue over the object and delight in my tanginess. This allows me the first sensation of what he's been teasing me with. It's pointed on one end and about the size of a large marble. He removes it quickly then and his clothes rustle.

Is he finally taking them off?

God, yes. Please.

I squirm on the bed, twisting the covers with my hands. How much more can I take? Is this fun for him, watching me go slowly mad?

"Don't move your hands, Skye," he says.

I release my fists and do as he says.

"Bend your legs so your feet are flat on the bed."

Again, I obey.

Then warm hardness nudges my slit. His cock. He's going to fuck me. Finally. Is he completely naked? I'm desperate to touch the warmth of his skin. I reach—

"I said don't move your hands!"

Fuck! Did I just screw myself out of an orgasm? I quickly move my hand back.

He teases my pussy again with his cock, sliding it back and forth from my clit nearly to my ass. *Please, Braden, please.*

But I say nothing. I keep my hands flat.

And I wait.

And wait.

He can't last forever, can he? He wants me as much as I want him, right?

Such a tease. Such a wonderful, aching tease…

Then a powerful thrust, and he's inside me, my emptiness finally filled. A vibrant groan wafts to my ears and enters me, a sound vibration that I can almost see in my mind's eye. I cry out, not in words but in pure emotion.

He pulls out, and I whimper at the loss, waiting for his next thrust.

Instead, though, he teases again, letting just the head of his cock breach my pussy. Tiny shallow thrusts, just enough to make me want him more.

Oh, he's a fucking expert at this. I want to scream and beg and lash out, but I keep my lips sealed.

"Fuck it," he finally says and thrusts into me, tunneling

through me with his cock made of hot steel.

I groan. It feels so amazing, so perfect, as if his cock were made to fit only me. My nipples are tight and hard, and I hope he'll move downward so his hard chest will appease them. My body is on fire, and he fucks me hard. The invasion spirals through me, and I'm close, oh, so close. If only he'd come forward, let his pubic bone hit my clit.

Such a tease!

This is what he meant when he said he'd control my climax. Bastard!

Then his lips are on mine, and my clit is getting the stimulation it needs. The fuse is lit. He thrusts and he thrusts and he thrusts—

A rocket of energy surges into my clit and my pussy contracts, pulsating against his plunging cock. Sounds come from my throat. Are they words? I have no idea. I'm blind, but colors and vibrations and kaleidoscopic images catapult through me as I jump from the precipice and leap into nirvana.

"That's it, baby. Give it to me. Give it all to me. It's mine."

Thrust, thrust, thrust—

"God, yes! So tight, baby. So good."

Braden's cock is so deep in me, and still I quiver around him, my climax reeling. In seconds, it slows, and I'm left with him pulling out and rolling off me.

And I've never been so satisfied in my life.

With a whoosh, Braden removes the blindfold. "You can speak now and move your hands."

But I have no words.

Chapter Twenty-Five

"Have I truly rendered you speechless?" Braden says, a glint in his eye. "Seems unbelievable." He's on his side, his head propped on his hand. He stares down at me.

I reach forward and push a stray hair over his forehead. "What do you want me to say?"

"You can start with, 'Wow, Braden. You rocked my world.'"

I laugh. "Isn't that pretty obvious?"

"See what happens when you give in to me?"

I smile but say nothing. Because I've stumbled upon a secret.

I *haven't* given in. I used my control to keep from speaking, to keep my hands in place. I used my control to be certain I ended this evening with an orgasm.

He may think he controlled me, but he didn't.

The glint in his eye remains, but a cloud hovers over us. Does he know my secret? Does he care?

Finally, I speak. "It was amazing."

He kisses my lips softly. "Go to sleep."

• • •

I wake to light streaming in through the wall of windows in Braden's bedroom. As promised, he didn't make me leave. But where is he?

I'm still stark naked. I wander to the bathroom quickly and then into Braden's closet. I grab a white shirt and put it on. What can only be 100 percent cotton is cool over my shoulders. I find my panties—still in one piece, thank goodness—on the floor and hastily don them. Then I leave the room.

This place is huge. My nose helps me find my way to the kitchen. Braden is sitting at the island drinking coffee and reading something on his iPad, while a woman—his chef, presumably?—stands at the stove frying bacon and eggs.

And I'm wearing nothing but black panties and one of Braden's shirts. Since it's doubtful a hole will open up and swallow me to save me this embarrassment, I clear my throat softly.

Braden turns toward me. "Good morning."

"Good morning."

"Coffee?"

"Absolutely. Thank you." I walk in and take a seat next to Braden.

The woman at the stove turns. She's young and gorgeous, with brown hair and eyes. "Good morning. I'm Marilyn."

"Hi," I squeak out.

"How do you take your coffee?" she asks.

"Black."

A moment later, a cup of steaming black coffee slides in front of me.

Braden turns to me. "Hungry?"

"No. I'm good."

"Are you sure? Marilyn always makes enough to feed a small army."

"That's because you have the appetite of a small army." Marilyn smiles and sets a full plate of bacon, eggs, and toast in front of Braden. "Sure I can't get you anything?"

"No." Seriously, if I try to eat right now, I'll puke.

This is the part I'm really bad at—the small talk after something intimate. I've never known quite what to say the morning after, and this time it's worse because first, I'm starting to really like Braden, and second, there's another person in the room—who knows Braden and I fucked all night long.

I take a sip of coffee and burn my tongue. I set the cup down quickly and spill a few drops on the marble counter. "Sorry," I mumble.

"Not a problem." Marilyn wipes up my mess with a flourish.

Braden places his iPad on the counter. "Could you excuse us for a few minutes, Marilyn?"

"Sure, Mr. Black. Just buzz if you need me." She exits the kitchen.

He turns to me. "What's going on?"

"Nothing."

"You're acting strange. Are you uncomfortable here?"

"No. Not exactly."

"You're the one who wanted to stay. To leave on your own terms."

I nod. "Yes."

"Okay. Just so we're both on the same page. You're welcome to stay as long as you like. I have a few hours of work to do."

"Oh. Okay. I should check in with work, too." I take another sip of coffee, being more careful this time. "Braden?"

"Yeah."

"I'm going to need something to wear home."

His lips curve up slightly. Just slightly, but I'll take it. "Of course. Find out where Tessa got the black dress, and I'll have it replaced. You can wear the cardigan I gave you last night."

"Okay… What about pants?"

He nearly smiles again. "I guess I didn't leave your dress in working condition as a skirt."

"No, you didn't."

He stands. "I'll find you something. Next time, bring a change of clothes."

Next time? A thrill surges through me.

"In fact," he says, "bring over several things. Or if you want to leave me your sizes, I'll have some stuff delivered."

He wants to buy me clothes? "That's okay. I have plenty. I can bring some over."

"Good," he says, his voice going darker, "because I plan to destroy a lot of them."

Chapter Twenty-Six

"I'm still wearing his sweatpants and shirt," I tell Tessa on the phone once I'm home. I turn the phone to speaker and hug myself. Wearing his clothes makes me feel…close to him, but it's more than that. It's like he let me take part of him home with me. "I can't bring myself to take them off."

"So the second time was just as good?" she says.

"Better." I can't stop the ridiculous smile that's pasted on my face. I look toward my full hamper. Time to do some laundry. I need clean clothes to take to Braden's. Which reminds me… "Oh, by the way…"

"What?"

I gather items from my hamper. "He kind of…destroyed your dress."

"What?" she says again.

"He ripped it off me. Literally."

No response for a few seconds. Is she in shock? Then, "When you say "literally" you mean *literally*."

"Yeah. I'm sorry, but he's going to replace it. I just need to know where you got it."

"Ross, I think." She sighs. "It looked better on you than me anyway. Tell him it was Chanel and I'll take the cash."

"Tessa…"

She laughs. "For God's sake, Skye, I'm kidding. Don't worry about the dress. If it helped you let go and get laid, I'm happy to donate some clothes to the cause."

"You're the best, Tess. I'm really sorry."

My phone beeps at me. "I've got another call. Hold on." I look at the screen. Addison.

"It's the boss," I say.

"Braden?"

I guffaw. "Of course not. It's Addie. I'll see you at lunch tomorrow."

I click on the next call. "Hey, Addie."

"I guess you had quite the time last night."

"It was okay. The post is doing well. I just checked it."

"The post is fine. What were you doing there with Braden Black?"

Huh? How did she know? "What are you talking about?"

"Please. Photos are up on the MADD website. There's a doozy of you and Braden sitting together at a prime table."

I throw a dirty sock to the ground in irritation. "Braden was at the benefit. We said hello. Remember? I met him at the office that day?"

"You looked pretty cozy."

I walk to the kitchen and put my Bluetooth in my ear. Then I fire up my laptop at the kitchen table and find the website. "We were just talking at a table." *And why is this any of your business?*

"I told you he's a douche, Skye."

"He seems nice to me."

Bingo! I find the photo. The caption reads, "Braden Black and friend." At least the dance-floor lighting makes me look glam. I don't recall anyone taking a photo, but of course, several photographers were working the ballroom.

"Are you sleeping with him?"

My cheeks warm and I actually feel my nostrils flare. "What kind of question is that?"

"A direct one."

No kidding. "Who I sleep with is my business."

"That answers it for me. He's bad news."

"I don't even know him, Addie." True words. *But yeah, I'm sleeping with him.*

"Take my advice," she says. "Keep it that way. See you tomorrow."

That's it. She ends the call. I get up from the table and upend my hamper onto the floor. I'm mad as hell, and now I have to do fucking laundry. But first, I need to talk to Tessa again.

"She's obviously jealous," Tessa says into my ear after I call her back. "I can't say I blame her."

"I don't think so," I say. "She can't stand him."

"She *says* she can't stand him."

I consider Tessa's words. Yeah, Addie and Braden have a history, but I've been working with her for more than a year and never once has she mentioned him despite his face being plastered all over the media.

"That's probably it," I lie. "See you tomorrow."

Whatever Addie's beef is with Braden, it's not my problem.

Addie isn't in the next morning when I get to the office. Monday mornings are always busy answering emails and checking all the posts for comments I may have missed over the weekend. I've got my nose buried in paperwork when someone enters the office.

"Good morning," a female voice says.

I look away from the computer screen. An attractive brunette stands in front of my desk.

"Hi there," I say. "May I help you?"

"I'm Kay Brown from the *Boston Babbler*."

The *Boston Babbler*—our local tabloid rag that follows Addie around as if she were the Grateful Dead. "I'm afraid Addison isn't in. Did you have an appointment?" I quickly access Addie's calendar.

"No, I don't."

"I'm sorry. I'm not sure when she'll be in."

"I'm actually here to talk to you, Ms. Manning."

I jerk in my chair. Did I hear her right?

"I'd like to talk to you about the photo of you and Braden Black at the MADD gala."

"My name wasn't on the photo."

"It only took a bit of research to identify you."

"A bit of research?"

"You're Addison Ames's assistant. You aren't hard to find."

"Exactly how—"

"I don't disclose my sources. Suffice it to say I know everyone in this city."

I nod. Including the event organizers, no doubt. "I don't have anything to say to you."

"So you're not dating Braden Black?"

I stand. "I believe I said I don't have anything to say to you."

"That *is* you in the photo, though?"

"No comment."

"Ms. Manning, you're going to be outed sooner or later. I'd like to be the first to get the scoop on Braden Black's new paramour."

"Paramour? Are you kidding me? No comment." I check my watch. "I've got a lunch date."

"It's eleven."

"Yeah, I eat early. Since Addie's not in, I need to close up the office. Please excuse me." I grab my purse and walk out from behind the desk.

Just as Braden walks into the office.

Chapter Twenty-Seven

"Kay," Braden says. "I can't say I'm surprised to see you here, since you've already called my office three times today."

"Mr. Black." She holds out her hand. "A pleasure as always."

He takes her hand and shakes it firmly. "If you'll excuse us, I need to talk to Skye."

"Of course. How long have you two been dating?"

I gulp. His answer to this question is far more important to me than it is to Kay. He certainly won't say we're sleeping together.

Then again, this is Braden. I've heard him say many things I never expected.

"We only met about a week ago," he says.

"And your date at the gala?"

"We didn't arrive together," he says. "Ms. Manning and I saw each other at the gala and talked a bit."

Another gulp. His response is clear and concise. I just wish he said we were dating.

"Your lunch date, Ms. Manning, is with Mr. Black?" Kay asks.

"No, it's—"

"Yes, it is," Braden says. "Are you ready, Skye?"

I clear my throat. At least this will get rid of Kay. "Yeah, I'm ready. I need to lock up."

"Of course." Kay walks out the door and then turns and looks over her shoulder. "I'll be in touch. With both of you." She turns and leaves.

"Thanks for the save," I say. "I thought she was here to see Addie."

"I figured she'd bother you this morning after she called my office and mentioned you by name."

"You came here to warn me?"

"In part."

"In part?"

"Yeah. I thought you might be up for an early lunch."

"Sorry. I'm meeting Tessa in an hour."

He narrows his eyes and his gaze seems to melt me. "Cancel."

Cancel.

One word. One unremarkable word in his deep, raspy voice, and I want to obey him without question.

I grasp the edge of my desk to keep from toppling over. "I can't. Tess and I always have lunch on Mondays." And most other days, for that matter, unless one of us is working over the noon hour.

My phone buzzes. It's Tessa. "Excuse me for a minute," I say to Braden. "Hey, Tess."

"You're never going to believe what happened. A courier just delivered a package to my office from Braden."

"Oh?" A sliver of jealousy knifes through me.

"Yeah. It's my dress, Skye. Or a perfect replica. I can't even believe it. I told you not to worry about it."

I clear my throat. "He said he'd replace it."

"If I didn't know better, I'd say this is the exact dress, but it can't be. It doesn't have a label."

"Hold on a minute." I mute the phone and turn to Braden. "She got the dress."

"Good."

"She says it's perfect. Did you get it repaired?"

"It was beyond repair, as you know."

"Then how did you…?"

"I gave the remains to my personal tailor yesterday, along with your Instagram photo. He was able to replicate it."

My jaw drops. "In a day?"

"I'm a very good customer." He smirks.

I hold back an eye roll and unmute the phone. "His tailor replicated it yesterday," I tell Tessa.

"Well, tell him a thousand thank-yous. I just took a closer look, and the fabric is much better quality than the original."

"You can tell him yourself." I hand the phone to Braden.

"Ms. Logan," he says.

Pause.

"You're very welcome. Any time."

Pause.

"Actually, there *is* something you can do for me."

Pause.

"Let me take Skye to lunch today. You can have lunch with her tomorrow."

Pause.

"I appreciate that. And you don't have to keep thanking me. Have a good day." He hands the phone back to me.

"Tess?" I say.

But she already hung up.

Braden stares at me, his eyes full of blue fire. "Seems you're free for lunch after all, Skye."

Chapter Twenty-Eight

"Tessa said you sent the dress to her office," I say to Braden after we order our meal at a cute little French bistro. "How did you know where she works?"

"That kind of information isn't hard to find," he replies.

"Not when you can pay for it," I say. "Just out of curiosity, how much did that dress cost you on such short notice?"

His lips twitch. I think he might smile, but he doesn't. "I never discuss personal purchases."

"Oh?"

"No. It's no one's business how much I pay for anything."

I can't argue the point. He's right. "Well, it was nice of you. Very nice."

"I said I'd replace it."

"I know, but I didn't expect you to actually replicate it. Why would you do that?"

Braden takes a sip of water. "Because I can."

I'm not sure what to say to that. I like that he doesn't discuss his purchases. That's cool, in my book. How much of Braden is nouveau riche, and how much is old-school blue-collar? I'd like to find out, but he's such a puzzle.

A puzzle I'd really like to put together.

Yes. I like him. I like Braden Black. A lot. I thought Addie was right at first, that he was a jerk, but now? He appeals to me, which frightens me, because he already told me he couldn't have a relationship with me. He didn't tell me why, and it's too soon to ask.

I want to date him. If I spent more time with him outside the bedroom, maybe I could figure him out. Maybe I could *make* him want a relationship.

"Skye," he says.

"Yeah?"

"It might interest you to know that I had my tailor make *two* dresses."

I swallow the sip of water I just took. "Oh?"

"I did. You'll be wearing that dress again, but the next time you'll be on *my* arm, and there won't be any question as to who you're with."

I suppress a smile. "Will you destroy it again?"

He stares at me, those blue eyes a hypnotic sapphire flame. "Yes. Definitely."

My cheeks warm, and I know I'm turning about twelve shades of vibrant red. "When exactly will I be on your arm?"

"You decide."

I let out a short laugh. "It's a cocktail dress, Braden. It might surprise you to know that I don't frequent a lot of formal affairs."

"You will now. I'm invited to a lot of them, and since you insist on dating, you'll be accompanying me."

"If I insist?"

His eyes darken. "I want you in my bed, Skye. If taking you out sometimes is the way to make that happen, I'll do it."

"What if I want more than that?"

"What more is there?"

"A...relationship."

He taps his fingers on the table. "I've told you I can't be in a relationship with you."

"Yeah, but you haven't told me why."

He wrinkles his forehead. Is he thinking about how to answer my question? Or is he getting angry? I can't tell. Braden always has a touch of anger about him. In truth, it's part of what attracts me to him—his darkness, the mystery that hovers around him like a dense cloud.

"The only reason I can give you is that I don't want a relationship."

"Why?"

He rubs his temple. "You're persistent. I'll give you that. But there is no answer."

"You mean there's no answer that will satisfy me."

"Semantics, as you like to say."

"I like you, Braden."

He doesn't smile, but his demeanor seems to lighten a bit. "I like you, too. I don't sleep with people I don't like."

"You didn't let me finish. I like you, but why me? You can have any woman out there. You must know that."

"I've told you."

"Yeah. You like my lips and my breasts. So do plenty of other men, and sexy lips and big tits aren't that hard to find."

"I won't deny that those are fine features of yours, but I also told you the thing I like most about you. Your need for control."

I take a sip of water and set my glass down more harshly than I mean to. "So I'm a game. If I give you control, you win. Is that it?"

"If you give me control, we both win."

"And how long do you expect this arrangement to last?"

I ask. “Until you get tired of me?”

That finally gets a chuckle from him. “As long as you want it to.”

“I find that hard to believe.”

“Why is that?”

I huff softly. “Because you can have anyone. You’ll get tired of me long before I get tired of you.”

“Don’t be so sure of that.”

“Why do you say that?”

“You’ll see.”

I’ll *see*? What the heck does that mean?

The waiter brings our meals, and I study the coq au vin on my plate. I inhale the scent of burgundy, chicken, and mushroom. It smells heavenly, but I’m not at all hungry after this conversation.

Why would I grow tired of Braden?

The question interests me not only because I can’t imagine it but also because he intimated I might at some point in the future.

He’s bad news.

Addie’s words.

Tessa felt Addie is probably jealous, and she has a point, but I’m not convinced. Addie and I aren’t exactly friends. Being friends with your boss is never a great idea, and in Addie’s case, it isn’t possible anyway. We come from two different worlds.

As do Braden and I.

Braden takes a bite of his sole and swallows. “Nothing to say? That’s not like you.” He rises and lays his napkin across the back of his chair. He removes his phone from his pocket, crouches down next to me, and snaps a selfie of us. “What the hell? Let’s get them talking.”

“You’re Instagramming?”

"Kay will have the whole city talking about us within a day, so why not? You're not embarrassed to be seen with me, are you?"

Seriously? "Of course not."

"Then there's no problem that I can see." He fiddles with his phone for a few seconds.

My phone dings in my purse.

"Tagged you," he says.

I pull out my phone. Same as last time. It's blowing up with notifications.

"You should make your profile public," he says.

"Why?"

"Because my followers will want to know you."

"I'm a private person, Braden."

"Not anymore."

I lift my eyebrows. He's right. Kay Brown accosted me at my workplace. She'll no doubt be the first of many. "I didn't sign up for this."

He laughs. A solid laugh, so unlike him, and I revel in the joyful sound.

"You did, though. You wanted to date, Skye. This is what dating *me* is like."

I keep my jaw from dropping open.

"In fact," he continues, "I'm on my way to do some charity work. Why don't you join me?"

"You do charity work?"

"Does that surprise you?"

"No." Though it does. Someone as rich as Braden can simply write a check rather than do the work. I'm glad he's willing to put in the time as well. Makes him even more attractive than he already is.

"I give a lot of money to charity," he says, "but there's no substitute for diving in and getting your hands dirty."

I look down at my work clothes. "I'm not really dressed to get my hands dirty."

"Just an expression, Skye. Though I do help with a community garden in my old neighborhood. But that's not what I'm doing today."

"Yeah? What are you doing today?"

"You mean 'what are *we* doing today?'"

I smile. "Okay, what are *we* doing today?"

"Wait and see."

Chapter Twenty-Nine

We end up at a food pantry in South Boston, which is where Braden grew up. Definitely not what I expected.

"I come here once a week for an hour and hand out food," he says. "Let's go."

We walk past the line of people waiting and into the building.

Several people rush to greet him.

"Nice to see you, Mr. Black," a young man says.

"Braden!" An older woman grabs his hand. "I see you've brought a friend."

"Cheryl, this is Skye."

The woman holds out her hand. "Nice to meet you, Skye."

"Cheryl's an old friend," Braden says. "We used to be neighbors."

"When he was just a little guy," Cheryl says. "We're all so proud of his success."

I'm in a kind of shock. Yes, Braden had humble beginnings, but why a food pantry? Why not just write a fat check and fund all the food pantries in Boston? Who is this man? Every time I think I've scratched his surface, he surprises me again.

"You all had a hand in it," Braden says to Cheryl.

"He's an amazing person," she says to me. "Never forgets his roots. His donations keep us in business. We're able to help more people than ever these days."

I smile. I'm not sure what to say. I like this side of Braden. I *really* like it.

Braden grabs a shopping cart. "This place means a lot to me. Come on, Skye. I'll show you the ropes." He takes the cart to the person at the head of the line. "I'm Braden." He holds out his hand.

A young woman carrying a toddler places the child in the buggy seat and then shakes Braden's hand. "Elise."

"How many people in your household, Elise?" Braden asks.

"Just Benji and me."

"And how are you today, Benji?" Braden goes to shake the little boy's hand.

The boy looks away.

"I'm sorry. He's shy."

"Not a problem. I was a shy kid myself."

He was? News to me.

"This is Skye," he says.

"Hi." I hold out my hand to Elise. "Nice to meet you."

Elise shakes my hand weakly. She's a pretty young woman wearing jeans and a sweatshirt. Her son is adorable, his light-brown hair combed just so.

"You'll need some powdered milk for Benji," Braden says. "We'll have fresh milk soon, once the new refrigeration unit is installed. I'm so sorry for the inconvenience. Refrigeration is down during installation."

The new refrigeration unit is being paid for by Braden, I bet. My heart warms, and a smile splits my face.

"Benji doesn't like milk," Elise says. "I wish he'd drink it."

"Not a problem. We can give you some sugar-free chocolate flavoring to put in the milk. Guaranteed to please." Braden leads the way down the first aisle.

I follow, walking next to Elise.

What's her story? I'm curious, but it's not my business. I'd also like very much to take a photo of her and Benji, but I don't dare ask for the privilege. Elise didn't come here to be photographed. She came here to get the help she needs. I've never been hungry, something I've taken for granted. Gratitude swims through me. I need to remember how lucky I am.

I smile at Benji, and to my surprise, he smiles back. He's a happy little boy, no different from any other toddler. Does he have a father in the picture?

"What do you like to do, Benji?" I ask.

He looks away then.

"He's not talking much yet," Elise says. "Benji, you should speak to the nice lady."

"Oh, no. That's okay. He's a beautiful child."

"Thank you." Elise smiles.

Braden pulls items off the pantry shelves and puts them in the cart. Powdered milk, canned fruits and vegetables, sliced bread, peanut butter, and jelly. Pasta and sauce, boxed macaroni and cheese, and some apple juice. Down another aisle he finds cereal, oatmeal, and instant coffee.

"Is Benji potty-trained?" he asks Elise.

"Yes and no. He still wears a diaper at night."

Braden turns down a new aisle and pulls a pack of toddler-size diapers off the shelf. "Anything else you need from this aisle?"

Elise shakes her head.

"Is there anything special that you'd like today?"

"No, I don't need anything," Elise says. "Just the food is fine."

I get it. Elise is proud. She comes here to feed her son and herself. She doesn't want to take anything more than necessary.

Braden doesn't push. He helps Elise bag her groceries, and then he and I pack them in the little red wagon she left outside the pantry.

"Do you live near here?" I ask.

"About twenty blocks away," she says. "It's a nice walk."

"There's a bus stop right there." I nod. "Let me give you—"

"No, thank you," Elise says. "Benji and I enjoy the walk. Thank you very much for the food."

"You're very welcome," Braden says. "You come back anytime."

Elise smiles and nods and then places Benji in the wagon among the bags of food. She begins the walk home. I watch them for a moment. Benji pulls a loaf of bread out of the bag and squeezes it. I smile. I never could resist squeezing a loaf of fresh bread, either. My mom got used to making sandwiches with misshapen slices.

"Thank you for bringing me here," I say.

"No need to thank me."

I look over my shoulder. Cheryl is leading another woman with a small girl hanging on her hand into the panty. Another volunteer takes a young man from the line.

"Why this place, Braden? You could volunteer anywhere."

"Because," he says, "my mother used to bring Ben and me here when we were little to get food."

My mouth drops open.

"Apparently I'm full of surprises today," he says.

An image pops into my mind of a volunteer leading a beautiful woman—for Braden's mother must have been beautiful—with a gorgeous little boy tugging on her hand.

Probably two little boys, as Braden has a brother. Did their mother wheel them home in a wagon? Did Braden like to squeeze a fresh loaf of bread?

"I think it's wonderful that you volunteer here and also support the pantry financially."

"It's the least I can do. Never forget where you came from, Skye. It's a part of you. Always."

We head to the Mercedes where Christopher waits. He opens the door for me.

Braden slides in next to me in the back seat. "I showed you a part of my past today. Now I'd like to know something about you."

Chapter Thirty

"What do you want to know?"

"Something that had an impact on you. Helped define who you are."

"Okay. But I want to say something first."

"Go ahead."

The words take a moment to come. "I didn't know you ever went hungry."

"Did you give it a second thought?"

"No, I didn't. I've never gone hungry, and I never realized how lucky I am. I'm going to try not to take things like that for granted anymore."

He trails a finger over my cheek, warming me. "Good. You should never take anything for granted. It can all be gone in a minute."

His words puzzle me. Does he really think his fortune can just vanish? "I'm sorry," I say. "The thought of you going to bed hungry makes me so sad."

"Don't be sorry, and please don't be sad. Everything in my past has contributed to what I've become. Just as it has for you. Maybe you don't have one thing you can pinpoint. But tell me something about your past. Something that helped shape who you are today."

Funny thing is, I can pinpoint the event that caused a shift in my personality. I've never told anyone other than Tessa. Mostly because it's embarrassing. Everyone expects a control freak to have some huge story. Mine isn't huge. It's not even interesting.

"Do I really have to go into this?"

"No. I'll never force you to tell me anything."

"Thanks."

Except now I want to. He shared something with me, and I want to share my experience with him. It was traumatic at the time. I can still feel my racing heartbeat.

Silence for a few minutes.

Then I speak.

"When I was seven, I was playing by myself in our cornfields." I close my eyes for a moment. The sweet scent of the plants drifts into my mind. Green giants to a little girl, and though I loved them, they became monsters that day.

"By yourself?" he asks.

"Yeah. I'm an only child, and none of my friends lived close by. I saw them only at school until I got older. Anyway, I got lost."

"In the cornfield?" He raises his eyebrows.

"Don't look so surprised. Our cornfields are huge. We have more than two hundred acres. I was only allowed to play at the very edge of the field where someone could keep an eye on me. Anyway, I got caught up chasing a praying mantis."

"Somehow, I never took you for an entomophile."

I'm impressed that he knows the word. Heck, I'm impressed that *I* know the word. "I was seven, Braden, with the attention span of a praying mantis myself. They're green, as you know, and it was a challenge to see it as it hopped from one stalk to another. I followed it with my camera I'd gotten for my birthday. I wanted to take its picture."

"You were having fun."

"I was. There wasn't much else to do."

"Except outrun tornadoes."

I give him a good-natured smack on his upper arm. "I won't deny taking shelter from a few in my day, but you can't outrun a tornado. You shouldn't try."

"Dorothy did."

"You watch too much TV."

"I don't watch any TV."

"That was a clear *Wizard of Oz* reference."

"I read books, Skye."

Of course he does. Why should that surprise me? He's not college educated but he's still brilliant. "Anyway, it hopped away from me again and again, and it was great fun to follow it, until I realized I had no idea where I was. I was shorter than the corn, and all around me was more corn. I freaked out. I can still feel my little heart pounding against my chest. It was like my whole body became my heartbeat. I started running in no particular direction and kept tripping over roots and stalks."

Even telling the simple story, the feeling of sheer terror and panic washes over me.

I inhale slowly to calm myself and then exhale. "I started screaming bloody murder, and eventually I ran into a scarecrow and knocked myself out. The next thing I remember is waking up in my bed with my mother next to me, holding a clammy washcloth on my forehead."

"So they found you."

"They did. I wasn't very far from the yard. It just seemed far to a frightened little girl."

I expect him to burst into laughter at my silly story, but he doesn't.

Instead, he says simply, "Thank you for sharing that with me."

Back at the office, Addie still hasn't come in. I'd texted her to let her know I'd taken a longer than usual lunch, but it looks like she hasn't even read the text. I check email and her posts quickly, making necessary adjustments. Then I regard my own Instagram account.

You should make your account public.

Should I?

I had several requests to follow after Braden's first post at Union Oyster House, but I ignored them. What would happen this time? And did I want it to happen?

I have to put off my decision because Addie walks in. "Hey," she says. "Sorry. Overslept."

Until two? I just nod. "Nothing much going on. The posts all look good."

"Any new offers?"

"Not today."

She shrugs. "Okay. I'll be in my office."

She seems a little off. Is she still upset that I was with Braden at the gala? Should I ask? Should I at least ask about Braden and why he's bad news?

I sigh. No. I'm here to do my work, not get gossip from my employer.

A few moments pass, and then—

Addie storms out and thrusts her phone in my face. "What the hell is this?"

Braden's post.

"We had lunch," I say.

She flips through several other posts and then thrusts the phone at me again. "And this?"

The post from Union Oyster House. "That was a week ago. You haven't seen it?"

"I don't follow him, or at least I didn't. I just followed him now, sitting in my office."

"Why?"

"Why? Because I'm curious. I care about you, Skye. I don't want you getting into something you can't handle. You're so young."

I'm twenty-four to Addie's twenty-nine, but I can't believe she mentioned my age. She usually hates thinking about how old she is. The big three-oh is just around the corner, and her current offers are reflecting that. A few weeks ago, she got an offer for a new brand of support leggings. She pouted for hours after that one.

"What's your problem with Braden?" I ask. After all, she brought it up.

"He's bad news. I told you."

"You're going to have to give me more to go on than that. Exactly *why* is he bad news? You said you had a thing with him a while ago. What happened?"

"I don't talk about that."

"Then how do I know he's bad news? None of his other girlfriends have said anything about him." That I know of, anyway. I don't read gossip rags.

"You should just trust me," she says.

What can I say to that? I have no reason to distrust Addison, but I also have no reason to trust her, especially if she sees herself as a woman scorned. I think back to our first conversation about Braden. Addie said they'd had a thing the summer after she graduated from high school. She was eighteen then, and Braden would have been twenty-four. The same age I am now.

He made his millions a year later, at twenty-five.

Addie knew Braden when he was a blue-collar construction worker. I stifle a laugh. Addison Ames was slumming after graduation. A last fling before college. Sowing her wild oats and all that.

"You and Braden were young when you were involved," I say.

"True. But a tiger doesn't change its stripes."

"Addie, there's a world of difference between a twenty-four-year-old guy and a thirty-five-year-old man."

"Not when both of them are Braden Black."

"How do you know?"

"I just know. Stay away from him."

Or what? The words hover on the tip of my tongue. What's the worst that can happen? She can fire me. I need the job, but I've made tons of contacts working for her. I could probably find something else fairly quickly.

Unless she blackballs me.

"We're dating," I say calmly.

"Braden doesn't date."

"Apparently he does now."

"Don't fool yourself." She flounces back into her office but then looks over her shoulder before she shuts the door. "Don't say I didn't warn you."

The door slams.

At least she didn't fire me.

I pull up my Instagram account and hit Public.

What can it hurt? I can always change it back.

Within seconds, though, I'm inundated with followers. Seriously, a thousand in ten minutes. What is going on? I haven't even posted anything about Braden, and I'm only tagged in two of his.

Ding! A notification pops up. Apparently I've been tagged in a comment to one of Braden's posts.

@krissmith4009: @stormyskye15 your lip color is gorgeous! What brand is it?

Without thinking, I reply.

@krissmith4009 Glad you like it. It's Susanne lip stain in Cherry Russet.

One of my favorites and my usual "everyday" color because it's beautifully neutral and goes with everything.

Almost immediately, I get a notification.

@krissmith4009 liked your comment.

I cock my head, expecting the xylophone rendition of *The Twilight Zone* melody to begin playing. Because I had lunch with Braden, someone out there is interested in my lipstick.

Surreal.

A half hour later, I have more than a thousand likes on the post of Tessa and me at the gala, plus quite a few comments.

You look gorgeous!

Beautiful ladies.

Wowza!

Who's your friend? You're both hot as hell.

Toto, I don't think we're in Kansas anymore.

Chapter Thirty-One

I'm Braden Black's girlfriend.

At least that's how one of my new followers describes me.

You're so lucky to be Braden Black's girlfriend! #envious

This new comment appears on the post of Tessa and me from the gala after I get home from work. I'm warming up some leftover beef stew when my cell rings. Must be Tessa. She saw the post. Without looking at the number, I put it to my ear. "Hi, Tess."

"It's not Tess."

Braden. How did he get my cell number? Ridiculous question. He's Braden Black.

"Hi," I say, trying to sound nonchalant.

"I see you're gaining quite a following."

"Yeah. It's pretty weird."

"Get used to it."

"I'll try. I can always put my account back to private."

"You can," he says, "but you won't."

"Why wouldn't I?"

"Just trust me. Do you want to get dinner?"

"I'm heating up leftovers."

"Enough for two?"

"Well, yeah, but—"

"Great. I'll be there in three minutes."

"In three minutes? What—"

"I'm right outside your building."

"How did you— Never mind. Christopher knows where I live."

"He does, but I didn't need him to find you. See you in a few."

I race to the bathroom and run a brush through my hair, fluffing it. My makeup is fine, but I've changed into sweats and a tank top and my feet are bare. Oh well. This will have to do.

A minute later, Braden is knocking on my door.

I open it.

My breath catches. He's clad in a black suit with a white shirt. He's removed his tie, though, and unbuttoned the first few buttons of his shirt. His eyes are heavy-lidded and his full lips slightly parted. I'll never tire of his male beauty. The fact that he rarely smiles only makes him hotter, for some reason unknown to me.

He walks in as if he owns the place. Come to think of it, that's how he always walks in any room. My modest studio is a large closet compared to his palace. I say a quick thanks to the universe that I made my bed this morning. That's a fifty-fifty possibility on any given day.

"Smells good," he says.

"Beef stew. One of my specialties. My mom's recipe, a staple from my childhood."

His lips quirk, and for a second, I think he's going to smile.

He doesn't. "I love beef stew."

"Good. Though I'm sure Marilyn could prepare you a

gourmet version that totally puts mine to shame."

"Marilyn has never made beef stew."

He loves beef stew but his personal chef doesn't make it? Puzzling. But I'm done with the subject of stew. "So much for small talk. Why are you here, Braden?"

"To join you for dinner."

"We just saw each other at lunch."

He raises an eyebrow. "I'll go if you'd rather I not be here."

"That's not what I meant." I want him here. I *really* want him here. I'm just confused as all get out. "Stay."

"All right."

"I just meant…you said you didn't want a relationship, but here you are."

"And…?"

"And…we've seen a lot of each other in a short time. Doesn't that make us…*something*?"

He rubs his jawline. "It makes you my girlfriend, Skye. Isn't that what you wanted?"

"Girlfriend?" I shake my head. Then it dawns on me. "You saw the comment on my Instagram post."

"I did. I'll ask again. Isn't that what you wanted?"

"I don't know what I want, honestly. I only know I want more than a purely sexual arrangement."

"Which is why I've agreed to date you."

"Then let's date."

"Isn't that what we're doing right now?"

I look down at my feet. "No. I don't normally date in bare feet and sweats. Why are you really here, Braden? Because I'm absolutely sure it's not to eat my leftover beef stew."

"Do you even have to ask?"

I warm all over. Then I gulp. "Yeah. I have to ask."

"I'm here to fuck you, Skye."

My knees wobble. "Then I definitely need to eat."

He smiles. Almost. "So do I."

I motion to my small table. "Have a seat. Dinner will be ready in a minute. Can I get you a drink?"

He removes his suit coat, hangs it on the back of a chair, and sits. "Wild Turkey."

I smile. "I always have that." I pull the bottle out of a top cupboard, grab a lowball glass, and pour him a double. Then I add one ice cube and hand him the glass.

He takes a sip. "Going to join me?"

"Not tonight, no." He's already changed my plans by showing up. Not that I mind, but I want all my faculties tonight. I busy myself dishing up the stew. I stopped at the bakery after work—not to look at erotic cakes, though it crossed my mind—and picked up another baguette. I slice it and set it on a plate. What's missing? Of course. Water. I pour two glasses and bring everything to the table.

"Dig in," I say.

He nods, spoons up some stew, blows on it, and then into his mouth it goes.

I wait, holding my breath. My stew is good. Though it's my mom's recipe, I've made it my own over the years.

"Delicious," he says.

I let out the breath, nod, and take a bite myself. It *is* good. Stew is one of those dishes that's even better as a leftover. The extra time for the herbs and spices to soften and blend makes all the difference. "Bread?"

"Yeah. Thanks." He takes a hunk. "Do you have any butter?"

"Oh, yeah." I rise and resist the urge to hit myself in the head. Who forgets butter? I find a stick in the fridge, unwrap it, and place it on my butter dish. "Here you go."

"Thanks."

A few minutes pass. Then—

"You're a good cook, Skye."

"Thanks."

"This is the best stew I've had in a long time."

"I'm glad you like it. I wasn't sure you were a stew kind of guy."

"Are you kidding? My mother made stew all the time while I was growing up."

"Right. It's easy to forget sometimes."

"What do you mean?"

"Well…" *Way to put your foot in your mouth, Skye.* "You grew up like I did. You didn't always have billions."

"You're saying stew is a poor man's meal?"

My cheeks warm. "I don't know what I'm saying. Forget I said anything."

"I still enjoy the simple things," he says. "A walk in the rain, watching the sun rise, a warm bowl of stew, and a slice of crusty bread. Money doesn't change who a person is."

"I didn't mean that it did."

"Okay. No big deal."

Maybe it *is* a big deal, though. "If you like stew so much, Braden, why don't you have Marilyn cook it for you?"

He doesn't hesitate. "It wouldn't be the same."

"As your mother's?"

He nods.

Braden's mother passed away before he made his billions. It's common knowledge. He's opening up a bit. A tiny bit, but I'll take what I can get.

"Tell me about your mother," I say.

He swallows his bite of stew, his eyes darting to the side. "I don't talk about her."

"Why?"

He meets my gaze this time. "It's too hard."

So much for that. "What about your dad? Can you tell

me about him?"

"You can google him and find out everything."

"I don't want to read it in some rag, Braden. I want *you* to tell me."

"I don't talk about my family."

What do *you talk about, then?* I don't say the words, though. Instead—

"What happened between you and Addison?"

He wipes his mouth with his napkin and stands. "Your stew is delicious, Skye, but I've had enough talking for one night."

Chapter Thirty-Two

Braden yanks me out of my chair, pulls me into him, and smashes his mouth to mine. His tongue invades me, tasting of Wild Turkey, beef stew, and cinnamon—an intoxicating mélange that both burns and cools me simultaneously. I melt into the kiss and explore every inch of his delicious mouth. Already my core is throbbing in time with my racing heart.

Braden pulls me closer, grinding his bulge into me. Has he been hard this whole time? While I was asking questions? Or is the kiss making him hard?

I don't care. I just need him inside me. I need another orgasm more than I want my next breath of oxygen. I'm already halfway there with his drugging kiss.

Yes, his kisses are like a drug I can no longer live without. I'm addicted to him, to Braden. To his body and his mind.

Be careful, Skye. He doesn't want a relationship. Don't fall in love.

I erase all thoughts from my brain and surrender to Braden's amazing kiss. It's not gentle, and though it's passionate, it's not a kiss of love.

It's a kiss of possession. Of power.

He's urging me to give up control once more.

My nipples harden, and I ache for his lips and tongue on them. Wetness surges between my legs, and the blood in my veins heats, sending every cell of my body into chaos.

Beautiful chaos.

I want him to fuck me.

I have no blindfolds here, no cool metal objects he can torment me with. No weird contraption hanging from the ceiling.

I have only a bed.

And Braden.

I thread my fingers through his thick hair, like silk against my skin. Our kiss deepens and it's like our mouths are fused together.

Need to breathe.

Don't want to break the kiss.

Need to—

He pulls away. "Bed."

I point. He drags me to the alcove where it sits and shoves me down. I bounce lightly on the mattress. He strips off his shirt. I gape at his perfect chest—those broad golden shoulders, the smattering of black hair, nipples brown and hard, his tight abs, and then that black hair narrowing down to his cock, still clothed.

He kicks off his shiny leather shoes and unbuckles his belt. In a flash, he pushes his pants and boxer briefs over his hips and steps out of them.

He's naked.

Gloriously naked, and I'm still fully clothed.

Usually it's the other way around.

He meets my gaze, his blue eyes full of sapphire smoke. "Get on your knees, Skye."

Tingles skitter through me. He wants me to suck him. I can do that. I've done it before. But on my knees? I can do it sitting on the bed. "Braden, I— "

"On your knees!"

The dark passion in his voice slides over me like melted caramel. I'm both terrified and aroused. I sit, immobile.

"Don't make me say it again."

I drive all thoughts out of my head and drop to my knees. His dick bobs in front of me, and I reach toward him—

"No," he says. "Stay still. Don't touch me."

I widen my eyes.

"I'm going to fuck your mouth like I fuck your pussy. You stay still."

"But it's better for you if I can use my hands."

"Maybe I'll let you do it your way sometime. Tonight, we do it mine. No hands. And no more talking."

That won't be hard, since his dick will be in my mouth. Does he realize I'm still dressed?

He nudges his cock over my lips. "God, your mouth is so sexy. Open for me."

I drop my lips into an O, and he slides his cock between them. Since I can't use my hands, I'm not steady. I take a chance and grab onto the backs of his thighs, relishing the firm muscle. He doesn't stop me.

He pulls out and then shoves himself back into my mouth, going as far as he can until he hits the back of my throat. I'm good at this. I don't gag, usually. But Braden stays embedded in my mouth for what seems like an hour. I hold my breath, but if he doesn't move soon, I know I'll—

He pulls out, and I relax the back of my throat. By the time it feels normal, he's sliding into me again. He holds it again and then pulls out. Is this good for him? Isn't it the thrusting that gets a guy going?

Before I can say as much, he's inside my mouth again, my lips embracing his erection. He goes faster this time, and soon he's doing what he said—fucking my mouth. It's uncomfortable at times, but I'm determined. If this is what he wants, I'll give it to him, and I'll give it to him better than Addison or anyone else ever has.

My jaw aches and saliva drips from my lips, creating a slick lubricant.

"Yeah, that's it, baby. Your sexy lips feel so good around me. Perfect. Just perfect. Fuck!" He withdraws quickly, and I inhale a much-needed breath.

"I need to come, but I want to come inside you." He grips my shoulders and brings me to my feet, turns me around, and slides my sweats and panties over my hips before nudging me onto the bed. My sweats are around my knees, so I can't spread my legs, but he thrusts into me, and the narrowness makes him feel even bigger than he is, like a rocket blasting through me.

"Damn, you feel perfect," he groans. "So good."

I gasp as he thrusts once, twice, three times—

"Fuck!" He propels into me, burning a trail through me as my clit bumps against the bed.

He slaps one cheek of my ass as he releases.

I try to grind into the bed to sate my clit, but I can't move with his weight bearing down on me.

No orgasm this time.

I can live with that. In fact, I feel wonderful because I gave him what he wanted.

He stays buried inside me for a few moments, breathing heavily. I don't move or speak.

I wait.

And wait.

Until he pulls out.

Then—

"Shit. Shit, shit, shit."

I look over my shoulder. "What? What is it?"

"I forgot the damned condom."

Chapter Thirty-Three

I swallow audibly. I forgot the condom, too. He and I both know I have one in my purse, just as he has one in his pocket. This is just as much my fault.

I've been on the pill since college, and I know I'm clean. I've had all the tests, and I haven't been sexually active in more than a year. He has nothing to fear from me.

Braden, however, has probably had myriad sexual partners. I turn over, pull my sweats and panties back up, and sit on the bed. "Do I have reason to worry?"

"Not from me. I get tested every three months."

"Every three months? Whatever for?" Then I clamp my hand over my mouth because I really don't want to know the answer to that question.

"Because it's good policy, Skye, that's why. What about you?"

"I'm good. Clean."

"That's not what I'm concerned about."

"What's the problem, then?"

"Pregnancy. I don't want a kid. You carry a rubber around

in your purse. Does that mean…?"

"Extra protection. I'm on the pill."

Still naked, he sits down next to me. "Thank God."

He's distant tonight. He's always a little distant, but tonight more so. I itch to cover his hand with my own, but something stops me, as if an invisible barrier exists between us despite the acts we just shared.

I let out a nervous laugh. "The good news is we don't have to use condoms anymore."

"I always use condoms."

Again, he puzzles me. Most men are thrilled not to use condoms. "Why? If we're both clean, and I— Oh." I press my lips together.

"Finish what you were going to say, Skye."

I inhale and let out a stream of breath slowly. "I'm not the only woman you're sleeping with, am I?"

"This week you are."

A wave of sadness explodes inside me. I do my best to stifle it. I will *not* cry in front of Braden. I have no hold on him. I don't want to give him up, but I won't be part of a harem, either, no matter what kind of silly emotion I'm feeling.

Silence for a few more seconds. Then—

He turns to me, his eyes serious. "That's never happened to me before."

"What do you mean?"

"I've never forgotten to put on a condom."

I'm not sure how to reply, so I don't.

He's still naked and not making any move to get dressed. Maybe I'll get that orgasm after all. I won't push it, though. Instead, in my head I'm dissecting his words.

I've never forgotten to put on a condom.

The operative word is "never." Braden has had a lot of sex. I mean, look at him. Plus, he's a billionaire. And he's never forgotten a condom until tonight?

His desire for me overtook his rational thought.

What other meaning can there be?

Though I'm tempted to smile, I don't.

Finally, I think of the perfect thing to say.

"Did you enjoy it?"

He huffs harshly. "Not using a condom? Hell yeah. You felt amazing."

"Then why use them?"

"It's hard to explain."

"Try."

"I'm not sure. It's kind of a..." He closes his eyes. A few seconds later, he opens them and meets my gaze. "We've done enough talking for one night. I owe you a climax."

The magic words.

I'm ready to strip and fall back onto the bed with my legs spread...but I don't. Instead, "I don't want you to sleep with anyone else while you're sleeping with me."

Yeah, I don't know what I'm thinking. I probably just gave up a climax when I'm still in single digits.

His gaze burns into mine. He was in a dark mood when he arrived, and it's become darker. I won't back down, though. As much as I want that orgasm, I deserve to be the only one in his bed, and not just because that's what I want. I deserve it because I don't want to be exposed to anything someone else might be carrying, condom or not.

"I told you. You're the only one I'm sleeping with this week. I haven't fucked anyone else since I started fucking you."

"Good," I say. "Keep it that way."

"Skye—"

"If I'm your"—air quotes—"'girlfriend,' I deserve to be the only one in your bed."

He stares at me, his expression shadowy and unreadable.

Finally—

"Okay."

My eyebrows shoot up. His answer is not what I expected.

"You're surprised," he says.

"A little."

"What kind of man do you think I am, Skye?"

"That's just it, Braden. I don't *know* what kind of man you are. You refuse to talk about anything personal. You're intelligent, obviously. You're an excellent businessperson. You do some charity work. But that's all I know other than what magazines report."

"You know I love oysters."

"For God's sake, Braden."

He sighs. "You know as much as anyone else does. Isn't that enough?"

"No, it's not, especially if I'm"—air quotes again—"your '*girlfriend*.'"

"Fuck," he says through clenched teeth. He grabs my breast and thumbs my nipple over two layers of fabric.

Sparks arrow between my legs.

He leans into me and kisses my neck, scraping his teeth over my skin.

I shudder.

God, I want that orgasm.

"You want to know about me?" he rasps into my ear. "Here's all you need. Since I laid eyes on you, I haven't been able to think about anyone else. Your mouth, your tits, your curious and controlling nature—everything about you beguiles me. Since I first fucked you, all I can think about is fucking you again. You're all I think about"—he bites my earlobe—"and it...*perplexes* me. Not much perplexes me, Skye. You're like a narcotic. I hunger for you." He inhales. "God, I love how you smell—like apples and sex. You taste even better. You want to be the only one in my bed? You don't even have to ask. You're the only woman I want right now. The *only* one."

A low growl vibrates from my throat as my belly flutters and my pussy pulsates.

He scrapes his teeth along the outer edge of my ear. "Now, let me give you that climax."

Chapter Thirty-Four

He lifts my tank top over my head and throws it on the floor. Then he unhooks my bra and discards it as my breasts fall against my chest. He cups them, kneads them, and then he buries his nose between them, kissing them and thumbing my nipples.

I'm still high from his sexy monologue. I want to return the sentiment, but I'm currently incapable of speech. Every cell inside my body is humming, ready to be expertly strummed by Braden's deft fingers and tongue.

He nibbles the tops of my breasts and then finally takes a nipple between his lips and sucks.

I inhale sharply. I'm so ripe. One touch to my clit and I know I'll implode on the spot.

"So beautiful," he says against my flesh.

"Braden, please…"

"Please what, baby?"

"I…I want to come."

"You will." He bites a nipple.

"Oh!" It's both painful and pleasurable.

"You like that?" he says.

"Yes. God, yes."

"Good. I could suck and bite your tits all day." He nibbles on my other nipple and then raises his head again. "On the other hand, that paradise between your legs is even more beautiful." He slides down my body, grasping my sweats, and glides them over my hips and legs.

Now we're both naked.

Perfect.

He spreads my legs. "God, yes. So beautiful."

I've never thought of that part of me as beautiful. Certainly not ugly, either. I honestly never gave its aesthetic value any thought at all. But I see the appreciative gaze in Braden's blue eyes. He truly does think it's beautiful—that *I'm* beautiful.

"I'm going to make you come, Skye," he says, his voice low and husky. "I'm going to make you come so many times that you'll be begging me to stop."

"No," I say, "I'll never beg you to stop."

"You will." He strokes his tongue over my clit.

I quiver beneath him. Already I'm close to climax. He tugs on my flesh and then closes his lips over my clit. Sensation skyrockets through me. Braden knows which buttons to push, and he's pushing them hard.

"You taste so good, baby," he says, lapping at me like I'm rich cream. "I'll never get enough. But this isn't about me." He glides a finger into my pussy.

And I shatter into millions of pieces—fragments of peace, of joy, of euphoria.

I close my eyes and revel in the tornado lifting me onto a soft cloud of desire and passion.

Braden's voice floats in the air—that deep timbre that slides over me and drives me wild. Words hover outside my grasp. He adds another finger, urging me on and then sucking on my clit. I climb the peak again and yet again.

Two orgasms and then three.

I'm exploding and relishing it. My clit becomes so sensitive, it almost hurts, but no, I won't beg him to stop.

I'll *never* beg him to stop.

I'm a woman who only recently experienced a climax, and I may go into double digits tonight alone.

His words form in the air and drift to my ears.

Tell me to stop, Skye. Tell me it's too much. Too much… Too much…

A soft chuckle.

You are obstinate. Fuck. I have to be inside you.

Then he's in me, his cock invading me with its granite heat. My pussy walls are still spasming, and the fullness completes me as he fucks me hard and quick, grinding over my clit so the climaxes continue.

"Braden!" I cry out.

"That's it, baby. Keep coming. Keep coming. You're so hot. That's it. That's it. Fuck!"

He pushes into me, so deep I can almost feel him in my soul.

I'm still spasming as he releases, and we come in tandem. Perspiration glistens on his forehead.

He stays on top of me, our bodies still joined, for a few timeless moments.

And for those few moments, I feel an utter completeness that is foreign to me.

Too soon, he withdraws and rolls onto his back. I snuggle against his shoulder and kiss his salty flesh.

"That was amazing," I say.

He doesn't look at me. "You didn't beg."

"No, I didn't."

"Any other woman would have begged me to stop. I know a woman's body. I know that many orgasms are a toll, pleasure morphing to almost pain."

He's not wrong.

"But you didn't beg me to stop. I'll say it again. You're my Everest, Skye."

I giggle. "I think you've already climbed me."

He opens his eyes and props his head in his hand to meet my gaze. "This isn't funny."

"I didn't say it was."

"You laughed."

"I was making a joke. About climbing on top of me?" I force a smile. How can he be upset about something so trivial?

"I get what I want, Skye. Always. No matter how long it takes."

I swallow.

"You gave in to me once. I want it again."

My body is so sated and relaxed, but still a tingle rushes toward my core. "And in return?"

"You get me. You're Braden Black's girlfriend."

I bite my lower lip. I can't deny my desire to be his girlfriend and his lover. I also can't deny how giving up my control in his penthouse that night resulted in the most exciting sensations I ever experienced.

"I think I'm already Braden Black's girlfriend," I say. "Instagram doesn't lie, after all."

I expect him to say something snide. Instead—

"All right. What else do you want?"

I answer quickly. "To be the only one. If you become interested in someone else, you have to tell me, and that will be the end. And I don't want you to use condoms with me."

He stays quiet for a few seconds that seem like hours.

Then—

"Done."

Braden falls asleep a few minutes later, and I lie in his arms, my body still ultimately relaxed but my brain working overtime.

I lost a golden opportunity. Why did I ask to be the only one? He already said he couldn't think of anyone but me and that I made him go wild. When he asked what I wanted in return, I could have said so many other things.

I want to know why you always use condoms even when there's no reason to.

I want to know about your mother.

I want to know the truth about you and Addison.

I kiss his shoulder and then his neck. I trail my fingers through the scattered black hair on his chest and then travel downward, over his sculpted abs to his nest of perfectly manscaped black curls. His cock lays flaccid. I touch the smooth flesh and let it rest beneath my fingers.

I kiss his shoulder again and release his dick.

"You are *my* Everest, Braden," I whisper. "I *will* figure you out."

Chapter Thirty-Five

I wake the next morning to a kiss on my forehead. I jerk upward.

Braden is already dressed, his hair damp.

"You took a shower?" I ask.

"Yeah. I've never used raspberry shampoo before. I like the fruity smell." His lips twist into a half smile.

I giggle without meaning to, and then I part my lips and inhale. His natural scent mingled with my shampoo smells like heaven.

"I didn't want to disturb you," he continues. "You were out."

A yawn splits my face. "I can't believe I didn't wake up."

"I can."

"You can? Why?"

"Multiple orgasms will do that to you." The words sound so matter-of-fact as he stares at his phone.

"What time is it?"

"Seven."

"Oh, good. I have plenty of time to get to work."

Still perusing his phone screen, he turns to me. "Looks like I have to go to New York for a few days."

"Oh," I say, trying not to sound melancholy. "Who will take care of Sasha?"

"Annika will. I'm texting her now. I'll be back Saturday morning. Saturday evening, I'd like you to accompany me to a benefit for the Boston Opera Guild."

I nod. "Sure. Okay."

He kisses my lips softly. "Wear the black dress."

Then he's gone, almost as if he disappeared in a poof of smoke. I yawn again and wipe the sleep out of my eyes.

Braden spent the night in my bed, in my tiny apartment. He stayed the night.

Now he's gone with only a chaste kiss. He's going to New York. New York, where beautiful businesswomen are everywhere. Where gorgeous models are everywhere. Today is Tuesday, and he won't be back until Saturday morning. That's four evenings where he'll no doubt be wining and dining other businesspeople.

Doesn't he need his "girlfriend" on his arm for the social parts?

Not that I can go anyway. Addie likes at least a month's notice before I take time off.

I sigh, get up, wander to the kitchenette to start a pot— I inhale. Of course. Braden already made a pot of coffee. He loves coffee as much as I do.

I smile and pour myself a mugful.

No time to ruminate on what—or *who*—Braden will do in New York. I have to go to work.

• • •

Addie's in early today because we have a shoot at ten. It's a smaller client, a local woman who makes her own pet products. Addie's chihuahua, Baby—yes, that's her name, even though she's a vicious little creature—is yapping in her kennel. Baby stars in all the pet-themed shoots. I love dogs, but this one gets on my last nerve. I never met a dog who didn't love me until Baby. The little monster growls at everyone except her owner, and she even snaps at Addie on occasion. And you can guess who gets the honor of cleaning up if Baby has an accident.

Still, Addie dotes on her and carries her around as if she were a real baby while I try not to gag.

I sit down at my desk, fire up the computer, and review the details for today's shoot. We'll go to Betsy's Bark Boutique and shoot a photo of Addie feeding Baby some of Betsy's homemade grain-free peanut butter treats. Betsy is an old childhood friend of Addie's, so she does the shoots gratis. Thank God *I* get paid. Getting a shot where Addie is convinced that both she and Baby look good sometimes requires dozens of takes.

I'm not looking forward to it.

The Bark Boutique is near the harbor. I call and confirm our transportation, and then I message Tessa, whose office is near, to meet me there after the shoot for lunch. As soon as I hang up, the phone rings again.

"Addison Ames's office," I say into the receiver. "This is Skye."

"Good morning, Skye, it's Eugenie from Susanne Cosmetics."

"Hi there. I'll transfer you to Addison." I put the call on hold and buzz Addie. "It's Eugenie."

"Who?"

"The social media promotions director at Susanne."

"Oh. Yeah. Thanks."

I wait until Addie picks up and then hang up the line.

I read through two emails and respond. Just as I'm about to click on another, Addie opens her office door and stomps out carrying Baby's kennel. She sets it down, opens it, and a yapping Baby shrieks through the office like a racquetball pinging off every wall.

"What the hell is going on, Skye?" Addison demands.

"Just responding to emails."

"Right."

"Addie, I have no idea what you're talking about." I hit Send quickly and close out of the mailbox.

"Eugenie," she says.

"What did she want? Is there a new color of lip plumper she wants you to model?"

Addie sits on the edge of my desk and looks down at me. I don't like the fact that she's on higher ground, so I stand.

She shoots daggers at me with her eyes. "Eugenie didn't call for me."

"Then why did she call?"

"She wanted to talk to *you*."

My jaw drops. "Me? Why would she—"

"I don't appreciate looking like I'm out of the loop," she snaps. "Why did you transfer her?"

"I honestly thought—"

"Apparently Susanne has gotten *hundreds* of orders for their Cherry Russet lip stain because of a comment you made on Braden's Instagram." Addie grabs my purse off the desk, opens it, and turns it over, letting the contents fall onto my blotter.

"What the hell are you doing?" I demand angrily.

She picks up the tube of lipstick. "What have we here? Cherry Russet lip stain." She hurls it to the floor, startling

Baby, who shrieks again.

I'm not only angry at Addison for touching my stuff, I'm flummoxed. Truly flummoxed. Why would anyone care what kind of lipstick I use?

"You have no right to—"

"Get over it," Addison says. "Your purse will survive, and as long as Baby is otherwise occupied, so will your lip stain."

I tamp down my anger long enough to try to figure out what's going on. "I don't understand. Did she call to thank me for the comment?"

Addie scoffs. "Do you really think the director of social media promotions for a top cosmetics company would call to thank someone for a comment?"

"Why else would she—"

"She wants you to do a post, Skye. She wants to pay you to promote the lip stain on your Instagram profile."

"Me? I'm no influencer."

"You are now. Apparently you're Braden Black's girlfriend, and that makes you an instant influencer." She scoffs again. "Oh, and to quote Eugenie, the stain is"—air quotes—"'*absolutely fabulous*' on you."

"I don't know what to say." I truly don't. I never wanted to be an Instagram influencer. I just want to take pictures. Really good pictures that move people. Not selfies wearing lip stain.

"This all makes sense now." Addie tosses my empty purse onto the desk.

"What are you talking about?"

"You. And Braden." She shakes her head. "He's just using you, you know."

A spear slices into my heart. Her words hurt, but I won't show her that. "We just met."

"He's using you. Trust me. He knows I'm getting older. He's trying to make you into a bigger influencer than I am.

Put me out of business."

"What?" I cock my head, incredulous. "You can't be serious. First of all, Braden has his own business. Why would he have any interest in taking down yours?"

"This has his stench all over it."

"Second," I continue, "I'm a nobody."

"For God's sake, Skye, you're Braden Black's *girlfriend*. You stopped being a nobody the minute he posted that first photo and tagged you in it."

The thought warms me but at the same time sends icy chills over my neck.

Is she right? Is Braden using me?

We got hot and heavy quickly. Too quickly, really, and he doesn't want a relationship.

Self-doubt washes over me. *No. No, no, no. He likes me. He can't stop thinking about me. He wants only me.*

"Call Eugenie," Addie says. "Do the post. Make a few bucks. But you'll never be me, Skye. You'll never be as big as Addison Ames." She marches back to her office and slams the door, leaving her dog still ricocheting wall to wall.

I don't want to be you, I say silently. *I never wanted to be you.*

Still, her words have carved out a piece of my heart.

I don't care about Eugenie or Susanne Cosmetics. I don't care about Addison's anger at the moment. I don't even care about her accusations that Braden is using me, though they're most likely true.

I care only about my heart.

And I may be losing it to Braden Black.

Chapter Thirty-Six

I coax Baby into her kennel and set her next to my desk. Then I gather the scattered items, including the Cherry Russet lip stain, and refill my purse.

I'm angry with Addie. Big-time. But I'm more befuddled than anything. Knowing full well it may cost me my job, I walk to her door and knock.

"What is it?" she yells angrily.

"I need to talk to you."

"I have nothing to say to you."

"Maybe not. But I have something to say to you."

"Nothing I want to hear."

"Please. It's important."

"Fine," she huffs. "Come in."

Addison doesn't look me in the eye. Instead, she stares at her laptop screen while sitting at her desk. She doesn't stand, so I take a seat on one of the leather chairs facing her.

"You need to tell me," I say, "what happened between you and Braden."

"I don't need to tell you anything."

"How else will I know if I'm making a huge mistake?"

"You can take my word for it." She still hasn't looked up from her laptop.

"I didn't even know you knew Braden until last week," I say. "Can't you just tell me?"

She closes her laptop and finally looks me in the eye. "He's bad news. The worst."

"You've already said that. What you haven't said is why."

"I've told you—I don't talk about it."

I raise my eyebrows. Addie is never one to mince words. She says what she thinks and doesn't usually give a damn about the consequences. "You don't talk about it? Or you *can't* talk about it?"

She stands. "Doesn't really matter which, does it? Our car should be here. Let's get this shoot over with."

To my surprise, we get the shoot done in minimal takes. Baby is abnormally subdued after the ride. Maybe Addie gave her a sedative. Betsy gives both Addie and me gift baskets of her dog treats as a thank-you for the shoot. This is new. Normally she only gives one to Addie. Addie regards me expectantly. Does she want me to give her my basket?

"Thank you so much," I tell Betsy. "I don't have a dog, but my friend does. She'll love this."

No, Tessa doesn't have a dog, but Braden does. This basket is for Sasha, which also gives me an excuse to go over to Braden's place while he's in New York. If only to smell his scent again—that perfect mélange of pine, spice, and leather that has grown as necessary to me as air.

Tessa meets me at the Bark Boutique as planned.

Addie left, thank God, so I introduce Tessa to Betsy.

"This is an adorable place," Tessa says. "Do you do a good business?"

"Pretty good. The posts from Addison help a lot." She smiles.

"It was great meeting you," Tessa says. "You ready for lunch, Skye?"

"Yup. All set. Want to join us, Betsy?"

"I wish I could. But maybe..."

"What?" Tessa asks.

"Would you like to have a drink later? After six, when I close?"

Surprising. I've been doing shoots for Betsy since I began working with Addie. She's never wanted to get together before.

"I wish, but I can't," I say. After all, I'm going to Braden's to deliver Sasha's basket.

"I can," Tessa says. "I never turn down a chance for a drink after work. I'll meet you here, okay?"

Tessa and Betsy just met, but my best friend has a way of putting people at ease.

Betsy smiles. "That'd be great. I'm looking forward to it."

Once Tessa and I hit a café for lunch, I fill her in on Addison's earlier antics.

"She did *not* empty your purse on your desk," Tessa says.

"She did. I'm still pissed about it."

"You should be."

"But I'm more confused. Why does she think Braden is bad news? She won't tell me. When I asked her if she doesn't talk about it or she can't talk about it, she changed the subject."

"You think she has an NDA or something?"

"I have no idea."

"It has to be something like that. Otherwise, why wouldn't she tell you? If she's concerned that you'll become competition for her because of your relationship with Braden, surely she'd want to get you away from him."

"Good point," I say, "and one I hadn't considered. You're right. She *can't* talk about it, for whatever reason."

"Or it's a big fat lie," Tessa observes.

"I don't think so. She and Braden both admit to having a thing years ago. Whatever it was, it didn't end well."

I don't tell Tessa that I think I'm falling for Braden. I'm hoping it will go away. After all, I've known him for all of a week.

The waiter delivers our lunches, and I take a quick bite of my chicken sandwich.

"When are you taking the doggie basket over to Sasha?" Tessa asks.

"Tonight. Betsy's treats are all organic and best enjoyed within a week."

Tessa swallows her bite of pasta. "Betsy seems nice."

"She is. Not the kind of person Addie normally—" I stop abruptly, a light flashing in my mind.

"What?" Tessa asks.

"Betsy's a childhood friend of Addie's. I wonder…"

"If they went to high school together?"

"Yeah. She must be some friend. Addie doesn't usually work for free, and she never charges Betsy for a post. If she's that good of a friend, she might know something about Addie and Braden."

"I'm on it," Tessa says. "Maybe she'll talk about Addie when we have our drinks tonight."

"Maybe." I take another bite of my sandwich, starting to feel a little guilty. I don't want to use Betsy for information. "Don't force her to talk, though."

"How on earth could I possibly force her? Besides, I wouldn't do that."

"I know. I just wish I could get Braden to tell me."

"Maybe it's nothing," Tessa says. "In fact, it probably is. This sounds like drama of Addie's making. Classic."

"You're probably right."

Between Tessa's drinks with Betsy and my trip to Braden's, this evening will be interesting.

Chapter Thirty-Seven

My nerves on edge, I grasp the doggie gift basket, nod to the doorman, and buzz Braden's penthouse.

No response for a few seconds. I buzz again.

"Yes?" says a female voice.

"Annika, is that you? It's Skye Manning."

"Hello, Ms. Manning. Mr. Black isn't home."

"I know he's in New York. I wanted to stop by because I have something for Sasha. A doggie gift basket from the Bark Boutique."

"How kind of you. I'll send Christopher down to get it."

"No, I— "

But she clicks off the intercom.

A few minutes later, Christopher steps out of Braden's private elevator on the far side of the lobby. "Ms. Manning."

"Hi, Christopher." I hold the basket to him. "Addison did an Instagram post today for Betsy's Bark Boutique, and Betsy gave us each a basket. Since I don't have a dog, I thought I'd give this to Sasha."

"That's kind of you. Do you want to take it upstairs with

me and say hi to her? Sasha will love it."

"Sure. Thanks."

A few minutes later, we step out of the elevator into Braden's lavish penthouse. Christopher whistles, and Sasha comes running.

"Hey, baby." I kneel and pet her soft head. "I brought you all kinds of goodies." I take the basket from Christopher's arms. "I'll just put this in the kitchen."

Christopher wrinkles his forehead but doesn't stop me. I set the basket on the island and untie the ribbon. "Come here, Sasha!"

She runs into the kitchen.

"Do you know any commands?"

"She knows them all." Christopher has apparently followed me to the kitchen.

"Great. Sasha, sit."

The dog plops down on her hindquarters.

"Good girl!" I hand her a small peanut butter dog treat. "There's some rawhide in here. Toys, too, it looks like."

After a minute of watching Sasha play, I look up at Christopher. "Could I use the restroom before I go?"

"Sure."

I walk slowly to the powder room, half expecting him to follow me, but he doesn't.

I spend a few minutes in the powder room, and then I flush the toilet and wash my hands. Before I open the door to leave, I dart my gaze downward to the magazine rack. It's filled with mail.

Strange. Does Braden read his mail in here? This is the first time I've actually been inside this room. In the past, I always used the bathroom in Braden's master suite.

None of your business, Skye. Walk away. Just walk away.

But do I walk away? No. I bend down and leaf through

the open envelopes. Nothing that catches my eyes until one near the bottom.

The return address.

Ames Hotels.

Without thinking, I grab it and stuff it in my purse. I don't know why. I honest-to-God don't know why.

But I'm out of the powder room and down the hallway toward the kitchen, my flesh tingling, before my brain kicks in. I should put it back, but if I walk back into the powder room, and someone on his staff sees me, I'll look suspicious. The basket still sits on the island, but Christopher is gone. I walk through the living room to the entryway. Christopher stands by the elevator, holding the end of a leash.

"Taking her on a walk now?" I ask.

"Yeah. She needs to go out every time she eats something."

"Oh. Sorry. I guess I shouldn't have given her that treat."

"No bother. I enjoy walking her."

"I should go, too," I say.

The letter is burning a hole in my purse. My nerves skitter across my skin. This was a huge mistake. I'd put it back if I could, but since I can't, I need to get home and see what it is. Why is Braden doing anything with Ames Hotels? He and Addison appear to hate each other.

And that bothers me more than a little. A thin line exists between love and hate. I'd much prefer him to be indifferent.

"That would probably be best, Ms. Manning."

I nod and walk into the elevator in front of Christopher and Sasha. I bend down to pet Sasha. She pants and licks my face. Then the elevator door opens, and Christopher waits while I walk out.

"Thanks, Christopher," I say.

"See you soon, Ms. Manning."

See you soon? That's a good sign.

I wave and walk out of the building, suppressing the shakes that threaten to consume me.

I just stole a piece of Braden's mail.

What the hell was I thinking?

A half hour later, I'm home, staring at the envelope from Ames Hotels.

It's already open. All I need to do is look inside. It's probably nothing. God, I hope it's nothing, because if it isn't, not only will I be heartbroken, but I'll also have to get it back to Braden's powder room somehow.

I can't do this. I can't.

My pulse thrums in my neck.

This isn't like me, to be so deceitful. I need to take this envelope back to Braden's house. Now. I pull one of my wire earrings out of my ear and stuff it inside my purse as well. Then I head back to Braden's. I can only hope Christopher is still on his walk with Sasha and Annika answers the intercom.

I'm literally shaking as I walk into Braden's building. I smile nervously at the doorman. I make my way to the intercom—

My cell phone rings.

Chapter Thirty-Eight

It's Tessa. Probably with news about her drinks with Betsy. Now what? I can talk to Tessa later, but if she has news, I need to know it now, before I attempt to put this piece of mail I so foolishly stole back in place.

I can't stay here in the lobby of the building. What if Christopher returns with Sasha? "Hold on a minute, Tess." I walk out of the building and continue walking. "What's up?"

"Betsy's really sweet."

I sigh. I already know that. "Oh?"

"Yeah. Don't hate me. But I have a dog."

"Why would I hate you? You know I love dogs. When did you get a dog, and why am I only now hearing about it?"

"Because she's a fake dog."

I make a face into the phone. "Huh?"

"I'm not sure how it happened, but she was talking so much about her business and how much she loves animals, it just kind of popped out."

"O…kay."

"Anyway, once she found out we have a love of dogs in

common—and I do love dogs; you know that—she opened up and we talked about…a lot of things."

My heart races. I'm still walking, now a block away from Braden's building. I dodge inside a small café and sit down at a table. "What did she say?"

"She and Addison have known each other since grade school. They didn't go to high school together. Addie went to some private school, but they stayed in touch and always got together over the summer. Betsy was kind of a charity case for Addie and her family. They paid for her to go to all the same programs Addie and Apple went to over the summer, except they didn't go away for the summer after graduation. Instead, Betsy stayed at Addison's house."

"So she knows about Braden."

"She does."

"Did she tell you anything?"

"Oh yeah."

I look down at my shaking left hand. I will it to still. "Don't leave me in suspense. How did they meet?"

"You're not going to believe this. One weekend when Mom and Dad were out of town, Addison and Apple threw a party at the mansion, and Braden and his brother, Ben, showed up."

"How would they know about a party at the Ames house?"

"Got me. Betsy didn't know."

"Okay. Wait, hold on a second." A server approaches. "Black coffee," I say. Then, to Tessa, "Go ahead."

"According to Betsy, Addie was all over Braden, but he didn't give her the time of day."

"What? They both cop to having a thing."

"They did, but it didn't start that night. Addie got obsessed with him. She couldn't understand how anyone could turn down an Ames heiress, and she was determined to lose her virginity that summer…to Braden Black."

"Oh my God…"

"She found the construction site where he was working and showed up there the next week. He rebuffed her again and again, but she didn't get the message."

"Seriously? She's a stalker?"

"She was then, anyway. Braden had a small apartment in South Boston, and Addie found the address."

I don't like where this is going. "And…?"

"Betsy stopped talking," Tessa says.

"Are you kidding me?" I wave thanks to the server when she sets my cup of coffee on the table.

"Yeah. She even covered her mouth and begged me not to tell anyone what she said, that she wasn't supposed to talk about it."

"What did you do?"

"I assured her I'd be discreet, of course, but that I tell you everything. She said that was okay but that you couldn't tell anyone. I assured her you wouldn't. I didn't want to push her any further. She's so sweet, and it's really not any of my business."

I take a sip of coffee. "Ouch!" The hot liquid scorches the inside of my mouth. I swallow quickly, burning a trail down my esophagus.

"What?"

"Nothing. I burned my tongue. Then what happened?"

"I said good night, we made plans to have drinks again sometime, and I promised I'd visit her boutique to get more treats for Margarita."

"Margarita?"

"My fake dog. Rita for short."

"All you could think of was Margarita?"

"What can I say? I was drinking a strawberry margarita."

I roll my eyes. Tessa and her froufrou drinks. "Slick, Tess."

"Hey, I was on the spot."

I sigh. "Yeah, okay. We still don't know what happened between them and why Addie is convinced Braden is bad news."

"But we do know that Addie is the one who pursued Braden."

"Which means she probably felt scorned when whatever they had ended."

"Right," Tessa says. "And hell hath no fury like a woman scorned."

We end our call, and I take another sip of my coffee. It's still hotter than asphalt on a summer day. I quickly lay several dollar bills on the table and leave the café. Now what? The stolen letter burns hot in my purse. I can almost feel its energy, like a homing signal is beeping from it.

All in my imagination, I know, but this was a huge mistake. Braden says he can't have a relationship with me. How can I expect him to change his mind if I paw through his personal mail? I trudge back to his building, half smile at the doorman, and press the intercom once more.

"Yes?"

My stomach twists into knots.

It's Braden's voice.

Chapter Thirty-Nine

"You... You're supposed to be in New York," I say without thinking.

Damn. Should have just rung the doorbell and ran. Except I'm not twelve.

"Skye? What are you doing here?"

"I dropped off some treats for Sasha, and I think I lost an earring. I just wanted to come up and look for it." The lie tastes like stomach acid in my throat.

"All right. I'll send the elevator down."

I move toward his private penthouse elevator and wait. When the doors open, I expect Christopher to walk out, but the elevator is empty. I enter and push the lone button for the penthouse.

Chills sweep over me as the cubicle ascends. Too soon, the door opens.

Braden stands waiting in the entryway. "Good evening, Skye."

"Hi." My voice cracks. Shit.

"Thank you for the treats for Sasha. I just saw the basket

in the kitchen."

"You're welcome. I got it free at a shoot, and of course I have no use for it."

"Nice of you to think of her," he says.

Things seem icy between us. But why? He showed up at *my* place unannounced. Why shouldn't I show up at his? "Why are you home so soon?"

"I was able to complete the business early."

"In one day?"

"Does that seem implausible to you?"

Does it? He's a billionaire. People probably continuously kiss his ass. No, it's not implausible. What's more implausible is that he had to be gone the rest of the week. Did he lie to me?

I have no right to ask, especially with a stolen piece of mail burning a hole in my purse.

And that's just it.

I don't want any lies between us. I can't control what he tells me, but I can at least control what *I* do. If I want him to eventually commit to a relationship, I need to show him I mean business. Honesty and trust are a big part of that.

"Braden"—I clear my throat—"I didn't lose an earring."

"Oh?" His blue eyes twinkle a bit. "Why are you here, then?"

"Because I…" I draw in a deep breath and hold it a few seconds.

"Spit it out, Skye."

Because I want you. Because I think I'm falling for you. The words are on the tip of my tongue, and they're not a lie. Just looking at him makes me yearn for him. But I thought he was in New York, so no way will he believe I came over here because I miss the smell of him.

I gather every bit of courage, pull the crumpled envelope out of my purse, and thrust it at him. "To return this."

He wrinkles his forehead and takes the envelope.

"I don't know what I was thinking," I say, words tumbling out of my mouth faster than I can think about them. "I brought the stuff for Sasha, and then I went to the bathroom. I saw all the mail in the magazine rack, and I couldn't help myself. When I saw the Ames Hotel envelope, I just… You won't tell me about you and Addie, so I thought maybe…"

"Maybe you could figure it out from this?"

"I didn't even look inside. I swear it. I felt terrible about it, and that's why I came back. I was going to come back up here and replace it in the powder room so no one was the wiser. But now you're here, and I…I don't want to lie to you, Braden."

He opens the envelope, withdraws the paper inside, and hands it to me. "It's a bid for an event my foundation hosted last year."

I glance over the words. The letter is dated more than a year ago. A quick look at the postmark would have given me this clue.

I can't believe it. Really can't believe it.

"You see," he says. "Nothing about Addison and me."

"I'm sorry."

"Do you really think I'd leave anything important sitting in my powder room?" he asks incredulously.

"No. I…" I sigh. He makes a valid point. "I wasn't thinking at all."

I brace myself. He's going to be angry. He might yell. He might call off our relationship—or whatever it is—forever, and if he does, I can't blame him.

"I'm sorry. I understand if you want to…"

He cocks his head. "If I want to what?"

"Not see me anymore."

He laughs. He laughs! So seldom does he laugh, and he

picks this moment?

I hold back a huff. "What's so funny?"

He pulls me against him, his lips pressing against my ear. "Nothing is funny about this."

"Then why did you—"

"You want to know why I'm home early? Because I couldn't stop thinking about *you*. I wanted you in my bed. I almost sent you a plane ticket, but I knew you wouldn't take off work with no notice. So I came home. I came home because I couldn't wait five fucking days to see you again."

I swallow as flutters rack my stomach and limbs, and my nipples harden against my bra. My pussy throbs between my legs. I squeeze my thighs together to try to ease the ache. "So...you're not angry with me?"

His blue eyes burn through me. "I didn't say that."

I swallow again. "Then you *are* angry?"

"Of course I'm angry. Who wouldn't be?"

I have no answer for his question, so I stay silent.

"The question is, what do I do about it?"

Again, I have no response.

"I could end things with you, but I didn't fly two hundred miles today to punish myself."

It would punish me as well, but I don't vocalize the thought.

"I could take you over my knee and give you a good spanking."

My body tingles. Do I want a spanking from Braden? No, I don't. Except that I kind of do.

"It's what you deserve," he continues. He advances toward me, like a wolf stalking his prey.

I walk backward, away from him, until my back hits the wall beside the elevator door. He closes in on me, his gaze smoldering.

"Your lips are parted in that sexy way," he rasps. "I want to kiss you so hard that your knees give out."

I inhale a slight gasp.

"That wouldn't punish you, though."

I stay silent and close my eyes.

"So no kisses tonight. I'm going to spank your creamy ass, and then I'm going to take what I came all this way for. And you're going to let me."

Am I?

He'll let me go if I tell him to. I know that. He won't do anything without my permission. But he won't ask. I see it in his gaze. If I want this to stop, I have to be the one to stop it.

"Braden…" I whisper.

"Yes?" His eyes laser into mine.

I squeeze my thighs together more tightly, but still my pussy aches with need. I'm wet. So wet already, without so much as a kiss. I won't get a kiss tonight. He's made that clear.

I inhale sharply. "Do what you need to do."

In a flash, I'm in his arms, and he's carrying me to his bedroom. He throws me on the bed and tugs off my shoes, slacks, and panties. I spread my legs, giving him full view of my arousal. Just his words, his smoldering gaze, his domineering countenance, make me wet. So wet.

He closes his eyes and inhales. "You smell like heaven. I'd love to taste you, Skye. Give you a hundred orgasms like last time, but that wouldn't be punishment. So I'm going to spank you. Then I'm going to fuck you hard and fast and take my own pleasure." He unbuckles his belt and unzips his fly. He yanks his pants and underwear over his muscled hips. His dick is fully erect, and a small pearl of clear liquid emerges.

He tosses me over onto my stomach, and before I can even anticipate what's to come, his palm comes down on my ass.

"Ow!" I cry out.

Another slap. Then another. I grit my teeth to stop from shouting again. I can take this. I want to take this. I want to give him what he needs. And I deserve it. I'm the one who did something wrong.

"Gorgeous," he rasps. "So pink."

The pain from his smacks turns to a tingling sting, a warming sensation. He slaps me again and then once more.

I brace for another—almost *crave* another—but he flips me back over so I'm lying on my back.

He pushes my legs forward and thrusts into me.

I cry out at the invasion—the burning invasion that makes me feel so complete.

He fucks me hard. He fucks me fast.

And with my legs pushed so far forward, his pubic bone doesn't nudge my clit.

Still, I climb the invisible mountain, edging toward the peak. *I can get there. I can get there…*

Except I don't get there.

He releases inside me, groaning, cursing my name, embedding himself in my body and taking his own pleasure.

Leaving me hanging.

My ultimate punishment.

It's no less than I deserve for violating his trust and stealing a piece of mail—a piece of mail that turned out to be useless anyway.

When he finally stops pulsing, he stays inside me for a moment, his eyes closed and his hands clamped onto my thighs. I lever myself against his strength, trying to move my clit forward. I'm still turned on. If I can just find something to grind against…

But he pulls out then and opens his eyes.

Leaving me wanting.

Which was his intention the whole time.

I say nothing. I told him to do what he needed to do. I gave him permission. My body may be on fire, but I'll never beg him for an orgasm.

At least not tonight.

He pulls up his pants and fastens them. "Have you eaten?" he says nonchalantly.

His voice is so calm, as if he didn't just spank me and withhold my orgasm. I'm still naked from the waist down, my legs still spread, his semen seeping out of me. "Well…no. Not yet."

"Get dressed. Marilyn is off this week, so I'll order something."

Chapter Forty

He leaves the bedroom.

I lie still for a moment. The phantom imprint of his hand on my ass still stings but in a good way. I stare at the unusual contraption above his bed. Does he ever use it? And what exactly does it do?

Still so much I don't know about this enigmatic man I've become addicted to.

I could lose my heart, and I'm not sure he'll ever be able to give me his. A wave of sadness sweeps over me. At least he desires me. I can live with that. For now. Indeed, I'm lucky his desire is so strong, otherwise my mail stunt might have cost me something much more than a missed orgasm.

I pick up my clothes and head to the master bathroom. I clean myself up and run Braden's brush through my hair. My lipstick is still intact.

Of course it is. He didn't kiss me.

Does he miss our kisses as much as I do?

Is this truly all physical for him?

How can I feel this much for a man I know nothing about?

Am I mistaking our physical chemistry for something more?

I don't have any answers for my own questions.

I leave the bedroom and find Braden at the bar pouring two Wild Turkeys.

"There you are," he says. "I ordered Thai food."

I nod. "Sounds delicious."

He hands me a glass. "Wild Turkey goes great with Thai."

I smile. "Wild Turkey goes great with everything." I take a sip and let the amber liquid sit on my tongue for a minute. The smoky caramel flavor soothes my nerves. I swallow, and it burns my throat. In a good way.

He takes a sip.

The silence grows in the room, like a rain cloud above us about to let loose at any moment.

Or is it just me?

Braden seems perfectly fine saying nothing.

"Braden?"

"Hmm?"

"I'm…really sorry about…you know."

"We don't have to talk about that."

"But we do. I don't want you to think I'm the kind of person who—"

"Skye, you did what you did. No amount of telling me what kind of person you are will change what already happened."

Brick to gut. Now what?

"Do you think I've never made a bad choice?" he continues. "Done something I regret?"

"No. I mean, I don't know."

"You don't get to the top without making mistakes along the way. I learn from every mistake, and I never make the same mistake twice. Do you see what I'm getting at?"

"Yeah. I won't do it again. I told you that already."

"I understand mistakes. I've made my share."

I nod. I'll never bring up the stolen piece of mail again. I won't bring up Addison, either—not tonight, anyway.

I take another sip of Wild Turkey. Christopher brings the Thai food into the kitchen. Braden murmurs his thanks and dismisses his driver. Then he pulls dishes and utensils out of cupboards and drawers. I'm surprised he knows where everything is. He dishes out a plate of food and hands it to me.

"Thanks," I murmur. I sit on one of the barstools at the granite island and wince slightly.

"Sore?" he asks, a twinkle in his eye.

"No. Just a little tender." I take a bite of the spicy curry.

Again, silence descends.

"Something interesting happened at work today," I finally say.

"Oh? What's that?"

I give him the short version of the call from Eugenie at Susanne Cosmetics.

"Are you going to call her?" he asks.

"I haven't decided yet. Addie won't like it. I'll probably lose my job."

"She hasn't fired you yet."

"No, but we had a shoot today. For the pet boutique where I got Sasha's gift basket. She needed me."

"She'll always need you."

"I'm not sure of that. Besides, the only reason Susanne wants me to do a post about the lip stain is because of you."

"So?"

"How can you be so nonchalant? I'm a nobody. No one gives a crap what kind of lip stain I wear except for the fact that apparently I'm your girlfriend now."

"So?" he says again.

I lift my eyebrows, shaking my head slightly. "What don't you get about this?"

"Here's what I get," he says. "This is an opportunity for you. Would you have this opportunity if not for me? Maybe not, but it's still an opportunity that has presented itself. Take it, Skye. You're a fool if you don't."

"A fool? How dare you—"

He gestures for me to stop.

I do.

"Don't get all excited. Anyone, including me, is a fool not to take advantage of what's thrown in his lap. Do you think I haven't taken every opportunity that's come my way? I won't leave you in suspense. I have, and some of them came along simply because I was in the right place at the right time. They had nothing to do with me."

"I can't believe that."

"Why not?"

"You're a self-made man, Braden."

"For the most part, that's true. But do you truly think I never had any help along the way? That opportunities fell into my lap simply because I'm me?"

"I've read all about you."

"The media never tells the whole story."

I pounce at his opening and smile. "Will *you*, then, Braden? Will you tell me the whole story?"

His lips twitch.

Yeah, I got him. He's trying not to smile.

"You *are* a challenge, Skye."

"You've said that many times," I say. "Has it escaped your notice that you're *also* a challenge?"

"I never said I wasn't."

"What will we do, then?"

He swallows a bite of food. "I've never backed down from a challenge."

"Neither have I."

"Then you'll do the post for Susanne Cosmetics."

I freeze, my forkful of food stopped midway between my plate and my mouth. How did we get back to that? Already I know the answer.

"You don't play fair," I say.

"Sure I do. I'm just more experienced than you are."

I can't fault his observation. "Posting about lip stain isn't exactly a challenge."

"Of course it is. It's something new. It's something you're not sure you're up for, but it fell in your lap. You can take your own pictures, Skye. Get credit for them. This is what you want."

"I want to take photos of things that move people. No one's going to be moved by me wearing Susanne lip stain."

"How do you know?"

"Because it's makeup, Braden. Who cares?"

"Your followers."

"The mobs who follow influencers aren't concerned about anything real."

"Do you know all of them?"

"Of course not, but—"

"Don't you see, Skye? You have the chance to grow a platform. To reach people. Once you reach them, you can introduce them to the kind of photos that *will* move them."

Chapter Forty-One

My mouth drops open.

No wonder Braden has come so far.

He's fucking brilliant.

"But," he continues, "never take the first offer. I don't care how high it is, counteroffer something higher."

"What if they tell me to go jump in the lake?"

"Then they tell you to go jump in the lake."

"But then—"

"Skye, show them you know what you're worth. They're not getting just Braden Black's girlfriend with you. They're getting an ace photographer, someone who can make their product look amazing. They know that, and if they don't, they will soon."

"Wait a minute," I say, my mind working overtime. "You didn't..."

"Of course not. I had nothing to do with them calling you. It may surprise you to know that I don't have time to call cosmetics companies and ask them to hire my girlfriend."

I nod. It sounds really ridiculous when he says it.

"Never be afraid to turn down the first offer. You're new at this, so they know they can lowball you."

Everything he says makes perfect sense. "You really are brilliant."

"I'm no more brilliant than the next guy," he counters. "I just know what my strengths are, and I know what they're worth."

"Braden..."

"Yeah?"

"Addison thinks you're behind all this, that you're trying to make me into an influencer and destroy her in the process."

He takes a drink. "That's what she said?"

"Yeah."

"And you believe her?"

"No." I shake my head vehemently. "Of course not."

He doesn't reply right away. Odd. Could there be something to Addie's theory?

Finally, he speaks, after draining the rest of his Wild Turkey. "Addison is a troubled woman."

"What's that supposed to mean?"

"I think you know."

"No, I really don't."

"Don't you? You've been working with her for more than a year. Isn't it clear that she has to be the center of attention? And when she's not, she sprouts claws?"

My mind races back to my conversation with Tessa. According to Betsy, Addie pursued Braden relentlessly, to the point of stalking him, eleven years ago. Classic Addie, wanting Braden's attention and...doing what when she didn't get it?

Neither Addison nor Braden will speak of that time.

Why?

"I see your point," I say. "Can you tell me more about her?"

He pours himself another Wild Turkey. "Nice try."

"I don't understand. Why won't you talk about your time with Addison? You were both young. Surely it couldn't have been *that* horrible."

"'Horrible' is too tame a word."

I swallow, my skin turning icy. What went on during that summer, and why won't they talk about it?

Jealousy rears its ugly green head, and though I know better, I blurt out, "How was she in bed?"

He stays silent.

"Tell me, Braden. Please."

"Why do you care?"

"I just…do."

"For God's sake, Skye. We were kids. Neither one of us knew what the hell we were doing."

"So you *did* take her virginity."

"Who said that?"

I don't answer. I can't violate Tessa's and Betsy's trust.

He advances toward me, and I quake before him.

"Why does any of this matter to you? Do you want to know if she was better in bed than you are?"

Yes. But I don't say it.

"Do you want to know about *all* my previous lovers? There are a lot of them, and I won't apologize for anything I did in the past."

I tremble without meaning to. "I'm not asking you to."

"Then exactly what *are* you asking, Skye?"

"I…don't know."

"I'll tell you what you're asking. You want to know how you compare to Addie, to everyone I've slept with." He takes a long drink of his bourbon. "I'll tell you only this. I've never cut a business trip short for any woman. Never…until now."

Heat courses through me, and my clit hardens and throbs.

He comes forward until only inches separate us, but he

doesn't touch me. "You challenge me. You perplex me. And damn it, Skye, you fucking *infuriate* me. You want to know how I feel about Addison Ames? Honestly?"

I nod shakily.

"I'm grateful."

"G-Grateful? Why?"

"If it weren't for her, I wouldn't know you."

I choke back a tear of joy. "Braden, I—"

"Shut the fuck up." His lips slam down on mine.

I open instantly and accept his devouring tongue. How long have I been here? This is our first kiss of the night. He denied me before, and now I ache for this forceful meeting of our mouths.

I spread my legs, straddle his hard thigh, and grind against him, easing the ache in my clit. Only it makes me want more. More kisses, his tongue on my nipples and between my legs, that orgasm he denied me earlier.

Braden finally breaks the kiss, turns me around against the kitchen island, and brushes my slacks and panties down my hips.

"Braden… Christopher. And Annika."

"This is my house, not theirs."

"But…"

"Quiet!" he roars.

Then his dick is inside me, pressing like a steam engine between my closed thighs and into my tight channel.

I cry out without meaning to.

He grabs my hands and places them flat on the marble countertop. "Don't move," he commands.

He thrusts into me again and again, the cold marble biting into my belly with each angry thrust. My clit isn't getting any stimulation except the indirect pulling from Braden's forceful plunges.

I want more. So much more.

But I can't move. He told me not to move.

If I could just find something to rub against. All I need is a slight friction, just enough to—

"I feel you searching," he says against my neck. "Don't, Skye."

"But I need—"

"Don't!" He smacks the cheek of my ass and then holds on to it, gripping me tight, keeping me still as he fucks me harder. "I told you to keep quiet. You'll get your orgasm, but on my terms."

I close my eyes, bracing myself against the counter, bracing myself against his thrusts. It's so good, so complete…and I can almost be happy with the sheer fullness of him inside my body.

"God, you're tight. Feels so good." He bites my neck lightly and then sucks at it. "Mine. Mine. Mine."

Mine.

I like the word. I like that he says it. I like everything about it. I want to be his. I want to be his even more than I want that elusive orgasm.

He releases my ass cheek as he pulls out of my pussy.

I gasp in surprise, looking over my shoulder. "You didn't—"

"All in good time. I needed to be inside you for a minute. Now I need something else."

"What?"

"Did you forget you're not supposed to be talking?" He slaps my ass, and then a jolt ripples through me when he taps my clit.

Again. And again. Until it's not a tap but a soft smack.

Each swat gives me just a taste of the friction I crave. Just a taste…and I want so much more.

Until the swats become full-blown hits. "Ah!" I cry out, urging him on and hoping I haven't earned punishment by talking. I tingle all over, and when Braden finally stops torturing my clit, he slides his tongue between my legs. He laps at the juices coating my thighs and then slides forward to my clit, swirling around it.

I close my eyes.

The intensity of the emotion coiling in my belly overwhelms me. I want a repeat of the last time we did this—of those multiple orgasms he forced me to endure.

And what an endurance it was.

He told me to beg him to stop that night, and though the intensity went from pleasure to almost pain, I didn't give in.

I didn't give up control.

My control is what he still wants.

Even now, as I revel in his attention, his tongue probing my pussy and my ass, finding every nerve that takes me to the brink, I hold back.

I promised him my control, and in return he promised to sleep with no one but me and not to use condoms.

I made a deal.

I'll stick with it, even though I've become a marionette, with Braden manipulating my strings.

Gah! Too much thinking. Pleasure rolls through me in soft waves, and I climb, reaching, reaching…

He slides a finger inside me while he licks my asshole. I moan in pleasure. The peak is in the distance, coming closer, closer…

Until his voice permeates through the haze.

"Skye," he says, his voice low. He thrusts his fingers into me and massages that spongy interior place inside. "Come. Now."

Chapter Forty-Two

I burst.

I burst like a geyser at Yellowstone.

I burst like a storm cloud exploding in rain.

I burst like a sun going nova.

I burst.

I burst into an intense nirvana.

Garbled words leave my mouth. My knuckles whiten as I clamp my hands against the edge of the marble countertop. My body tightens, loosens, tightens again as electric current seems to race through me, my arteries and veins its power lines.

"Braden!" I cry out. "Yes, Braden, Braden!"

He pushes me further into euphoria, continuing his chant. *"Come. Now. Come. Now."*

It's never-ending.

Perfect and never-ending.

He pulls another climax out of me and then another. Everything in the universe throbs with my clit, my pussy, my whole body. I'm limp against the granite countertop, completely at his mercy.

"That's right," he says. "Keep coming. Give me another one."

I explode. Truly, as if I'm his to turn on and off by the sound of his voice, I shatter, pulsing, jumping off the precipice again and again.

"Give me more, baby. More."

Again I respond to his command. I fly. I fly again. And again.

Orgasm after orgasm rolls through me, twisting my world and smashing my perception. I'm high and then low, hot and then cold, all the time emotion rocketing through me.

"Keep going," he urges.

One more begins in my clit, races outward to my limbs, heating my blood. My legs no longer hold me up. If Braden loosens his hold, I'll collapse.

"Again," he says.

But I'm used up. I can't.

Until you beg me to stop.

That's what he wants. I brace myself as another climax tries to emerge. I close my eyes, allow it to take me, and I soar once more into the clouds, this time finding an inner peace I've never felt. I'm in a dream. A beautiful erotic dream, so colorful and intense.

"One more, Skye."

I'm still drugged, still floating in dreamland, but my body is done. I can't take anymore. He told me not to talk, but I have to get the words out. To tell him…

"Can't," I grit out.

"You can."

"No. Please. I can't. Stop."

In a flash, he replaces his fingers with his cock, ramming into me as I fall from my last orgasm. He thrusts and thrusts and thrusts, his groans a hum of vibration around the bubble of lust encircling us.

He fucks me hard and fast, again and again, until he plunges deeply into me. "God! Skye!"

I feel every puff of his breath against my neck, every pulse of his cock as he releases.

And I keep my hands glued to the countertop.

After a few minutes, he pulls out, and I hear him zip and snap his pants.

Still, I don't move.

"You may move now," Braden says. "Christopher will drive you home."

Christopher—as I suspected, he has been here the whole time—had a front-row seat for our little interlude. He probably wasn't watching, but he sure as heck could hear every little detail.

I choke back the sadness and confusion that threatens me. Didn't Braden just say he was grateful to Addie because she led him to me? "You said you'd never kick me out of your home again."

"That's true. I did." He walks out of the kitchen but looks over his shoulder. "You're welcome to stay as long as you like. I left my business meetings to get back here, so I have a lot to do. I'll be in my office working."

Semantics. That's all this is. He's not "kicking me out," but he's leaving me. He's done with me for the night. Though he is here because of me, and he probably does have work to do.

His invisible bindings are pulling me in two different directions.

I check my watch. Ten o'clock, and I have work in the morning. I can stay here and sleep in one of his extra bedrooms, but I don't have any supplies. I haven't brought any extra clothes over yet.

He hasn't given me a choice at all.

He found a loophole. Braden is a billionaire businessman. He's probably very good at finding loopholes.

I hop off the counter, dress, gather my purse, and head toward the elevator.

"Home, Ms. Manning?" Christopher says.

The thought of riding with Christopher when he knows exactly what just happened—not just our encounter in the kitchen but what happened afterward as well—makes me nauseated.

"No, thank you. I'll call an Uber."

"Mr. Black wants me to drive you home."

"Please. Don't bother."

"It's no bother." He calls the elevator and rides down with me.

Once in the car, I gather my nerve. "Christopher?"

"Yes?"

"How well do you know Braden?"

"As well as any employee knows his employer, Ms. Manning."

"Please. Could you call me Skye?"

"If you wish."

"I wish."

"Very well...Skye."

When we reach my apartment building, Christopher gets out of the car and opens the door for me.

"Thanks," I say.

"Mr. Black wants me to see you to your door."

"Oh." First time for everything. "Okay."

Christopher and I enter the building and take the elevator to my floor. When we reach the door to my studio, I pull out my key.

"Allow me." He takes my key, opens the door, and hands

it back to me.

"Thanks, Christopher. Good night."

"Skye?"

I turn.

"He's a good man."

"I know that."

"He cares for you."

I lift my eyebrows. "Does he?"

"Yes."

"How do you know?"

"I've said all I can. Good night."

Chapter Forty-Three

Addie's still sulking the next day at work. Not surprising. I've made up my mind to call Eugenie, but I can hardly do it while Addie's in the office. Instead I do the usual—read and respond to emails, check yesterday's sponsored post, and delete a few comments that are borderline negative. Then I respond to comments on some of her fake personal posts, all of which were staged by me. I check email again. Addie has an offer from a new restaurant in downtown Boston. It looks like a place for the young and hip. Good. She'll be happy about that. I forward the email to her.

Then, on a whim, I log out of Addie's Instagram and into my own.

"What?" I say aloud.

My following has increased from two hundred to over twenty thousand seemingly overnight.

I never logged out of Addie's account yesterday, so I had no idea what was happening on my own. No wonder Susanne is interested.

I'm nowhere near Addie's ten million followers, but still...

This is unbelievable.

All because I'm Braden's girlfriend.

If my newfound followers only knew how close I came to screwing that up last night. I always push. I always try to take charge of every situation.

Addie walks out of her office. "I have an appointment."

I scan her calendar. "I don't see anything."

"It's personal."

"Okay. When will you be back?"

"I don't know."

"Did you get the email I forwarded? From that new restaurant?"

"I'll deal with it later." She walks out the door.

Okay, then.

Now that Addie's gone, I'll call Eugenie.

My heart begins to race. Why am I nervous? They called *me*, after all. I'm just returning a call. Braden said not to take the first offer, but I'm no negotiator. I'm a photographer, an artist. Not a businesswoman or attorney. How am I supposed to control this phone call when I have no idea what I'm getting into?

Just do it.

I hear the words in Braden's voice in my mind.

I exhale and dial the number.

"Susanne Corporate," a voice says.

My heart is thudding. "Eugenie Blake, please."

"May I tell her who's calling?"

"Skye Manning, from Addison Ames's office."

"Thank you. I'll see if she's in."

A few seconds pass.

"Skye, how are you?"

"Hi, Eugenie. I'm fine. I'm so sorry about yesterday's mix-up."

"Not a problem at all, and perfectly understandable," she says. "Addison was a little taken aback, I'm afraid."

A little taken aback? Try jealous rage. "We worked it out."

"I'm glad to hear that. I love how the Cherry Russet stain looks on you."

"Thank you. It's my favorite."

"I can see why. And I must say, you're starting to amass quite a following on Instagram in record time."

"I wouldn't call twenty thousand followers anything big," I say. "I've started dating Braden Black. That seems to be the catalyst."

"Yes, what a lucky woman you are!"

I'm not sure what to say to that, so I just say, "Thank you."

"The fact that you've gained that many followers within days is very telling. We think you're going to be huge. Anyway, we had a run on the Cherry Russet after you responded to that comment on Mr. Black's post, so we're prepared to offer you five thousand dollars to do a series of three posts on your own account highlighting our products."

Five thousand dollars? For a few posts? Sounds like a mint to me, but Addie gets six figures for some of her posts. I'm tempted to take it and run, but Braden's advice erupts like a volcano in my mind.

Never take the first offer.

The problem is, he didn't tell me how to ask for a higher offer. I race through our conversation. Maybe he did. He said counteroffer something higher. So instead of turning Eugenie down, I say I'll do it for *this* amount.

But what is *this* amount?

I'm new, and I only have a fraction of Addie's followers. I can't demand six figures. What's reasonable? Fifteen thousand? Twenty? Fifty?

How I wish Braden were here to advise me.

"Skye?" Eugenie says.

"I'm here. Just thinking. I truly appreciate the offer."

"Of course. Take your time. Would you like to call me back later?"

Call her back? And give her time to rethink giving five K to a nobody? No way. I clear my throat. "I appreciate your faith in me and my following." I echo the words I've heard Addie say to clients so many times. "But I'm afraid I can't do what you're asking for less than fifteen thousand."

Silence for a few seconds. Damn. I've blown it.

Then, "You drive a hard bargain, Skye. We can offer ten, but I'm afraid I can't go any higher without the VP of marketing's okay. If you're willing to wait, I can check with her."

Now what?

Maintain control, Skye. You heeded Braden's advice. You got her to go higher.

I can take the ten thou, or I can take the chance that the VP of marketing will up it to fifteen. She may say yes. She may say no. There's also a third option. She may very well tell Eugenie that I'm asking way too much as a newbie and not to bother with me anymore.

I can't take that chance. Not yet, anyway.

"That's very generous of you," I say. "I'm happy to do the posts for ten."

"Wonderful. I'll email the contract to you. We're thrilled to be working with you."

"I'm thrilled as well. Thanks so much for the opportunity."

"You're very welcome, Skye. We'll be in touch."

I end the call and lean back in my chair.

My heart is still pounding, but I feel good. Darn good. I got twice the original offer.

I can't wait to tell Braden.

Fifteen minutes later, the contract lands in my inbox.

Addison has one of the hotel attorneys review all her contracts, but unfortunately, I don't have that option. I can call an attorney and pay for the services out of the $10K I'll be getting, but who do I call? How do I know who's good?

I sigh.

I know the answer.

Braden. Braden has access to the best attorneys in town. He can tell me who to hire.

Why is my belly fluttering? I've never phoned him before, but I showed up at his place unannounced last night. A phone call is nothing. I hastily search the number and call.

"Black, Inc."

"Braden Black, please."

"May I ask who's calling?"

"Skye Manning."

"Just a moment."

Then, "Good morning, Skye."

My thighs quiver at the sound of his voice. "Hi, Braden. I'm sorry to bother you at work, but I got the contract with Susanne Cosmetics, and I was wondering if you knew a good, reasonably priced lawyer who could review it for me."

"Email it to me. I'll review it."

"But you're not—"

"An attorney? True, but I've reviewed my share of contracts. I also have four attorneys here in the office who can help me with the legalese if necessary."

"Braden, I didn't call you to give *you* work. I'm perfectly willing to pay an attorney."

"I have the best attorneys here at corporate."

"None of which I can afford, I'm sure."

"Did I say you had to pay?"

"No, but—"

"Forward it to me. I'll be in touch. Goodbye."

That's it? Classic Braden.

It's almost noon. I print the contract and then phone Tessa quickly to cancel our lunch date. Luckily I get her voicemail. I'll spill everything to her eventually, but at the moment I need to hurry. Braden may not be in his office for long.

He wants me to forward the contract? I'll forward it.

Personally.

Chapter Forty-Four

Everyone in Boston is familiar with the Black Building, but very few have been inside, including me. That's about to change.

I stand outside the silver skyscraper. It wasn't always the Black Building. Black, Inc. bought it five years ago when the company went public. A new building is in the works—the building that Peter Reardon and his father want to design but apparently won't. For now, Black, Inc. is housed here.

I enter the vast lobby. I walk through a metal detector while an armed guard peruses the contents of my purse. Then I head to the reception desk where I sign in and receive a visitor badge.

"Who are you here to see?" one of the receptionists asks me.

"Braden Black."

"Do you have an appointment?"

"No. I'm his...girlfriend."

The young woman's eyebrows nearly shoot off her forehead at the word "girlfriend." Then, "So you're the one."

"Apparently," I say.

"I should give him a quick call."

"If you'd like."

She pauses a moment, looking me over. Finally, she says, "Go ahead up. Thirtieth floor. I'll let the receptionist up there deal with you."

I'm not sure what to make of her words. I head to the elevator and press the requisite button. I'm transported to the thirtieth floor so quickly that my feet feel like they're buried inside the floor.

I draw in a breath and exit the elevator.

Sure enough, another receptionist—this one black-haired and gorgeous—sits right outside.

She looks up as the elevator doors close. "May I help you?"

I clear my throat. "I'm Skye Manning, and I'm here to see Braden Black."

"Do you have an appointment?"

"No." I hold her gaze with as much bravado as I can muster, even though my knees are shaking a bit.

"I see. His lunch was just delivered. Let me see if he's okay being disturbed."

I nod.

"Mr. Black," she says into her headset. "Skye Manning is here to see you." *Pause.* "All right, thank you." She locks her gaze on mine. "Go ahead back. Take a right and keep going. It's the corner office."

"Thank you." I force my feet to move as if I know what I'm doing. The hallway is long and narrow and seems longer and narrower the closer I get to Braden's office.

Until I'm facing his office, and his closed door nearly smacks me in the face.

I knock more forcefully than I feel.

"Come in."

I open the door.

The office is huge, with glass windows overlooking the city, much like his bedroom overlooks the bay. Braden sits behind a dark cherry desk, a gourmet feast spread out before him.

"Skye," he says simply.

"I brought the contract." I pull it out of my purse. "I thought maybe we could look at it together."

"That couldn't have waited until tonight?"

"We didn't make any plans, and I thought—"

"You'd interrupt me at work?"

"You're not working. You're eating."

"I'm always working, Skye. Close the door, please."

I shut it quietly, walk forward, and hand him the contract.

"Leave it on the desk. Have you eaten?"

I set the document on the corner of his massive desk. "No."

"Would you like half of mine?"

"No, that's okay."

"So you want to sit here and watch me eat?"

"Well…I guess."

He stands, gathers his containers of food, and moves them to the table across the room. He walks back to his desk and pushes a button on his phone. "Claire, could you bring in another plate, please?"

A few seconds later, someone—Claire, presumably—knocks at the door.

"Come in," Braden says.

The door opens, and in walks a woman, blond and blue-eyed and wearing a skin-tight navy sheath. She sets the plate she carries on the table.

"Thanks, Claire."

She nods and leaves the office, closing the door behind her.

"Sit down and help yourself. They always deliver enough for two or more people."

"I didn't come here to—"

"Eat, Skye. You'll need energy for what I have planned for you this afternoon."

"I—"

"You barge into my office with a contract you could have easily emailed me, looking sexy with your red lips parted. You think I'm not going to fuck you after that?"

"I... I didn't mean—"

"You promised me your control, Skye, yet you hold on to it in any way you can. Don't think I don't know why you showed up here. It was in complete defiance. I told you to email the contract, so you did what you do. You got around my instructions."

"You told me to *forward* the contract, Braden. You didn't say to email it. So I forwarded it. In person."

"You knew exactly what I meant."

I don't bother arguing the point. He and I both know he's right. "So I got around your instructions. Just like how last night, you got around our agreement never to kick me out of your place. You said I was welcome to stay, but you made it very clear you were done with me for the evening."

His lips tremble. Does he think this is funny? My neck burns with the anger creeping up on me. I wait for him to acknowledge my point, but he doesn't.

"I never promised to give up my control outside the bedroom, Braden."

"That's true," he says, "but you're forgetting one very important detail."

I whip my hands to my hips. "What's that?"

"Any place can be a bedroom."

Chapter Forty-Five

My legs tremble. I don't for a second doubt that Braden is sincere. After all, he fucked me in the kitchen last night where Christopher or Annika could have walked in anytime. Already my core is on fire.

Then a knock on the door.

"Come in," Braden says.

In walks Claire, her long blond hair flipped all over one shoulder. "The *Babbler* just came out online. I've ordered copies but figured you'd want to see this now, so I printed it. Let me know how you want to handle it." She hands him a paper and then leaves, closing the door.

Braden scans the paper. He sighs and hands it to me, saying nothing.

I gape at the headline.

Braden Black Dating Kansas Native and Budding Influencer

Budding influencer? I only got the offer from Susanne Cosmetics today. Kay Brown works quickly.

I blink a few times, hoping the headline will disappear.

"What the heck?"

"Did you think this would stay quiet for long?" Braden asks.

"But I didn't tell her anything."

"Do you think that matters?"

"Why do you keep asking me questions?"

"Let me put it to you this way. Neither of us said a thing. We didn't have to. Read the article."

I glance down.

Boston's own billionaire Braden Black of Black, Inc. was seen nuzzling—

"Nuzzling?" I say, perplexed.

"To lean against," he says.

I roll my eyes. "I know what it means, Braden. Jesus. We weren't nuzzling."

"Just read," he says.

Boston's own billionaire Braden Black of Black, Inc. was seen nuzzling a new love interest at the recent MADD charity event. She is Skye Manning, a self-professed farm girl and aspiring photographer who works for mega-influencer Addison Ames. "She's smitten," a source close to Manning says. "I've never seen her so infatuated."

Yeah, I'm going to be sick.

Black, known for his womanizing ways, hasn't dated anyone seriously since his short relationship with model Aretha Doyle ended last year. "I wish him all the best," says Doyle. "He and I remain close friends."

They do? First I've heard. Then again, since no source I know would say I'm smitten, this is probably another lie.

Black and Manning met at Ames's office recently and have been inseparable since. They've dined together in public several times and Black will escort her to the Boston Opera Guild Gala this Saturday evening at the Ames Hotel Downtown.

Aspiring photographer Manning is reportedly thrilled by the attention. Several of Ames's clients have reached out to her personally asking for Instagram posts. As she's familiar with the business, she's poised to become the next sweetheart of Instagram. "She's over the moon," the source says. "Not only is she on the arm of Braden Black, but she's getting the attention she craves for her work."

Black's office had no comment.

I gulp. "Braden, I never said any of this."

"I know."

"And I have no idea who this purported source is."

He nods.

"How can they lie like that?"

"Easy," he says. "They found a '*source*' who's borderline credible and got him or her to say what they want. Happens to me all the time."

"Not this time. You had no comment. It makes me look like I'm chasing you."

His lips quirk. "And you're not?"

"Braden! I'm being serious. I've had *one* call from Susanne Cosmetics, not several calls. This isn't right. And how do they know we're going to the opera gala?"

He chuckles. "Do you really think I announce where I'm going and who I'm going with?"

"Someone knows. Christopher? Annika?"

"I trust my staff implicitly."

"Then who?"

"A *source*, most likely."

I look around nervously. Is this office bugged? Is there a hidden camera? Braden wouldn't film me without my knowledge. Would he?

"You're getting carried away," he says.

"What do you mean?"

"I know what you're thinking. The same thing I thought the first time this happened to me. You're wondering who's watching you. Who's listening to you. Who among your circle of friends could have sold you out. The answer? No one."

"Then how—"

"I already told you. They find a source who doesn't want to be named. Surely you've read tabloids before."

"Actually, I haven't," I say.

"Do yourself a favor, then. Don't ever start reading them. It will slowly invade your mind, and it's not worth it. No one gives the *Babbler* any credence."

"Then why did Claire bring it straight to you?"

"I have to keep up with what the rags are saying about me. Doesn't mean I give it any value whatsoever."

"Then why—"

"If anything is said that could affect business, I have to be aware and file the necessary defamation lawsuits."

"Well, I want to know who this source is."

"Journalists don't have to reveal their sources."

"This isn't journalism, Braden. It's gossip. Fabricated gossip."

"Potato, po-tah-to, as far as the courts are concerned. Besides, look at the facts. We *are* dating. We *did* sit together at the MADD event. We *are* going to the Opera Guild Gala. And we've pretty much been inseparable since we met."

"Except they make me sound like a lovesick schoolgirl who's after Addie's job. She's going to have a field day with this."

"Maybe she won't see it," he says.

I laugh. Seriously laugh, because what Braden just said is funny in a ridiculous way. "Addie won't see it? The woman thrives on attention. She googles her name all the time. How will she *not* see it?"

He doesn't reply.

"I'm nothing like Addison," I say indignantly.

"If you were anything like Addison, do you think I'd have the slightest interest in you?"

"Honestly? I don't know, Braden, because you won't tell me what happened between you two."

"Skye, you do try my patience." He stands, pulls me out of my chair, and into his body.

I part my lips.

"Fuck, you're so sexy." He kisses me. Hard.

In an instant, I forget about the *Babbler*, about the source, about Addie and Braden and whatever happened all those years ago.

I know only his lips sliding against mine, his tongue probing between them, his vibrating groan humming into me. My nipples are hard and taut, aching to be freed from their confinement. His erection pushes into my belly.

I want him.

Here, in his office, I want him.

He breaks the kiss and inhales deeply. "God, what you do to me." He whips his tie off his neck and fingers the fabric.

I gasp sharply.

"Silk isn't the best for binding," he says. "The knots are sometimes too tight, which can be a problem if I need to untie you quickly."

I lift my eyebrows, my heart pounding. Binding? Me? In his office?

"However, it's all I have at the moment." He unbuttons his shirt and removes it. He stands in a white tank.

And God, is he sexy.

I have no idea what he has in mind. I know only one thing.

Whatever it is, I'll do it.

Chapter Forty-Six

"Take off your clothes, Skye."

I eye the door.

"No, it's not locked," Braden says.

I part my lips, my whole body tingling.

"No one will interrupt us. They know the penalty for entering without knocking."

Arousal billows through me; pinging flows straight to my clit. The door isn't locked, and somehow, that excites me.

"I've never bound your wrists before," he says.

I shake my head.

"Are you ready?"

Am I? I have no idea, which doesn't explain why I nod.

I want whatever he wants, which is unbelievable but no less true.

"Take off your clothes, Skye," he says again.

I tremble as I obey and then stand naked, in full view of anyone who might be scaling the building. What if the window washers are working today?

"Now hold your wrists out. Together."

I do, and he wraps his tie tightly around them and secures it with a knot I don't recognize. Not that I'd recognize any kind of knot.

I gape at him. His shoulders are tan and magnificent, all his corded muscles visible beneath the tank. I long to reach forward and touch him, skim my fingertips along his warm flesh, but I don't dare move.

My wrists are bound. I can still walk, I can still touch, but something in me makes me remain still until Braden tells me where to go next.

"You look beautiful, Skye."

I smile nervously.

"Bound for my pleasure," he says.

My flesh tingles as he regards me, as if his eyes are lasers that tantalize me. I don't know what he's going to do, and that both frightens and excites me.

And that unlocked door…

"Walk to the window, Skye, and face it. Hands above your head."

I'm so naked. So exposed. But I obey, pressing my bare breasts against the glass, my bound wrists resting on the pane above me.

Braden's belt clinks. Then his zipper.

He's behind me, pushing into me. He grasps my bound wrists and holds them clamped against the window. "Don't move," he whispers against my ear.

Then, in one quick thrust, he's inside me.

I can't help it. I cry out.

"That's it, baby," he says. "Take it. Take all of me."

He pulls out and pushes back in.

My cheek and breasts are crushed against the glass. Braden's hand stays clamped onto my bound wrists, rendering me immobile.

With his other hand, he grips my hip as he fucks me. "Good girl. Don't move. Let me take what's mine."

I melt into the glass, closing my eyes against whatever is on the other side. Can someone see me? I don't care. I care only about Braden inside me, taking me, filling the empty ache I never knew I had until I met him.

It's a hard and primal fuck. No kisses to my neck, no nibbles on my ear. Just a raw taking, and I'm so willing to be taken.

"That's it." He pumps faster. "Yeah, baby, just like that."

He glides his hand from my hip around and touches my clit gently. I gasp. Then not so gently.

I explode.

Quick as lightning, he withdraws and spins me to face him. My body still throbs from the orgasm as he lifts me, my ass pressing against the glass window.

"Put your arms around my neck," he commands.

I look down at the binding. How—

"Do it!" he grits out.

Still reeling from the climax, I lift both my arms and ring them around his neck. I'm suspended now, flat against the window, and my arms bound and around him. He spreads my legs as wide as they'll go, his arms under my thighs like a makeshift swing. He's holding all my weight, pushing me up and against the glass. Anyone looking up can see my naked ass. Anyone…

But the thought flees my mind as he plunges into me.

Though he was just inside me, I'm tight from the climax, and this new position feels amazingly different. He burns into me, charges into me, thrusting and thrusting.

"Fuck," he groans. "Feels so good."

"God, yes," I say. "Please."

I want him to touch me. Touch my clit. Give me another orgasm.

But he doesn't. Instead, he leans into me, our chests touching, and rocks his cock gently back and forth into me.

It's deliciously erotic, a new sensation, and—

"Braden! I'm coming!"

"That's it, baby." He pulls back slightly and plunges deep.

He withdraws and then thrusts.

A fuck. A good, hard fuck.

The orgasm rolls through me, and as my body releases, I shout. I scream. And I don't give a damn who can hear me.

Braden shoves his cock into me one last time, pulling another climax from me as he gives in to his own.

Together we soar through the window and over the skyscrapers of Boston.

I open my eyes, and the colors are so much more vivid. Downtown isn't gray and brown. It's silver and gold and bronze, the sun casting luminous rays over the buildings and down onto the cars and passersby below.

I close my eyes once more and surrender to the feelings bubbling through me even as I remain immobile.

Inside I'm flying, waving my arms, and laughing. Feeling vibrant and free.

So vibrant and free.

When I finally open my eyes again, Braden withdraws, panting.

I want to turn, to see him—his face glistening, his hair in disarray, his muscles taut and tight.

But I don't move.

He told me not to move.

Finally, he touches my wrists and brings my hands down, turning me to face him. Without saying a word, he loosens the knot and removes his tie from my wrists. He rubs them. "Okay?"

I nod.

"Tell me."

"Yes. I'm okay."

"Good."

Did he fuck Aretha Doyle against the window in his office? Anyone else? I want to ask, but I don't. I won't do anything to spoil this moment.

"Braden?"

"Hmm?"

"That was…amazing."

He nods. "It was."

Now what?

"I mean, *really* amazing. Anyone could have seen us."

His lips curve slightly upward, as if he wants to smile but is holding back.

"What?" I ask.

"The windows are tinted on the outside, just like my apartment. We can see out, but no one can see in."

"Oh." Oddly, I'm a little disappointed. I almost wish he hadn't told me.

"Did you like being bound?" he asks.

"I'm…not sure."

"You're not sure? You said yourself it was amazing."

"I meant the sex."

"Your wrists being bound was part of the sex."

"It was everything, though. Being in your office. The unlocked door. The window."

His blue gaze penetrates mine. "You like to be watched."

Do I? "No, not really. It was more—"

"You just admitted it. You never cease to amaze me, Skye."

"I guess I never thought about it. It was knowing anyone could walk in. The suspense. It was…"

"Erotic," he says. "Erotic and a little frightening because you were taking a risk. Did you like being tied up?"

My cheeks warm. "Yes. And being tied up with *your* tie,"

I say without thinking.

Why does stuff always sound funnier in my head?

"Would it surprise you to know I'd like to bind all four of your limbs, have you splayed out, naked, for me to do whatever I want?"

My body quivers as heat sparks from my core outward. Tied up? Really tied up?

My mind goes again to the strange contraption hanging from the ceiling above Braden's bed. Is now the time to ask about that?

Maybe, except that I'm unable to form the words.

"Skye?"

"No," I say, trembling.

"Good," he says, "because I want to do all that to you and more. Have you ever been fucked anally, Skye?"

I gulp. I shouldn't be surprised at his question. He's made it clear he likes to play with my ass. "No."

"Do you remember the instrument I stroked you with while you were blindfolded?"

"Yeah. It felt cool against me."

"Did you enjoy it?"

"Yes."

"Do you know what it was?"

"How could I? I was blindfolded."

His lips twitch. Again, I feel like he wants to smile but he's holding back.

"It was an anal plug."

"What's that?"

"A tool. To prepare you for anal sex."

"Braden, I—"

"Don't worry. We won't go there yet. Not until you're ready."

I may never be ready for that, but I don't say so. I don't

want to say or do anything that might deter Braden's interest in me.

"Go ahead and get dressed," he says, "and we'll go over your contract."

As I dress, Braden picks up his shirt and opens a door on the opposite side of the room. At least a dozen crisp white shirts hang inside. He takes one, puts it on, and then stuffs his original shirt in what looks like a laundry bag.

Why does he have so many clean shirts in his office?

Does he fuck a lot of women in here?

I tell myself it doesn't matter. That he's promised to sleep only with me as long as we're together.

But it *does* matter.

Jealousy slides through me, not in a raging way but subtler, like a tiny bug inside me that I can't swat away.

Since Braden won't talk to me about his past relationships with Addie and others, I fear the bug will never leave me in peace.

Chapter Forty-Seven

Back at the office, I electronically sign the contract that Braden approved and email it to Eugenie. I check email. Better check yesterday's post again. I log in—

The password doesn't work. I must have mistyped. Before I type it again, the phone rings.

"Addison Ames's office."

"Skye?"

"Yes?"

"It's Eugenie. I just received the signed contract, and we're thrilled to have you on board."

"Great! I'm looking forward to it."

"We'd like you to do the first post as soon as possible. Today if you can."

"All right. Do you have any—"

The door to the office opens and then slams. In walks Addie, the *Babbler* in her clenched fist. "What the hell is *this*?"

"Skye?" Eugenie asks.

"I'm sorry. Could I call you back? I have a...situation here."

"Hang up the damned phone!" Addie slams the tabloid

down on the desk.

"Sure," Eugenie says. "But get back to me within the hour, please."

"I will." I end the call.

"Poised to become the next sweetheart of Instagram?" Addison glares at me.

"I already know about the article. I never said any of those things, and I have no idea who their alleged source is."

"Your BFF, no doubt?"

"Tessa? Of course not. Tessa wouldn't lie about me."

"Even if they offered her some money?"

"They *pay* their sources?" I shake my head.

"I don't know," she says, "but I wouldn't put it past them. Just how many calls have you gotten from my clients, Skye?"

"One. Just the one from Eugenie."

"That's not what this says." She points to the rag.

"You can believe me, or you can believe some *source*," I say. "Your choice."

"It doesn't matter who I believe. You're the competition now, which means you have a conflict of interest. You're fired, Skye."

I widen my eyes. "Excuse me?"

"You heard me. I'm a professional, so you'll get two weeks' severance pay, but you're done here. I already locked you out of my account."

That explains why the password doesn't work. "What about tomorrow's shoot?"

"I'll handle it myself. Or I'll hire a new assistant. You're not indispensable, no matter how much you think you are."

"All right," I say.

"You'll lose in the long run."

"What's that supposed to mean?"

"Braden. He'll destroy you. He may make you into a huge

influencer, but one day you'll be wishing you took my advice and stayed away from him."

"How can I take your advice when you won't give me any details?"

"Figure it out for yourself. I'm done." She stomps into her private office but looks over her shoulder. "Pack up your shit and get out of here." She slams the door.

My flesh goes numb. It's over? Like this? This was never my dream job, but I did good work for Addie. Not just good work. My *best* work. It sucks not to be appreciated.

I don't have a lot of personal things at the office. Everything fits easily in a reusable grocery bag. Before I go, however, I print out Addie's email contact list before she locks me out of that as well. I won't go after her clients, but a lot of those contacts are also *my* contacts, and I'm not about to lose them.

I return Eugenie's call as soon as I reach my apartment.

"I'm so sorry for the interruption," I tell her. "Trust me that it will never happen again."

"Not a problem. Will you be able to do the first post today?"

"Absolutely. Do you have anything you specifically want me to include?"

"No. This is all you, Skye. Just wear the Cherry Russet and mention it. Otherwise, be creative. I've already contacted payroll. Since you chose automatic deposit, your first half should hit your account by the end of business tomorrow."

"Thank you."

"As per the contract, the second half will clear after all three posts are published."

"I understand. Thank you again. I truly appreciate the opportunity."

"You can be huge, Skye. We know you're the brains behind Addie's posts. Be yourself and use your talent. You'll outshine her in no time."

I'm not in this to outshine anyone. But I don't say the words.

"I'll get the post up before seven p.m.," I promise. "Oh, and from now on, please contact me on my cell." I recite the number.

"Awesome. Talk soon."

Eugenie has my number. Excellent. Only problem? All my other contacts will attempt to call me at Addison's office. That's a problem. If she's answering the phone, she'll no doubt try to blackball me.

You'll outshine her in no time. Why would Eugenie say that? Is *she* Kay Brown's source?

I laugh out loud. The social media director for a major cosmetics company certainly has better things to do than give out false information to a gossip rag.

You can be huge, Skye.

Eugenie talked about me being the brains behind Addison, about using my talent and being myself.

But the truth is, Braden is the only reason anyone cares what kind of lipstick I use.

Braden.

Once he's out of the picture, no one will care what I think anymore.

I sigh. That's a fact. But I have another fact to consider.

I'm now unemployed. I need a steady stream of income, and if this will give me income, I have to do it.

I'm a photographer. An artist. I'm going to get creative and give Susanne Cosmetics a post that's not only catchy and informative but also a work of art. I'll use this to my advantage, as Braden suggested. It's a chance for me to put my talent as a photographer out in the world.

If only I had a photography studio where I could

manipulate the lighting.

Of course, studio shots can sometimes look sterile.

A photo in my apartment would be more personal, but again, I have a lighting issue.

This requires some thought.

I go to my bathroom and touch up my hair and makeup until I'm satisfied. Not bad. Not bad at all.

My contract is for three posts featuring the Cherry Russet lip stain. What do I love most about it? It's dark enough for a dramatic effect at night but neutral enough for everyday wear.

Casual, formal, and dramatic—perfect.

I'll begin with casual. I look good, so I leave the apartment and walk outside. It's not the greatest day for an outside shoot, so I walk a couple of blocks to Bean There Done That. I peruse the setting. Lighting is good, especially if I can get a table where the sunlight shines in opposite. I quickly order a cinnamon mocha latte and find a table that works.

I don't have an assistant to hold the phone for my "selfie." This is all on me. Good thing I have a lot of experience taking influencer photos.

I take about ten selfies—smiling, serious, even feigning laughter in one.

And that's the one I choose.

It's spontaneous and lively. Perfect for my casual theme. I do a few quick edits until I look as good as I'm going to.

Now for the copy. I almost always wrote Addie's copy unless the client writes it. I understand Addie's voice.

I'm not Addie, and I don't want to be.

I must find my own voice, and my own voice will be authentic, not fake.

What to say?

How do I feel about the lip stain?

I love it. It's my go-to. And that's all I need.

Love my Susanne Cherry Russet lip stain. It's my go-to for every occasion. Perfect for a casual afternoon! @ susannecosmetics #sponsored #lips #lipgloss #kissproof #kissablelips #youknowyouwantsome

Hmm. Five hashtags is a little much. I delete *#kissablelips*. I add Bean There Done That for my location. Perhaps they'll see the post and want me to do one for them. I actually *like* coffee.

My heart races as my finger hovers above the Share button.

I analyze the post once more. Perfect photo? Check. Decent copy? Check. A nice mixture of marketing and fun hashtags? Check.

I swallow, gathering my courage.

And I hit Share.

Within a minute, comments appear.

Gorgeous on you! #orderingnow

Love the color!

You look so happy!

Totally getting this for my wife.

More and more of the same. Emojis, too.

Until—

@realaddisonames #fuckyou

Chapter Forty-Eight

Delete.

Easy enough.

Until—

@realaddisonames #youllneverbeme

I'm tempted to leave that one and let my followers see who Addison truly is, but I delete it as well.

I wait for her next move.

Nothing. At least for now. If it continues, I'll simply block her, though I hope it doesn't come to that. She said herself that I'm the competition now, and it's always a good idea to keep an eye on the competition.

Then a comment that takes my breath away.

@bradenblackinc You're gorgeous. See you tonight.

My face splits into a wide grin. We didn't make any plans for tonight, so I assume he'll call me with the details. I continue reading comments as quickly as they appear while I finish my latte. I'm so into the comments that I jerk when my phone dings with a text. It's from Eugenie.

Perfect! Love the post. I want to see another tomorrow and the last one over the weekend.

I text her back.

So glad it works for you. Will do.

My next post is formal.

Hmm. Would Eugenie be willing to wait until the weekend when I'm at the opera gala with Braden?

I hastily text her back, and she agrees.

Good.

I have the perfect idea in mind for dramatic as well. I'll pose by Braden's window looking out over the moonlit harbor. That means I'll need to be at his place over the weekend. Since we're going to the gala, we'll most likely end the evening at his place. No problem.

I check my watch. Maybe Tessa can meet for a drink and I can tell her all my news. Hmm, still about an hour before she gets off work. I know the perfect way to kill some time. I fire up the laptop and do some searches.

"Addison Ames" "Braden Black"

Lots of hits, but all recent and all articles where they're both mentioned but not together. I skim through several, but I'm looking for what happened eleven years ago.

I add the year to the search.

Nothing. Nothing about the two of them together in that time frame.

What went on that summer?

I fear I may never know.

I check my watch again. Tessa's just getting off work, so I call her.

"Hey, Skye."

"Hey, yourself. You busy? Want to go for a drink?"

"Actually, you won't believe this."

"What?"

"I've already got plans for a drink. With Betsy. Believe it

or not, she called me. You're welcome to join us."

"I'm not sure that's a good idea. She's a friend of Addie's, and Addie and I sort of…well…let's just say I'm no longer working for her."

"What happened? Is everything okay?"

"Yeah, I'm fine. It's a long story. Maybe I *will* join you. Addie can't possibly have blackballed me all over town yet." I quickly give Tessa the scoop.

"Seriously? She's leaving nasty comments on your posts? She's so immature."

"True story," I say. "Where are you meeting Betsy?"

"Esteban's for happy hour. Please come."

"I think I will. I'll see you there."

"Four grande margaritas and two Wild Turkeys." The server sets down our drinks—two each, as it's happy hour. "And chips and guacamole."

So far I've learned that Betsy isn't as fond of Addie as she first let on to Tessa. I wait patiently. The two margaritas should get her talking. I sip my first Wild Turkey slowly. Tessa and Betsy trade dog stories. I have to hand it to Tessa. She can lie about a fake dog as well as anyone.

Tessa and Betsy are both on their second margarita before I'm even halfway through my first drink. Not surprising. I listen with one ear, eating a few chips now and then.

Until—

"Skye!" Betsy shrieks.

I suppress a jerk and widen my eyes. "Yeah?"

"Seriously? You're dating Braden Black?"

I nod. "Yeah."

"Wow. Addie didn't warn you?"

"Oh, she did, but she wouldn't go into any detail, so why should I listen to her?"

Betsy's cheeks turn pink. "I shouldn't talk about it."

"Okay," I say. "We don't have to talk about Addie or Braden at all."

Betsy smiles timidly and finishes her second margarita. "It was all so long ago. And look at what they've both accomplished since then."

"Yes, they're both huge successes," Tessa says. "Which means whatever happened had no effect on them whatsoever."

"Of course it didn't," Betsy says. "No one knows, and no one can ever find out."

"Really?" Tessa lifts her eyebrows. "How is that?"

Betsy gestures to the server. "Another, please. You guys want another?"

I'm still only halfway through my first, so I shake my head.

"Sure," Tessa says, filling a plate with chips.

"Excuse me." Betsy rises. "Little girls' room."

Once she's gone, I grab Tessa's arm. "I need to get out of here."

"No, trust me. It's better that you're here. Your presence appeals to her conscience. If there's really a danger to you, she won't be able to keep it to herself."

"Braden isn't dangerous."

"I don't think he is, either, but Addison does, and Betsy knows why. She and Addie aren't exactly friends."

"I gathered that from what she was saying when I arrived. Why does Addie do her posts for free, then? That's not like Addie at all."

"I don't know, but I'm pretty sure we can find out tonight if we play our cards right."

Five minutes pass.

Then ten.

Twenty.

I sigh. "Either she's got some chronic diarrhea or she ditched us."

"Shit. You think?" Tessa asks.

"One way to find out." I rise and head to the bathroom.

Only one stall is occupied. Oh well. I can't fault Betsy. She's known Addie forever and probably changed her mind about talking.

I don't have to use the toilet, so I quickly check myself in the mirror and turn to leave—

When I hear a sniffle coming from the occupied stall.

I look at the feet. Black army boots. I didn't check out Betsy's shoes, but I'm betting the boots go with whatever boho-chic outfit she's wearing. It's a brown and green flowing number.

"Betsy?" I say.

Another sniffle.

"Are you okay?"

The door to the stall opens and Betsy walks out, her face tear-stained and her eyes red.

"Oh my God. What happened?"

She shakes her head. "I can't tell you, Skye. I wish I could, but I can't."

I touch her shoulder. "It's okay. You don't have to say anything."

"But I want to. I really want to. You deserve to know. But I made a promise a long time ago. A promise I regret now. Addie's not who you think she is."

I think she's a self-absorbed heiress, but Betsy may not know that. "I thought you two were friends."

"We are. Or were. Or…I don't know what the heck we are, to be honest."

"It's okay. I'm sure Addie's posts help your shop."

"They do, but she doesn't do it for me."

I lift my eyebrows. "Oh?"

"I mean, she does, but not because we're old friends. She does it to…" She sighs. "She does it to keep me quiet, Skye."

"Quiet about what?"

"About that summer. I told Tessa she could tell you."

"She may have mentioned something."

Betsy spews out the story I already heard from Tessa about the illicit party at the Ames house, Braden's attendance, and Addie's obsession with losing her virginity to him.

"Wow," I say.

"I know."

"But Braden isn't the problem," I say. "Seems like Addie's the one who pursued him. So why does she say he's bad news?"

"There's a lot more to the story," Betsy says.

"Was it ever in the news?" I ask. "Because I can't find anything about the two of them that year."

"No, nothing was in the news."

"Then what happened?"

Betsy blows her nose into a paper towel. "I'm so sorry. I've said all I can." She runs out.

Chapter Forty-Nine

Now what?

Before I leave the restroom, my phone dings with a text from Braden.

Braden: *Where are you?*

Me: *Esteban's. Having a drink with Tessa.*

Braden: *I'm at your place. Why aren't you here?*

Right. His comment on the post said *See you tonight*. Still, we didn't make official plans.

So I reply.

Me: *Because I'm at Esteban's having a drink with Tessa.*

My heart gallops as the dots jump while he writes. Then—

Braden: *Be there in fifteen.*

I smile for a few seconds, but then I scramble out of the restroom. If Braden shows up, Betsy will have a meltdown. I return to the table. Tessa is sitting alone.

"Where's Betsy?"

"Gone. She came back and looked awful, threw some bills down, mumbled a quick apology, and then ran out. What the heck happened in the bathroom?"

I give Tessa the lowdown. "To make matters more complicated, Braden is on his way here."

"What for?"

"Apparently he wants to see me tonight."

"I can make myself scarce. I didn't need this fourth margarita anyway. Good thing I took the T to work today."

"You can stay."

"That's okay." She stands. "Call me tomorrow."

"Will do."

She walks away but then turns and looks back. "By the way, I saw your post. It's gorgeous!"

I warm. "Thanks. I think."

"You can do this, Skye. I believe in you." She winks and leaves the restaurant.

I look over the bill and count up the money Betsy and Tessa both left. I pull out my wallet, and—

"I've got it." Braden sits down and takes the check from me.

"You don't have to. They left money."

"I saw Tessa on the way out," he says. "I told her you'd be returning her money."

"What about Betsy's money?"

"Who's Betsy?"

"Betsy… Huh. I don't know her last name. Anyway, she owns the Bark Boutique where I got Sasha's gift basket."

"You can return her money, too."

"That's generous of you, but you don't have to—"

"I know I don't have to, Skye. I want to. This is pennies to me."

I smile. "Okay, then. I'll let you, because I'm now officially unemployed."

He shakes his head. "Why am I not surprised?"

"I don't know. I still have no idea what went on between you and Addison."

He throws a credit card on top of the bill. "Nice try. Still not going there."

The server arrives and grabs the bill and credit card. "Can I get you anything, Mr. Black?"

"Yes, a Wild Turkey, one ice cube, and a menu please. Ms. Manning and I will be dining."

"You want to eat here?" I ask, flabbergasted.

"Why not?"

"It's not exactly fine dining."

"So? You seem to forget I come from South Boston. I grew up on beans and stew."

"Boston baked beans?" I can't help asking.

"One and the same."

"No chains like this when I was growing up, but we had some great little mom-and-pop restaurants in the nearby small towns. Not fine dining, but delicious food where everyone knew everyone else. We had this amazing Mexican restaurant run by a couple who'd emigrated twenty years previously. The best Mexican food ever. The stuff here can't compare."

"Esteban's is yuppy Mexican food," he says. "But it's still decent."

"True."

The server returns with the menus. I glance over mine.

"Eat hearty, Skye," he says. "You're going to burn a lot of calories tonight."

As soon as we enter Braden's penthouse, he attacks me next to the elevator, kissing me hard and deep. I respond immediately, my whole body quaking in anticipation of what's to come.

Then his phone buzzes, and he breaks the kiss.

"Ignore it," I whisper.

"I can't. I'm sorry. I'm expecting an important call."

"At nine thirty?"

He doesn't answer, just pulls his phone out. "Black," he says, walking toward the living room.

I straighten my clothes and follow him, but a few seconds later he walks away and into his office, closing the door.

None of my business. I get it.

I head to the kitchen for a glass of water. I down it quickly. Two Wild Turkeys and Braden's kiss have me dangerously dehydrated.

About fifteen minutes later, Braden returns. "I'm sorry," he says. "I have to fly back to New York."

"Right now?"

"Yeah. I shouldn't have left early. My bad."

He left early because of me. Am I supposed to feel bad about that? Because I don't. Not in the least. I say simply, "Oh."

He stalks toward me. "I seem to make questionable decisions because of you, Skye."

I say nothing. Just shiver from his nearness.

"I want you to think about something while I'm gone."

I shiver. "What?"

He pushes something into my hands. It's a silver chain with some odd-looking baubles at each end. "About wearing this to the gala on Saturday."

I wrap it around my neck and secure it like a lariat necklace. "All right. It will go nicely with the black dress."

Braden laughs.

A serious uproarious laugh.

I smile because I love seeing him laugh. "What's so funny?"

"It's not a necklace."

My cheeks warm. I remove it from my neck and hold it

out to him. "What is it, then?"

"Those things on each end are nipple clamps, Skye."

My nipples tighten and my areolas shrink around them in response to his words. My jaw drops as I examine the baubles on each end. They resemble tiny clothespins with a screw-on device reminiscent of some of my mother's old clip-on earrings.

"I control how tight the clamp is," he says. "And when I give the chain between them a good yank… Well, you can imagine."

I hand the chain back to him and clear my throat. "I'll… think about it."

His gaze darkens. "Think about it a *lot*, Skye."

I nod, trying not to tremble.

"I'm sorry about tonight. Christopher will drive you home."

"When will you be back?"

"Saturday afternoon, as originally planned. I'll pick you up at your place for the gala at six p.m. sharp. I'll bring the chain and put it on for you."

I'm hotter than ever now, and he's leaving.

Maybe tonight I'll try masturbation again.

I nod. "Braden?"

"Yes?"

"I… I'll miss you."

He smiles. "I'll miss you, too, Skye. More than you know."

Chapter Fifty

I allow myself some indulgence the next morning. I sleep in a little. No job to go to, so why not? I fire up the laptop and check my Venmo account. Sure enough, Susanne Cosmetics has sent me five thousand dollars, half of the contract amount.

At least I'll be able to pay my bills for the month or two—after I put a third of it away for taxes. Being self-employed comes with its own issues.

I don't normally exercise during the week, but I have time, so I head to the yoga studio and pick up a morning class. After a quick trip for groceries, I return home at one p.m., fix myself a sandwich, and sit down at the computer.

First, I check my phone. Did I inadvertently silence the ringer?

No, it's on. No calls.

No one else asking for me to do a post.

Okay. No reason to panic. I've got another five thousand dollars coming after Saturday.

Time to check my post.

I delete a few comments that are borderline negative and

respond to quite a few. No more comments from Addie. She probably figured I'd block her, and if I did, she'd no longer be able to keep tabs on me.

Of course she could always open up a dummy Instagram account.

So could I, if I ended up having to block her.

Perhaps she is truly taking the high road. For now at least. Probably not, but a girl can hope.

I play around on Instagram for a little while until my phone dings with a notification. Hmm. Apparently I have a direct message. No one has ever messaged me on Instagram before.

I click.

The message is from Tammy Monroe. Never heard of her.

Greetings, Skye! I see you're a new influencer, and I love your name. I'm the marketing director for New England Adventures, and we'd like to contract you for an Instagram campaign. We'll call it Skye Takes to the Sky. You would take a ride in one of our hot-air balloons and post over the beauty of our New England countryside. Please contact me if you're interested.

A post from a hot-air balloon? Definitely intriguing, except for the fact that it scares me to death. I quickly call Tessa at work.

"So do it," she says. "You've flown before."

"Inside an airplane. Sure."

"What's the difference? You're not afraid of heights."

"You're right," I say. "I'm not afraid of heights. I'm afraid of plummeting to my death from the basket of a hot-air balloon."

She laughs. "It's perfectly safe."

"Have you ever done it?"

"Well, no, but— "

"Then you don't know." An idea pops into my head. "You should go with me."

She laughs again. "I'd go in a minute, but they haven't asked me."

"I'll see if I can bring a friend."

"Hold on. This is only your second offer. Don't get a reputation for making unreasonable demands."

"What's unreasonable about wanting my best friend with me?"

"Just be careful is all I'm saying. The offer could go away if you start asking for favors."

"This isn't black and white, Tess. There are gray areas here. If they want me, they'll be willing to negotiate."

"You don't even know what they're offering yet."

"Good point. I've got to go. I'll be in touch."

I end the call and quickly respond to Tammy, letting her know I'm interested to hear more and giving her my cell phone number.

Within fifteen minutes, my phone rings with a number I don't recognize.

"Hello."

"Skye Manning?"

"Yes."

"Tammy Monroe from New England Adventures."

"Hi there. Thank you so much for messaging me."

"You're very welcome. Let me tell you what we've got in mind. We want to take you up on one of our hot-air balloons and have you shoot posts from the air. They don't have to be selfies. We want to show your followers the wonders they can see if they take one of our balloon rides."

My heart beats faster. Take actual photos of beautiful scenery? "That sounds great."

"Have you ever been in a balloon before?"

"I'm afraid I haven't."

"Then you're in for a treat. It's a breathtaking experience."

"I don't mean to sound rude, but…it is safe, right?"

She laughs. "You're not rude at all. We get that all the time. It's very safe. All our pilots are certified by the FAA."

"The FAA certifies balloon pilots?"

"They do. They all have balloon pilot licenses, and they err on the side of caution. If there's any indication that weather could be a factor, they won't go up."

"All right."

"You've flown before, I assume?"

"In a large aircraft, yeah."

"I promise you that you'll love our rides."

I clear my throat. "If the photos don't have to be selfies, why do you even need me? Send me the photos and I'll post them."

"Because the experience needs to be authentic."

She's right, of course. If I'm going to be an influencer, I'm going to be authentic. I won't be Addison, who posts about coffee when she hates it.

She continues. "We can set you up for a test ride. If it's truly not your thing and you decide you can't do the posts, no hard feelings."

Test ride. That sounds good. "Would you mind if I bring a friend along?"

"Not at all. What day works for you?"

"Anytime. I'm flexible." Being unemployed certainly gives one flexibility.

"How about tomorrow? The weather's supposed to be great. Say about eleven a.m.?"

"I'm not sure my friend will be able to get off work."

"All right. Saturday morning, then? Though of course it will depend on the weather."

"I'll have to check with her."

"Sure. Call me back when you know. We're excited about

working with you."

"Thank you. I appreciate the opportunity, Tammy. You'll hear from me soon."

I sigh and lay my phone on my small table. Then I berate myself. I didn't ask about what they were willing to pay me for the posts. Braden would no doubt want to give me another spanking if he knew I made such a faux pas.

I'm new at this, for sure, but how could I have forgotten to ask about money?

This from someone who values control.

I hastily call Tammy back.

"Tammy Monroe."

"Tammy, Skye Manning."

"That was quick!"

"Yeah, change of plans. I'll go up tomorrow without my friend, if you're still amenable to that."

"Of course."

I clear my throat. Will asking about money ever become easy? "How many posts are you looking for, and what type of compensation can I expect to receive?"

"We'd like to begin with one post and see how things go. We're willing to compensate you with the balloon ride, which is a three-hundred-dollar value, plus two thousand dollars on top of that."

Hmm. Much lower than the Susanne offer.

Never take the first offer.

Wisdom from Braden.

"I'm afraid that's too low for me."

"You're new at this, Skye."

"I understand that, but I'm a professional photographer and I have a deal with another client for a lot more."

"We're a small operation. We can't afford to pay what Susanne Cosmetics pays."

"Fair enough," I say, "but I can't accept less than four thousand dollars for one post."

"Two thousand."

"Three."

"I'm sorry. I can't go higher than two. We just can't afford it."

What would Braden do?

Hell, I have no idea. Two grand is nothing to him. To me, it's nearly a month of expenses paid. The day I have Braden's money is the day I can turn down an offer.

Unfortunately, that's not today.

"All right, Tammy. I'll take two thousand. Email me the contract." I provide her with my email address.

"Wonderful! We'll see you tomorrow. Eleven sharp."

"I'll be there, and thank you again for this opportunity."

Yeah.

I just agreed to go up in a balloon tomorrow for two thousand dollars.

I'm officially out of my element.

Before I contemplate my folly further, someone knocks.

Chapter Fifty-One

I open the door. No one is there, but a package lies on the floor. I pick it up and take it inside.

It's wrapped in plain brown paper with a note attached. I open the envelope.

This will go beautifully with your black dress. Wear your hair up and paint your lips red. Bloodred. I'll pick you up at six.

No signature, but it's clearly from Braden.

I open the package. Inside, nestled on white cotton, lies a black pearl choker. I suck in a breath. The pearls are perfectly round, not knobby like cheap freshwater pearls. It's gorgeous.

I pull the pearls from the cotton cloud and hold them up to my face.

I'm wearing the Cherry Russet lip stain, and it looks good, but bloodred will really pop against all the black, especially if I do a smoky eye.

How does Braden know that?

And underneath my dress…the nipple clamps joined by the silver chain.

Do I wear a bra? Will the clamps show through?

And why am I worrying about any of this when I may fall out of a balloon tomorrow?

Before I think further about that, though, I grab my purse and leave my apartment, heading to the mall. I make my way to the Susanne Cosmetics counter. They just paid me ten grand, so I should throw them some business.

"May I help you?" a salesgirl asks.

"Yes, please. I need a bloodred lipstick."

"What you have on is very flattering," she says.

"This is the Cherry Russet lip stain. It's my go-to. But I'm attending a gala this weekend and my boyfriend wants me to paint my lips bloodred."

"Oooh!" she nearly shrieks. "Sounds exciting! Let me see what we have." She pulls out a tray of samples and picks one up. "This is the vamp lip stain."

I take the sample and try it on the back of my hand. "It's a little more blackish red. He said bloodred."

"Try this." She hands me another.

I rub a little next to the vamp. It's less black but still too dark. I read the label. New York Heat. Interesting. I'm about ready to open a vein to show her what color blood actually is, but she hands me another.

"This one is called Hotshot. It's probably not dark enough, but give it a try."

I spread a line of Hotshot on the back of my hand next to the other two. We have a winner. "This is perfect."

"You think?"

"Yeah. Blood is red. A piercing red with a slight tinge of blue."

"Hmm. You're right. How do you know so much about color?"

"I'm a photographer. Color is my business."

"Interesting. Do you want to take one of these, then?"

"This is lipstick. Do you have a similar color in the lip stain? I'd rather not have to constantly reapply."

"Let me see." She pulls out some lip stain samples and hands me one. "This is probably the closest."

The sample is called Night on the Town. At first glance, it looks bloodred, but the real test is what it looks like on me. "Do you have some lip stain remover? I'll try this one on my lips."

"Sure. Here you go." She hands me a sample and a cotton ball.

I quickly remove the Cherry Russet and apply the Night on the Town.

Oh yeah. Bloodred at its finest. I can see why Braden requested it. On my fair skin and against the black dress and pearls, my lips will be a focal point.

"I'll take a tube of this one," I say.

"Absolutely. Anything else?"

"I'm good for now. Thanks."

She rings me up, and I leave the mall, bloodred lips and all. I get more than a few glances as I make my way home. Suddenly, I'm fearless. Who knew bloodred lips were so potent? I'll definitely be wearing this lip stain on my balloon ride.

When I return home, the contract is waiting in my inbox. I read through it quickly. Braden's not here to consult, and I don't want him berating me for doing a post for so little money, so I read through it myself. Pretty straightforward. I sign it electronically and send it back to Tammy.

Only to get an email almost instantaneously.

Hi, Skye,

Seems we need to cancel your balloon flight tomorrow. I misspoke when I said we had availability. I've penciled you in for Monday, same time. Let me know if this doesn't work.

I quickly email her back to say it's fine, and I'm relieved. Now I don't have to deal with the balloon ride just yet. Monday will give me a chance to read up on hot-air ballooning so I know better what to expect.

I check my Susanne post. Still all good. I now have nearly a thousand comments. Addie gets a thousand comments in the first hour, not the first twenty-four, but I'm new at this. I never got into it to overtake her. Still, though, out of curiosity, I go to her profile.

A new post pops up.

It's a selfie, slightly blurry, so she must have taken it herself.

Ecstatic that I'll be going up in a hot-air balloon tomorrow! @ newenglandadventures #sponsored #takingtothesky #ballooning

My jaw drops.

This can't even be real. How did she know about my deal with New England Adventures? Is this why Tammy canceled my ride for tomorrow? And why I haven't received the countersigned contract yet? *#takingtothesky*? Tammy called my campaign "Skye Takes to the Sky."

This all seems too convenient.

I pace around my apartment. What to do? I won't call Addison. I could call Tammy, but I won't. I'll never beg for a job, and I won't ask her to tell me whether she and Addie have been in contact. I'm a professional, and I can't risk getting a bad reputation in the business. I absolutely will not be a whiner.

Think positive, Skye. For all I know, Addison will go up in a balloon and attempt to take the photos herself, which means they'll suck. Once Tammy sees my photos, she'll know who better represents her company. Except that Addie is a known influencer and has way more followers than I do. Plus, she may hire a pro to take the photos.

I draw in a deep breath.

Addie can easily be bluffing, and even if she's not, I refuse to let this get to me. I will always stay focused. I'll look on the bright side. Even if my contract with Tammy falls through, the positive is that I won't have to go up in a hot-air balloon.

Oh…but think of the gorgeous photos of the quaint New England countryside I could take.

Now I want this contract more than ever.

I check my inbox.

Still no word from Tammy and no countersigned contract.

I sigh and check my watch. Five thirty. Good. Time for a Wild Turkey. No reason to be concerned. In two days, Braden will be back, and I'll go to the gala on his arm.

And after the gala, I'll give him my control.

I needn't have worried. The next morning I wake to three Instagram messages, all from local establishments asking me to post on their behalf. None of them is a big corporate company like Susanne, but I don't mind starting small. I contact each one and make arrangements. These are all smaller deals, between five hundred and two thousand dollars, but I take them all and don't negotiate. *Bam*. I've made another four thousand dollars, and two of the posts I can do today.

I catch another yoga class and take a quick selfie afterward.

Who loves yoga? I do! Check out the relaxing atmosphere at Wildflower Yoga. #yoga #treatyourself #youknowyouwanto

I'm not getting paid for this one, but within a few minutes I already have more than a hundred likes and fifty comments. Unreal. I shower, change, and then head to the bakery to do a post.

Yes, the bakery with the erotic cakes. I'm a frequent

shopper there—love their baguettes—so that's what I choose to pose with.

Need bread? Check out Le Grand Pain! Best baguettes around! (And if you need a special cake for your bachelor/bachelorette function, LGP can hook you up!) @LeGrandPain #sponsored #bakery #bread #baguettes #getyourglutenon #breadisgoodfood #soiscake

I leave a thou richer along with three freshly baked baguettes.

Not bad for a half hour's work.

I'm beginning to like this influencing thing, even if Braden is the only reason anyone cares what I think. I did a little research last night on what influencers can expect to be paid. Turns out Addie gets a lot more than most influencers, so the fact that I scored $10K from Susanne is quite a coup.

I'm hungry, and there's a little café near the harbor I've been wanting to try. I hop on the T, and twenty minutes later I exit the station and immerse myself in the harbor area.

This is the beauty I see lit up at night from Braden's window. In a strange way, I feel his building watching me as I walk down a side street. I stop to peruse the antiques in a shop window, and then—

Betsy's Bark Boutique.

Right here, where it always is. I still have Betsy's money in my purse, so I impulsively open the door and go in. Betsy is helping a customer, so I look at her selection of handmade dog collars while I wait.

A few minutes later, she approaches. "Hi, Skye."

"Hi, Betsy. I wanted to return your money from the other night." I hand her the bills. "Braden ended up picking up the entire check."

"You came all the way here for that?" she asks.

"I also came for lunch. I've been meaning to try the new

deli and café down the street."

"Oh, good. I'd hate to think you made a trip just to give me a few dollars."

"Why? It's your money."

"You could have easily kept it and I'd never know."

I lift my eyebrows. "I'd never do that."

"No, you wouldn't." Her eyes become glassy, as if she's looking through me.

"Betsy? You okay?"

"Yeah," she says quietly, eyeing her other customers. "I should apologize to you, for…you know."

"For what?"

"For breaking down in the bathroom. You didn't need to see that."

"It's okay."

"Just be careful, Skye."

"Be careful of what? Braden?"

She nods.

"I don't understand. Everything the man does is scrutinized by the press and the public. He hasn't had a tiny blemish on his record in the last ten years. How am I supposed to believe he's bad news, as Addie says, when the worst thing I've read about him is that he's a womanizer?"

"Isn't that bad enough?"

My heart speeds up a little. "He's not the first billionaire who likes women, and as long as he's faithful to me while we're together, I don't see why it should matter."

"He's faithful to you?"

"We haven't been together long, but yeah, so far he is."

She clears her throat. "Addison came into the shop this morning."

"Oh?"

"Yeah. She doesn't want me talking to you."

"Why *shouldn't* you talk to me?"

"She's all uptight about you and your new Instagram posts. She's being weird. I haven't seen her like this since…" She shakes her head.

"Since when?"

Betsy shakes her head. "Nothing. If you're not going to buy anything, I need you to leave, Skye."

Chapter Fifty-Two

I follow Betsy to the counter and set my baguettes down. "I don't have a dog, but I'll buy some treats for a friend's dog." I place a bag of small bone-shaped cookies on the counter.

She rings me up quickly. "Eleven dollars and thirty-eight cents."

I insert my credit card into the chip reader. "What are you scared of, Betsy?"

She doesn't look me in the eye. "I'm not scared of anything."

"Look at me."

She hesitates a few seconds but then meets my gaze and speaks quietly. "I like you, and I like Tessa. We all clicked so well, and I'll miss you guys, but I can't do this."

"Do what?"

"Hang out with you guys anymore."

"Why?"

"I just can't."

"Whatever Addie has on you—"

"She doesn't have anything on me. It's me, Skye. I'm the

one who has something on *her*."

I raise my eyebrows. "Then what do you care what she says?"

"She's a huge influencer. She could ruin me."

Betsy's hands tremble slightly. Only slightly, but I notice. She's frightened of Addison. But why?

"Maybe she's afraid you'll ruin *her*," I say quietly.

Betsy looks around the store. Two customers are browsing. One leaves. When the other chooses a few items and then pays for them, Betsy thanks him politely and then locks the door to the shop, placing the CLOSED sign in the window.

"Closing for lunch?" I ask.

She nods.

"Want to join me?"

She nods again.

"You just said you don't want to hang out with me anymore."

"I said I *can't* hang out with you anymore. Big difference."

I nod. I get it. "You're right. I'm sorry."

"I like you guys a lot. It's been a while since I've met any new friends. My shop keeps me busy. I only have one employee and he's part-time. He works a couple of evenings a week. The shop is doing well, but without Addie's influencing, I'm not sure I'd stay afloat. Every post she does brings in a huge influx of business."

"You're local. Why not expand?"

"I can't afford it."

"Sure you can. Expand into online shopping. Addie brings business to big companies like Susanne who have stores all over the world, plus their website."

She widens her eyes. Has she truly never thought of this?

"Do you think it would work?"

"Everyone shops online these days. And people *love* their

dogs. They're always looking for ways to pamper them."

"True. I do great business during the holidays. You wouldn't believe how much people spend."

"Think of how much more you can sell online. You can set up an Etsy shop, too!"

She hesitates. "There are a million online pet stores out there."

"But there's only one Betsy's Bark Boutique."

She smiles. "You think I can do it?"

"I do. We can discuss it over lunch."

I return home after lunch. I didn't press Betsy to talk about Addie, and we spent the whole lunch talking about expanding her business. She returned to her shop excited, with an agreement from Tessa—we called her—to run some numbers.

My cell phone rings.

"Hey, Tess," I say.

"You'll never guess what I did."

"Probably not."

"Well, Betsy's a doll, and I've been feeling super guilty about lying to her about having a dog, so I took a late lunch after you guys called and went to the shelter. I found Rita!"

"You adopted a dog?"

"Yeah. She's an adorable little terrier mix. I pick her up tonight after work. Want to come along?"

"Absolutely. But what about your apartment?"

"I can have a pet."

"You can?"

"Yeah, and it'll get me out to walk, which is good. Besides, she's already two, so house training won't be a huge thing."

I laugh. "It just so happens that I picked up some treats today at Betsy's."

I spend the rest of the afternoon working on my posts until I leave to meet Tessa at the shelter.

I both love and hate the shelter. I adore seeing all the dogs, but I end up wanting to take every single one of them home with me, and I can't.

Today is particularly difficult. I fall in love.

A small puppy sits alone, away from the rest of her litter. She seems to cry to me, and her sad brown eyes sear into my soul. She's black with white markings, probably a heeler or border collie mix.

She's my dog. I feel this so deeply, but my building doesn't allow dogs.

"Can you take her as well?" I ask Tessa.

"You know I can't handle two dogs."

"Please, Tess? My heart is breaking."

"Call Braden."

"No way."

"He's super into you. He'll probably take her, and you can visit her all the time."

I give her idea brief consideration. Braden's still in New York. It's after six, though knowing him, he's probably still working. Or he's out to dinner on business.

In the end, though, I can't do it. I can't be the needy girlfriend who begs for a puppy.

A shelter worker brings Rita out for Tessa. She's white and gray, maybe a Scottie or highland mix, and her tail wags nonstop. She's so happy to be going home, and I can think only of my sweet Penny.

Yeah, I've already named her. I'm a glutton for punishment.

"I need to get out of here," I tell Tessa.

"Okay. I get it. I've already done all the paperwork, so we can go." She puts Rita on the leash she brought, and we leave.

I planned to go home with Tessa and help her get Rita settled, but I can't. I beg out.

I lost my heart to a sweet little pup.

Just like I'm losing my heart to Braden Black.

And I still don't know the secret he and Addison are keeping.

What the hell have I walked into?

Chapter Fifty-Three

I haven't heard from Braden, but I assume our date for the gala is still on.

I do my makeup and sweep my hair into a slightly messy bun. Then I don the black dress. I paint my lips with Cherry Russet to do the "formal" post for Susanne. I go into my hallway, take a quick selfie, and type in the copy I wrote earlier.

Wearing my Cherry Russet lip stain by @susannecosmetics again. My go-to color is perfect for everything from a day at home to a formal evening! #sponsored #lips #kissme #formal #littleblackdress

I return to the bathroom and remove the Cherry Russet. Only then do I paint my lips bloodred and fasten the pearls in place.

I'm transformed.

And a knock sounds on the door.

Shudders rack my body as I open the door, my hand trembling.

My jaw drops.

Braden stands in the doorway, clad in his black tux and

looking delicious. A plain black mask covers his eyes, and in his arms he holds a bouquet.

Of roses.

Bloodred roses.

They match my lips perfectly.

He walks in swiftly, closing the door behind him.

His dark demeanor fills my small apartment. He owns this room. He owns me.

He's going to kiss me. I see it in his eyes. I feel it.

He comes closer to me, and I inhale his spicy, woodsy scent. His leans toward me, his firm lips ready to take mine—

Only a millimeter away, and he stops.

"I won't," he says gruffly. "I won't ruin those perfect lips. Not yet."

I sigh. "Please."

"Not yet," he says again, this time in his dark voice.

I tremble before him. My body responds to everything Braden. I'm ready to give in right here and right now. To hell with the gala. Let's just fuck.

"I missed you," I say softly. "Why didn't you call?"

"I was busy," he says.

"You couldn't find two minutes?"

He grabs my cheeks. "Baby, if I'd called, I wouldn't have been able to stop myself from getting on a plane and flying back to you."

I inhale swiftly. His words send an erotic thrill through my body.

"I couldn't do that. I did it once, and I nearly lost a deal because of it. I had to take care of business."

I nod. I know he was busy. But God, I'm hopelessly into him. Hopelessly in lust with Braden Black.

Hopelessly falling for a man who has a secret he won't divulge.

He doesn't love me. He doesn't want a relationship. He doesn't—

"Christopher's waiting," he says. "Let's go."

I grab the bag I packed.

"What's that?" he asks.

"Oh." My cheeks warm. "You said for me to bring over some clothes and stuff."

"And you assume we'll be going to my place?"

"Yes," I say boldly.

"You assume correctly." He stares at me, his eyes blazing sapphires against a sea of white foam. "Remove the top of your dress."

I slip one strap over my shoulder, going deliberately slowly. He sucks in a breath. I hold back the smile that wants to split my face as I slide the other strap over my shoulder and urge the fabric downward. The only thing standing between him and my breasts is a strapless bra.

We stand there, gazes locked, until—

"Fuck it." He crushes his lips to mine.

My lips are already parted, and he thrusts his tongue between them. My whole body responds. My nipples protrude, and I remember the nipple clamps. Did he bring them? Already I tense in anticipation.

He unclasps my bra deftly and tosses it to the floor. Then he cups my breasts, thumbing my hard nipples as he deepens the kiss. Our mouths are one, giving, taking, licking, kissing. I reach downward, toward his crotch, and grasp the bulge beneath his slacks.

He groans into me, a low melodic hum like the beginning of a rolling clap of thunder.

I revel in his warm mouth, his spicy flavor, his velvet tongue twirling around mine. I arch, my clit throbbing, searching for something to rub against. Yes, his thigh. His hard and taut thigh. I grind into him, still holding his clothed erection—

He breaks the kiss and inhales sharply. "Damn, Skye."

I steady myself, force my jelly legs not to tumble over.

He pulls the chain from his pocket. "Your tits are so beautiful, your nipples so hard. God, I want to suck and bite them until you can't stand it."

"Go ahead," I say boldly.

"Later. For now..." He positions one of the clamps around a nipple.

I jerk.

"Easy," he says. "This won't hurt."

"It won't?"

"Not unless you want it to."

The stainless steel is cool on my skin. He tightens the tiny screw slowly, squeezing my nipple. The bold sensation arrows straight between my legs.

"Good?" he says.

I nod, my lips parted.

"You look incredible right now," he says. "So fucking sexy."

I don't know how I look, but I know how I feel. I feel sexy. Amazingly sexy. The steel can't compare to Braden's warm fingers or lips, but it's a constant pressure, a constant pinch, and oh my God, it's so good.

He adjusts the second clamp around my other nipple. "Beautiful," he says, his eyes heavy-lidded. "So beautiful. Are you ready, Skye?"

"Ready for what?" My words come out on a sigh.

"For this." He yanks on the chain between the clamps.

"Oh!" The feeling is intense and pure, as if he's biting both nipples at once. I'm wet. So wet. So ready for his cock inside me. I reach toward his bulge, but he brushes my hand away.

"Time to go, baby."

Is he fucking kidding me? "Braden…"

"I know. This will keep you on edge tonight. Right on edge and under my control. You aren't to touch that chain, Skye."

"But it's on me. How can I not?"

"Because you won't. If you do, I'll know."

"But how can you—"

"I will know. Trust me." He pulls my dress upward. "I want you to go without your bra tonight."

"But the clamps will show."

"No, they won't. Your nipples will show, which is hot. They'll be hard all night and will jut out farther than the clamps themselves. No one will be the wiser."

"But—"

"And I'll be able to subtly pull on your chain whenever I want."

I gulp. "That will…"

"Drive you wild. I know. That's the point." He leans down and bites the shell of my ear. "Then maybe you'll know how completely out of control I get just thinking about you."

My legs nearly stumble, but he steadies me.

"Go now. Fix your bloodred lips."

I nod and walk to the bathroom. My lips haven't run, thank goodness. Susanne lip stain is good stuff. They do need a touch-up, though, which I do, hands shaking.

When I return, Braden has put the flowers he brought me into a vase. They sit on my small table.

"Thank you," I say, "for the flowers."

"You're welcome. Are you ready?"

I nod. Every time I move, the clamps and chain move. Just the slightest twitch sends a thrill through me.

Damn.

This is going to be a long night.

Chapter Fifty-Four

When we arrive at the gala, Braden and I are treated like true VIPs, which, I guess, he is. I don't feel like a VIP, but we're led to the best table in the room, right in the front, where a bottle of Dom Pérignon and a platter of berries sit waiting.

"They think we like this better than Wild Turkey," Braden whispers to me.

I giggle. I've never had Dom Pérignon, obviously, and I'd like to try it. The server opens the bottle and pours two flutes for us, handing the first to me.

Braden takes his and clinks his glass to mine. "To control," he says, casting his gaze down to my breasts.

To control? An odd toast, since he's been trying to get me to give *up* my control since we met. Then I realize what he means.

His control, as evidenced by the clamps and chain binding me to his will. Just his gaze sends jolts through both my nipples. He hasn't touched the chain, and already I'm bending to his desires.

"To control," I echo and take a sip of the champagne. It's crisp and dry and elegant, and the bubbles effervesce against my tongue and seem to explode as they crawl down my throat.

It's wonderful.

The room is already full of guests. Braden doesn't attempt to speak to anyone, and soon I see why. People seek him out, come to him, schmooze him. He doesn't have to do the schmoozing.

Peter Reardon and Garrett Ramirez sit a few tables away from us. Has Braden broken the news that their firm won't get his big contract? I have no idea. Peter catches my eye, and I smile. He looks away quickly.

Braden chivalrously introduces me to everyone who speaks to him. I'm in a haze of surreality until I realize I should be listening and taking note. If I'm going to be an influencer, I need all of Braden's bigwig contacts.

"George," Braden says, "meet my girlfriend, Skye Manning."

An older man holds out his hand to me. I know nothing except that his name is George.

"A pleasure, Ms. Manning," George says.

"Please, call me Skye."

He nods and continues his conversation with Braden. I listen, but soon the words become a jumble in my mind. The din of conversation hangs around me, almost visible. Men in tuxes abound, and fashion for women ranges from conservative long-sleeve maxi dresses to skimpy cocktail numbers much like my own.

Is anyone else wearing nipple clamps? I find myself staring at women's chests and wondering. I force myself to stop.

"Tell me about yourself, Skye."

I jerk. Who's speaking?

George is making eye contact with me. Who is George

again? Braden must have mentioned who he is and what he does.

"I'm a photographer," I say.

"Interesting. What kind of photography?"

"Mostly social media at the moment, but my dream is to photograph for *National Geographic* someday."

"Interesting," he says again. Clearly, he's not interested at all. He returns to his conversation with Braden.

And it dawns on me.

I'm arm candy.

Arm candy wearing nipple clamps.

I take another sip of champagne and look around the room once more. Would anyone notice if I wasn't here? A few men glance my way, but no one will dare approach me with Braden at my side. Not that I want them to, but I'm isolated.

I touch Braden's arm gently. "Excuse me for a moment."

He nods.

I leave our table and walk around the room. At one edge of the space, silent-auction items are set up. I skim over them and take some photos. May as well do an Instagram post. This is my job now. Then I take a selfie.

At the Boston Opera Guild Gala! #operaguild #formalball #supportthearts

I can't think of any other hashtags, so I post. After all, this isn't a paid post. Almost immediately I get a query.

Love your lips! What color are you using?

I reply instantly.

Night on the Town lip stain by Susanne. Perfect for an elegant evening!

I walk back through the room and notice Peter and Garrett again. Since they're the only people in the room I know, I amble to their table.

"Hi, Peter. Hi, Garrett," I say.

They both stand.

"Skye." Peter looks around, his eyes twitching a bit. "Nice to see you."

"Something wrong?" I ask.

"No."

"How's Tessa?" Garrett asks.

"She's good."

"Great," he says.

"You should go," Peter says.

"Why?"

"Because Black is shooting daggers at us."

I look toward the front table. Braden is indeed watching. I smile.

He doesn't.

Peter sits down. "Nice to see you, Skye. Bye."

"Seriously?" I say.

Garrett sits down as well. "Just the way it goes. Tell Tessa I say hi."

"Have you called her?"

"Well…no. Not given the…you know. Circumstances."

"What circumstances are those? Oh, for God's sake. Never mind."

I roll my eyes and make my way back to Braden's table. He excuses himself from the crowd around him and takes me aside, walking me swiftly out of the ballroom and to a secluded hallway.

"What was that?"

"I was talking to Peter and Garrett. They're the only two people here I know."

"You know a lot of people. I've introduced you to everyone I've talked to."

I hold back a huff. "That doesn't mean I *know* them."

"You know them as well as you know Peter Reardon."

"Not really. Peter and I have danced. We've had a drink."

He grips my shoulder, not hard but in a way that makes me know he's serious. "For God's sake, Skye. Are you trying to drive me to distraction?"

I wiggle against his hold. "I'm trying to have a good time here."

"Being with me isn't a good time?"

"That's not what I mean, and you know it. I just—"

He grabs the chain beneath my silky dress and yanks.

"Oh!" Sensation jerks into my nipples and then outward, landing in my pussy.

"Don't forget who you came with," he says, his voice low and dark.

"I haven't forgotten. I—"

He yanks the chain again, this time slightly harder. The intensity deepens, and I nearly lose my footing.

"Dinner is being served now. We're going to go back to the table, eat, and then we're leaving."

"But it's a ball. Aren't we going to dance?"

"No," he says. "We're leaving after they thank me for my generous donation, which will happen right after dinner."

"But—"

"No buts, Skye. You've already driven me out of my mind tonight. It's time for me to return the favor."

Chapter Fifty-Five

He takes my arm and escorts me back into the ballroom. The crowds have dispersed a bit as most people take their seats for dinner. Servers bring out plates covered in silver domes.

I'm following Braden, not looking where I'm going, when someone steps in front of us.

"Don't you two look stunning?"

I know the voice. And the snark. I meet Addison's gaze.

"Nice to see you," Braden says shortly.

"And you, as always," she says curtly and then tugs on my other arm and whispers in my ear, "Nipple clamps? Classic Braden."

I warm in both embarrassment and anger. Did he use nipple clamps on Addie eleven years ago? Even if he did, should it matter?

Braden whisks me quickly to our table where we sit down. Servers place plates in front of us almost immediately.

"Don't let her get to you," Braden says to me.

I nod.

She already got to me, however. Nipple clamps. The little jewels that give me so much pleasure are now tainted. And how does she know? They're not visible. Only my erect nipples are—I made sure of that in the mirror—and I'm not the only one here with erect nipples. Not by far. Plus, somehow she found out about my post with New England Adventures. I still haven't received the countersigned contract from Tammy.

"Braden," I say.

"Yeah?"

"She's trying to ruin me." I quickly explain about New England Adventures.

"I'll take care of it," he says.

"No! That's not what I meant. I don't want you to get involved. This is *my* problem."

"All it'll take is a quick call to your balloon place."

"Please. No. That's not why I told you."

"Then why *did* you tell me?"

Because you're my boyfriend. Because I need to talk to you about stuff in my life. Because if something is bothering me, it should matter to you. Because, because, because.

I don't say any of this.

"Skye, when you tell me about a problem, I find a solution. It's what I do."

"I'm not asking for a solution. Please. I'll handle this myself."

"Are you sure?"

"Definitely sure. Let's just have dinner."

The salmon *en croute* with asparagus and walnut sauce tastes like sawdust. Even the bourbon Braden brings me doesn't help my mood. Addie has ruined this night for me. Even the scads of likes and comments on both my posts today aren't helping. I silence my phone so I don't have to keep hearing the dings.

Dessert is served, and the emcee, some bigwig with the opera guild, takes center stage.

"Thank you all for being here tonight," he says.

I recognize him. It's George, the guy Braden introduced me to early in the evening.

"I'm happy to report that we've surpassed our expected donations for the evening thanks to our generous benefactor, who has doubled all our receipts. Please give a hand to Boston's own Braden Black."

Braden stands to thunderous applause. His demeanor is stoic, as usual. He takes the applause gracefully and sits down after several seconds when it begins to wane.

George continues speaking, and Braden turns to me.

"Time to go," he says.

"Now? While he's talking?"

"Yes. Now. Before I tear that dress off you right here."

To my surprise, Christopher isn't waiting for us. A limo is. A chauffeur I don't recognize opens the door, and I step into the back while Braden follows. The interior is decorated in red and black leather. I inhale the earthy and slightly sweet fragrance.

"Where's Christopher?" I ask when we're secure in the limo.

"He has the night off."

"Oh."

"You didn't really think I could wait until we got to my place to have you, did you?"

I gulp. "I…didn't think about it."

He moves toward me, softly brushes my straps off my

shoulders, baring my breasts, and then gives the chain between them a good yank.

I cry out.

"That's right. I've been thinking about those nipple clamps all night, Skye. Every time I looked at you. Every time someone *else* looked at you."

"No one looked at me," I say.

"Not blatantly, no. They wouldn't dare. But they looked, baby, and every time they did, I thought about what I'd do to you tonight in this limo. What I, and no one else, would be doing to you."

"What are you going to do?" I ask.

He yanks the chain again. "I'm going to drive you as wild as you've driven me all evening." He crushes his mouth to mine.

I open instantly as he continues to pull on the chain in tandem with the thrusts of his tongue.

With one swift movement, he has me on his lap, my dress around my waist and my clamped nipples in full view. We kiss and we kiss and we kiss, as the rhythm of his yanks on the chain becomes discordant and nonsensical. It's thrilling.

Need to breathe. But God, I don't want to break the amazing kiss. Finally, he pulls his mouth away from mine, his lips swollen and glistening.

"God, those tits," he says. He lifts my skirt and rips my panties off me. Then, holding me to the side, he unbuckles his belt, slides his pants and boxer briefs over his hips, all with his one free hand. His cocks juts out, hard and beautiful as always, the blue vein marbling through it throbbing in time with my heartbeat. Am I imagining it, or are we that in sync?

"Have to have you now." He grips my hips and pushes me down on his erection.

Full. So full and complete. I'm ready. Wet and ready. All

evening, the nipple clamps teased me, kept my body on edge, made me alive with anticipation.

"Ride me, Skye," he says huskily.

Is he truly letting me take charge? Before he changes his mind, I begin to fuck him hard and fast. I don't care that the driver is right behind the wall. He doesn't seem to care, either. I moan, gasp, cry out his name, all the while knowing the chauffeur can hear us.

Braden's fingers never leave the chain between my breasts, yanking it in the same discordant way as I fuck him, so I never know when it's coming.

My boobs bounce as I fuck him harder and harder.

"Damn. Those tits," he says again, yanking on the chain. Then he grips my hips, taking over the thrusting. This is his rhythm now, and as he takes over, he twists the chain between my nipples tight, parachuting into an intense climax.

A moment later, he's releasing, slamming me down onto him. So sensitive are the walls of my pussy that I feel every contraction of his cock.

When we both finally come down from our high, I can't move. I'm immobile, my black dress around my waist like a belt.

He embraces me, holding me close—something he's done very seldom. I warm all over.

"We'll be home soon," he says. "I have a surprise for you."

Chapter Fifty-Six

A surprise? I'm not sure whether to be excited or frightened. I'm both, and it's an exhilarating mélange of emotion.

The limo arrives, and the driver opens the door for us. Braden thanks him and we walk into his building. He calls the elevator.

I say nothing as we ascend. Nothing as the door opens. Nothing as—

"Oh my God!" I clamp my hand over my mouth.

Sasha runs toward us, and she has a friend.

It's Penny—my puppy from the shelter. I grab her and hold her, letting her pepper my face with sweet puppy kisses.

"You like her?" Braden says.

"I love her! I adore her. How did you know?"

"Tessa called me."

"But...you know I can't keep her. My apartment doesn't—"

He places two fingers over my lips. "I know. She'll live here with Sasha and me until you get a new place."

A new place? I don't plan to move anytime soon. But I don't care. Braden rescued Penny for me.

For *me*.

The warmth of love I feel for this man overwhelms me. If I had any doubt about where my feelings were headed, this act of sheer kindness toward an innocent puppy—to make me happy, no less—negates it.

I'm in love with Braden. Truly in love.

No relationship? I can't let myself think about that at the moment, not with this lovely little puppy panting in my face and kissing me.

"Thank you!" I squeal. "Thank you so much."

Penny squirms out of my arms and jumps to the floor, chasing Sasha.

"Annika is paper training her," Braden says. "And she'll go out with Sasha on walks with Christopher and me. She'll be house trained in no time."

"She's three months old," I say. "It won't exactly be no time."

"I've had dogs all my life," Braden says. "I know what I'm in for."

I smile. He probably does know, even more than I do. At the farm, we didn't have to do much house training of our dogs. They had the run of the land and potty trained themselves. We taught them how to sit and come, and that was about it. Braden has always lived in the city, and city dogs must be trained.

"She seems so happy now," I say. "Yesterday at the shelter she sat in a corner and didn't interact with her littermates. She gave me such a sad look that said, 'Please take me home.' I was distraught when I couldn't. And then Tessa..." I smile, tears welling in my eyes. "I can't thank you enough, Braden. Truly. This is the nicest thing anyone has ever done for me."

Braden smiles. A big smile showcasing his perfect teeth. A smile I've so rarely seen. The darkness that is always present disappears for a moment as he looks at me, looks at the dogs.

He's happy.

Braden Black is happy.

I want to bottle this moment and save it forever. Hold it close to my heart and never let it go.

I love you.

The words hover on my tongue, but I can't bring them forth. He most likely won't return them, and I can't risk that devastation.

"Do you have a name for her?" Braden asks.

"Penny. I named her at the shelter."

"Oh? Tessa didn't tell me."

"Because I didn't tell *her*. I kept it to myself. I didn't think I'd ever see this baby again." I pick Penny up once more and snuggle her soft fur against my cheek. "I love her so much."

Again, Braden is smiling. And God, he's so handsome. So magnificent. I'm not sure I've ever seen him look more devastatingly beautiful.

And I make a decision. A true and honest decision for tonight and for however long he'll have me.

I'll give him what he craves.

I've said it before, yet still I've struggled against it.

No more.

He's earned it.

My control.

I'll give it up to him for good. Tonight.

Braden takes Penny from me and ushers Sasha out of the room and up the stairs, where I presume Annika or someone else will tend to them. I've never been up those stairs, and though I'm curious, my curiosity is tamped down by my pure love for the man before me.

Can he love me back?

Will he love me back?

A man doesn't rescue a puppy for a woman he feels nothing for, does he?

I don't dwell on it. I want to be in Braden's bed. I want to show him how I feel even if I can't tell him.

I want to give him what he desires.

"Braden," I say.

He fingers a few strands of my hair. "Hmm?"

"Take me to bed. Please."

Chapter Fifty-Seven

He doesn't hesitate. He sweeps me into his arms and marches to the bedroom. The lights from the harbor illuminate the dark wood and bedding. Later, I'll do my last post for Susanne standing by this window.

Now, though?

I don't think about work. I think only of the man whose arms hold me as if I'm light as a feather.

"I'm yours," I say. "Do whatever you want to me."

His eyes darken. "That's a tall order, Skye. Are you sure?"

"Absolutely sure."

He lifts his gaze to the contraption above his bed. "Anything?"

I nod, trembling. "What is that thing?"

"It's no longer functional," he says.

I hold back a sigh of relief.

"It was a harness, where I could suspend a partner, but I found that sort of play wasn't particularly enjoyable for me."

"Oh? What about your partner?"

"Depended on the partner."

I opened this can of worms, and I suddenly wish I hadn't. I'm about to give up control for good to this man, and I don't want to think about all the other partners he's had in this room.

"Why is it still there, then?"

"I just haven't gotten around to having it removed yet."

"Why not?"

"Because I met a woman who invades my mind every fucking second." He sets me on the bed. "And all I can think about is all the dark and dirty things I want to do to her."

I swallow. It's okay. I want these things as much as he does. I want to give in.

"Did you like it when I bound your wrists?" he asks.

I nod, my body thrumming.

"How about these?" He tugs the chain between the clamps. "Do you like these?"

I nod again, inhaling swiftly against the torturous pleasure the clamps inflict on my nipples.

"Say yes, Skye."

"Yes. I like them. A lot."

"Did you like it when I covered your eyes?"

"Yes, Braden."

"What else would you like me to do to you, Skye?"

I suck in a breath. "Whatever you want."

He raises his eyebrows, sits down on the bed next to me, and fingers the odd notches on the runs of his headboard. "Do you know what these are?"

"No."

"I had this headboard specially designed. I have bindings that secure here and here, and same on the footboard. They'll hold you in place, all four of your limbs, render you completely helpless, Skye. What if I want to do that to you? Tie you up spread-eagle and then have my way with you?"

My body pulsates. "Then I want you to."

He stands and walks to his highboy, opens a drawer, and pulls out what appears to be a riding crop. "What if I want to use this all over your body while you're tied up?"

"I want you to do it."

He sets the crop down and picks up a stainless steel object. "This is the anal plug I used on your body while you were blindfolded. What if I want to put this in your ass and then fuck you?"

I clear my throat. I'm determined to finish what I've started. "I want you to."

He sets down the plug and picks up something else—something I don't recognize at all. It looks like a collar but has a silver ring with four prongs sticking out of it. I shiver.

"This is a spider gag, Skye. Do you know what it's for?"

"No."

"It holds your mouth open so I can fuck it. What if I want to use this tonight?"

I've come too far to back down now. "Then I want you to."

"Are you sure?"

"Braden," I say, "let me be clear. I'm giving myself to you. I'm giving you the control you so desperately want. If you want to put a collar on me and lead me around on a leash like Sasha or Penny, do it. I'm yours."

"For good this time? I get your control in this room?"

"Yes, Braden. I yield to you. I give up control." He's opened up my dark side, and at this point, I fear nothing from this man.

Nothing.

I want him. I want it *all.*

He groans, pushes me onto my back, lies on top of me, and dry thrusts his cock against me. "See how hard I am for you? See what you do to me? All these things I love to do, all these toys—I don't even need them with you. All I need is your lush little body, your gorgeous parted lips, those luscious tits. Your control. But mostly I just need *you*, Skye. I can fuck you all damned night."

I open as he slides his lips against mine, pushes his tongue into my mouth. We're still fully clothed, but I feel as though we're already making love, our bodies already joined in that most intimate way. He deepens the kiss.

I'm in love with this man. So freaking in love.

Can he possibly return my feelings?

He breaks the kiss, gasps sharply, and gives the chain between my breasts a hard yank. I arch my back, my whole body reacting to the tingles that flow outward from my nipples. Then he grasps the fabric of my dress and rips it, tearing it from my body.

"Braden!"

"I already told you. I'll have this dress remade as many times as it takes."

My nipples are red and hard from the nipple clamps that still grip them. Only my black panties are between Braden and me now.

"Grip the rungs of the headboard, Skye," he says darkly.

I don't hesitate to obey. I grip the wood firmly.

"Don't let go," he commands.

"I won't." He rises and walks back to his highboy.

What does he have in store for me? I want to know, and just as desperately I don't want to know.

But I'm all in now.

I'll take what he gives me, and I'll take it gladly from the man I love.

He returns with a piece of rope. "Nylon," he says, "doesn't cause rope burns."

I nod as he deftly ties my wrists in place, using the strange notches on the rungs. I pull against my restraint to no avail. I'm secure in his bindings. Secure in what he has in store for me.

He walks back to the highboy and returns again, this time with a piece of black silk. He covers my eyes.

"Do you remember the last time I took your sight?"

"Yes."

"That was to heighten your other senses. But that's not why I'm doing it this time."

I don't respond.

"This time, I'm taking it because I can. Because you're giving it to me."

"Yes."

"You can't move your arms. You can't see. What else should I take from you?"

"Whatever you want, Braden."

He yanks the chain between my breasts once more. I arch into the sensation, my feet flat on the bed as my hips rise. I pull against the restraints, my fingers itching to run through Braden's silky hair, to trail over his masculine jawline and scrape over his stubble, to touch his hard shoulders and corded muscle.

Rustling wafts to my ears. He's undressing, I think. Soon. Soon he'll touch me with those warm hands, those firm lips, that beautiful hard cock.

But nothing.

Nothing, until—

Whip!

A lash comes down on my breasts, jiggling the chain and clamps and sending an intense sensation through me.

Another *whip* and then another.

"The tops of your breasts are rosy pink, Skye. So beautiful. Do you want me to do it again?"

"Yes, please. Whatever you want."

The lash comes down once more and then again. I gasp and then sigh. Gasp and then sigh. Gasp—

"Oh!" Something pricks my nipple. Then again, on the other one.

What happened?

Then softness, wetness, a suck of one nipple. The prick wasn't a prick at all. Braden pulled the clamp off without loosening it, and now he's licking and sucking the already sensitive bud. I'm so ready for his dick, I think I might die a slow death if he doesn't get inside me soon.

But he continues his torturous teasing, licking and nipping at my nipples, and then—

"Oh!"

Something cold makes my areola shrink so tightly, I think I might pop. He hasn't told me not to speak, but I stay silent anyway.

He has my control. I give it up freely, and it feels…

It feels *free*.

I feel free.

Free as a bird soaring through the blue skies. Who knew giving up power could be so freeing? How do I feel so unbound when I'm bound?

The icy trail extends over my breasts and then down my belly, where it pools in my navel for a few seconds. Then down, over my vulva, and onto—

I jerk, arching. The tip of the ice melts against my clit, and it's an influx of heat and chill together mingling in an intense spiral. Tiny droplets trickle over my labia, chilling and blazing at the same time.

"Braden!" I cry.

"Baby," he says huskily. "We've only just begun."

Chapter Fifty-Eight

The coldness slips inside me then, and I lift my hips against the invasion. Then his mouth is on me, replacing the chill with his hot tongue.

He devours my pussy, licking and sucking, moving upward to my clit as if he knows exactly when I needed it, but then leaving it before I can reach the precipice I long for.

He's good at the tease, at the anticipation. He enjoys it… and truth be told, so do I.

He leaves my pussy then, and I whimper at the loss, but warmth crawls up my body, and I brace myself, ready for him to thrust his hard cock inside me.

I whimper again when the thrust doesn't come.

Instead, a soft caress to my earlobe and then a raspy whisper.

"I know your secret, Skye."

"Wh-What secret?"

"You only come when you give up control."

My eyes shoot open under the blindfold. All I see is black.

"That surprises you?" he says softly.

I say nothing. Though I never thought it before, his words make perfect sense. All those years I tried for an orgasm only to fail time after time. Only when I relinquished control to Braden did I have success.

Wow. Talk about an epiphany.

"I've given you climax after climax, but only when you yield to me. You told me tonight that your fight is over. That I have your control."

"Y-Yes," I say.

"Do you know what that means to me?"

"N-No."

"It means you're mine, Skye. In this bedroom—in the *dark*—you're mine."

"Yours," I echo. "Yours in the dark."

Then he thrusts his cock into me.

I arch into the invasion, trying to open myself to take more of him.

"So much more I want to do to you," he says against my cheek. "So much more. And now that I have your control, I will. But for now, I want to fuck you like this, while you can't touch me, can't see me. Your tits are so beautiful, your nipples red from the clamps and your chest pink from my crop. Colors I gave you, Skye. Colors that prove you're mine here in the dark."

"Yours," I say again as I wrap my legs over his hips. His perfect rear end is hard against my calves.

Thrust. Thrust. Thrust.

I revel in the fullness, the completeness, of him inside me. So good. Better than good, even. Something feels different this time—something I can't put my finger on.

Until it explodes into my mind as if it were always there.

I'm letting myself feel the emotion behind the physical.

I love him. Does he love me? I don't know, and for this brief time, it doesn't matter. I'm going to feel the emotion. Let myself go. Throw myself into this coupling with my whole heart and damn the consequences.

I love him. He may not be making love to me, but I'm making love to him.

I want to trail my fingers over his broad shoulders and strong back. To scratch him. To mark him.

Mine.

Tonight—at least right at this moment—he's mine.

His balls slap against me, and the smacking sounds from my wetness drive me further toward the brink.

The brink.

The peak.

The precipice.

Still, I don't get there. Don't quite make it. Until—

"Come, Skye. Come for me."

A pleasure bomb explodes in my pussy and wafts outward, outward, outward…

Tapestries of color and sound whirl in my mind's eye as I leap into oblivion. Perfect oblivion.

"That's it, baby. Show me. Show me how you come for me."

"Braden!" I shout. Then more words, some jumbled, some completely unintelligible. Because it's all fantasy now. I don't even pull against my restraints anymore, because everything suddenly makes sense. Perfect sense. All everything and all nothing at the same time.

All.

Just *all.*

I give it all to Braden. Not just my control but my heart. I already knew I was in love, but now? I'm lost without him. Lost without giving all of me to him.

He gives me one last thrust and releases, and as I feel him

contract, filling me, I know this is what I've been searching for. This.

Just *this*.

"You're beautiful," Braden says, stroking my cheek. "You have an amazing 'just-fucked' look."

He removes my blindfold and releases my wrists.

I instinctively rub them, though I feel no chafing or pain. He took good care of me.

I look out his amazing floor-to-ceiling windows at the twinkling harbor.

This.

It's all *this*.

This is how I'll take my last photo for my contract with Susanne Cosmetics. I'll wrap a sheet around me, leave my hair in "just-fucked" disarray, and have Braden shoot me profiled against the window.

"Will you?" I ask after I tell him my plan.

"I will. You just can't post that you're at my place."

"I wouldn't do that," I say. "Our private life is private."

"Don't be surprised if the *Babbler* does some kind of exposé."

"Good point. I'll wear a robe instead of a sheet."

"God, no, Skye. Wear the sheet. You'll sell so much lip stain that Eugene what's her name won't know what hit her."

I rise, go to the bathroom, remove the Night on the Town, and apply the Cherry Russet. I run my fingers through my hair so the disarray is an arranged mess. Perfect.

I set up the shot, find the place where the lighting is perfect, and then hand my phone to Braden. "Stand right here. I want a profile shot against the harbor. Make sure you get a good shot of my lips."

"Wait," he says.

"For what?"

"You'll see." He walks to his closet, rummages around, and returns with a black object. He hands it to me. "Wear this."

"A mask?" It's satin with black feathers and a large crystal jewel fanning out from one side. I'm almost afraid to touch it because it looks so delicate. I simply stare at it a few minutes.

"Trust me," he says. "Go to the bathroom and put it on. See what you think."

I nod and traipse into the bathroom, securing the sheet around me. I place the mask over my eyes…

And I'm transformed. My eyes pop against the blackness. But my lips? They don't pop. No, that's too tame a word. The russet red seems more vibrant than it is, almost as if the rest of me has faded into black and white.

Braden is right.

I adjust my mussed hair just a bit to accommodate the mask and then return to the window where Braden waits, still holding my phone.

"You look breathtaking," he says.

"Remember, it's the lip stain I'm selling."

"I'll take several," he says. "We'll get a good one."

I take my place at the window.

"Smile," he says. Then, "No, don't. Part your lips in that sexy way."

I chuckle and then move my mouth into my normal expression. I hope that's what he means.

"Perfect." He shoots several photos and regards the screen. "The second one, Skye. Use the second one."

I take the phone from him and peruse the photos. Though I prefer the fourth, as my lips are more visible, I see Braden's point. In the second, my gaze seems focused on nothing in particular, as if I'm contemplating the harbor. Or the night. Or the mask I'm wearing. Or the fact that I've just been fucked incredibly well. Or anything. The "what" doesn't matter. What matters is the ethereal look of the photo. It perfectly captures a perfect moment.

Second one it is. I do some quick edits and post the photo.

Cherry Russet lip stain by @susannecosmetics. Perfect for all life's moments. #sponsored

No hashtags other than the required one. Just the copy.

It says it all.

Braden walks toward me and wraps his arms around me. We look out at the beauty of the harbor, the moon shining down and casting silver sparkles on the boats below.

"I have more in store for you," he whispers, "now that I control you in the dark. Will you follow me, Skye? Trust me to give you all kinds of pleasure?"

I smile against his shoulder. "I will."

He kisses my forehead. "I can't believe what I'm about to say."

I pull away slightly and meet his gaze. He's looking at me. Truly looking at me, and I feel, almost for the first time, that he's actually *seeing* me.

"What?" I ask.

"Maybe"—his voice is low, hypnotic—"maybe we can give this relationship thing a try."

Waves of happiness surge into me, and I can't help myself. I say the words.

"I love you, Braden."

Seconds pass. Seconds that seem like hours while my heart races. Until—

"I love you too, Skye."

Chapter Fifty-Nine

An email arrives Monday from Eugenie.

Skye, those posts were fabulous, especially the last one. You looked radiant, and sales for Cherry Russet are off the charts! Plus, we're getting orders for Night on the Town, as well. I've deposited the remaining five thousand dollars in your account, along with a thousand dollar bonus for the extra post about Night on the Town. I want to meet with you in person to talk about our next deal. We're so pleased! I'll be in touch to set up dates for you to fly to New York. Thank you so much!

I smile and hug myself. Addison may have ruined my balloon shoot, but Eugenie is pleased. I take a quick look through my posts. The photos are good. No, not just good. They're great, and I've gained another ten thousand followers. I have far to go before I pass Addie's ten million, and I may never get there. If I don't? That's okay. I'm taking good photos. They may not be changing the world yet, but someday I'll shoot a photo that people remember always.

I'm free of Addison Ames, I'm earning money, I have an adorable new puppy, and I'm in love with an amazing man who loves me back. I still know so little about Braden, but he rescued Penny for me. He saved a puppy. For *me*.

Really, what more do I need to know?

After I shower and dress, I take the T to Bark Boutique early on Monday. Won't Betsy be surprised when she learns I have a new puppy?

When I get off the T, my phone dings. A text from Braden.

Be ready tonight. I'm going to take you where you've never gone before.

Sparks sizzle beneath my skin. What does he mean? Is it literal? Is he taking me somewhere? I doubt it. It's probably a new adventure in the bedroom. He could mean anything, and I don't want to know almost as much as I want to know. Surprise heightens the anticipation. Already my body is on fire.

I quickly type a response.

Can't wait!

Then I enter Betsy's shop. She smiles and beckons me over to the counter.

"Skye, what are you doing here?"

"I need everything. A collar. A dog dish. A kennel. Treats and toys."

"For Tessa's dog?"

I smile. "No, for mine."

"You got a dog?" she squeals.

I nod. "She's the sweetest little rescue pup, about three months old. Her name is Penny."

"But you said your place doesn't allow dogs. Are you moving?"

"Not for a while. My lease isn't up for six months, but she's staying at Braden's until then."

Betsy's face drops. "Oh."

"What's wrong?"

She shakes her head. "I've been over and over this in my

head, Skye. There's no way around it. I can't tell you what I know."

"I didn't ask you to."

"But you did."

"Yeah, before. But the past doesn't matter to me anymore, Bets. I love him."

She shakes her head again. "Fuck."

"What?"

"You love him."

"Yeah. And he loves me."

"He does?"

"Yeah." I hug myself. "He told me Saturday evening. Actually it was early Sunday morning."

"Oh, Skye..."

"It's okay. The past doesn't matter. I don't care what happened between him and Addison. Nothing matters except now, and right now, I need supplies for my adorable new puppy. Can you believe that Tessa called Braden and told him about the pup, and he went right over and got her for me?"

"That does seem sweet of him," she says.

"It was. I'm so happy."

"I'm glad you're happy, Skye. I want you to be happy."

"I am. Now, show me everything I need for a pup."

"I will. But first we need to talk."

"Okay..."

She walks to the door and locks it, putting the CLOSED sign in place.

Uh-oh. My heart thuds.

She's going to tell me. Finally.

And it's not going to be pretty.

"Come with me." She leads me to the back room of the shop where a table and chairs are set up. "Have a seat. Do you want a drink?"

"Do I need one?"

"Maybe. But all I have is soda and bottled water."

My mouth is suddenly dry. "Water, please."

She pulls two bottles out of a mini fridge and hands one to me. "You really love him, huh?"

"I do. I have for a while, but if possible even more now. He rescued a puppy for me, Betsy."

She nods. "I'm going to tell you something, and you have to promise me you won't tell anyone. Not even Tessa."

"I'm not sure I can promise that. I may have to talk to Braden about it."

"If you have to talk to Braden, you can't tell him where you heard it."

"All right. Deal."

"You know that Addison pretty much stalked Braden that summer."

"Yeah."

"She found his apartment and waited for him there. Got him to invite her in."

"Okay."

"She tried to seduce him, but he wouldn't bite at first."

"Good for him."

"At *first*, Skye. He did eventually bite. They had sex that night."

"Just that night?"

She shook her head. "No. They ended up screwing all summer, and Addie found out that Braden has…certain *tastes*."

The phantom sensation of the silver clamps courses through me, and my nipples tighten. My nerves scrape along the edges of my flesh. Whether it's from the memory of the clamps or the apprehension about what's to come, I'm not sure.

"What kind of tastes?"

"He likes to dominate in the bedroom."

Relief sweeps through me. "I know that."

"You do?"

"I've been with him a couple of weeks now. How can I *not* know that?"

"And you're okay with it?"

"He's respectful, so yes, I'm okay with it." More than okay, actually, but Betsy doesn't need to know that.

She nods. "Good. I'm glad to hear you say that."

"Was he not respectful with Addie?"

"I honestly don't really know. Turned out that Addie was a natural submissive and pretty much let him do whatever he wanted to her. She never used the safe word."

"She had a safe word?"

"Yeah. Don't you?"

"No. I guess I never thought I needed one."

"Maybe you don't. Addie definitely did. She got into the submission role—"

"Wait. Is Addison still like this? Submissive? Because I've sure never seen it."

"I have no idea, but unless you've been in the bedroom with her, you really wouldn't know."

"Okay. I just got a visual I didn't want. Go on."

"They tried a lot of things, and Addie was always game for more. She used to tell me all about it, and I admit I was transfixed by her stories. They did some kinky stuff, and she was happy to let him do whatever he wanted."

"Like what?" I ask, not sure at all that I truly want to know.

"It started innocently, with just a little bit of bondage."

I flash back to the time Braden tied my wrists with his silk necktie. That seemed innocent enough at the time. Then he bound me with rope to his headboard. Innocent? Maybe...

A little bit of bondage.

"Addie liked it, wanted more. They were both young and inexperienced, and they went places neither of them was ready for."

"What kind of places?" I swallow audibly.

"I'm not sure, but Addie was shaken after something they did."

"Was she hurt?"

Part of me doesn't want to know. Part of me doesn't want to even entertain the notion that the man I've lost my heart to—the man who rescues puppies—is capable of harm to another human being, even if it is Addison Ames, a woman who seems determined to become my nemesis.

"No," Betsy says, "but she was never the same afterward. And then…"

Silence for a few seconds, until I can no longer bear it.

"What? And then what?"

"Oh my God… I hate having to tell you this."

"What? Just tell me, Betsy, for God's sake. Don't leave me hanging. What?"

"When she refused to get kinky with him again"—Betsy closes her eyes, pauses, and then opens them—"he dumped her cold and broke her heart. She was never the same. It took her forever to rebuild her confidence—not until her Instagram took off, really."

Addie lost her confidence? Seems out of character for her. Except…she seems threatened by my new following, which is no danger at all to her. But I'm gaining my following because of Braden…

Is it all related somehow? I frown, not sure what to say.

Betsy pauses a moment and then goes on. "He likes his sex dark, Skye. Depraved."

Dark, yes. I know this well. But depraved? Braden? He's

never seemed morally corrupt to me. I clear my throat. "Go on."

Betsy wrinkles her forehead. Is she surprised at my reaction? Or disappointed. "He's relentless," she continues. "He'll push and push until you finally let him do anything he wants. Then he breaks you. It's a game to him."

I maintain my composure as best I can. "Are you sure?"

She nods aggressively. "Yes. He makes women think he cares for them, takes what he wants, and then he's gone."

She's far too excited about this. Maybe not excited so much as anxious. Frightened. For me.

Of course, Betsy got this information from Addie. And no one knows how well Addie plays to her audience better than I do. This could easily be Addie seeing herself as a woman scorned, trying to badmouth the man she loved who didn't love her back.

Still, Braden won't talk to me about this part of his past, so I have no point of reference. How far did he and Addie go? I'm not naive. Braden has a very dark side—a side I'm extremely attracted to. He's told me some of his desires but not all of them. I know he wants more.

How much more?

How far will he push me?

And why am I trembling with excitement at the thought?

Betsy sighs and leans forward. "Look. Just promise me you'll be careful, okay? This isn't just some sexy fantasy. Braden Black is dangerous."

My phone vibrates in my pocket. Without thinking, I pull it out.

It's a text from Braden. My skin numbs, and the anticipation I felt earlier morphs into an apprehension that both inflames me and petrifies me.

Everything's ready for tonight. Are you?

Acknowledgments

I first met Liz Pelletier over a decade ago through Colorado Romance Writers. I had published a few books and had earned a couple bucks, and Entangled was only a seed in Liz's entrepreneurial mind. We chatted at meetings and partied at conferences. (What happens at conferences stays at conferences!) I kept writing, and Liz founded Entangled a year or so later.

Fast forward ten years. I attended one of Liz's workshops and we got to talking. A few weeks later, *Follow Me Darkly* was born.

We've come a long way, baby! Thank you so much, Liz, for your confidence in me and my work, for your friendship and guidance, and of course for your brilliant editorial eye. It's been a blast!

Thanks also to the rest of the Entangled crew. Stacy Abrams, you know how to use a semicolon correctly, and I'm devoted to you for that reason alone but also for your eagle eye as a copy editor. Heather, Jessica, Katie, and Curtis—thanks so much for your contributions to this project. And Bree Archer...this cover art—so dazzling and provocative! Perfection!

Thanks to the women and men of my reader group, Hardt and Soul. Your endless and unwavering support keeps me going.

To my family and friends, thank you for your encouragement.

Thank you most of all to my readers. Without you, none of this would be possible.

I truly hope you loved *Follow Me Darkly*. Braden and Skye will return soon!

Skye and Braden's story continues!
Be sure to preorder *Follow Me Under*,
available January 26th, 2021.

#1 *NEW YORK TIMES* BESTSELLING AUTHOR

HELEN HARDT

FOLLOW ME UNDER

A NOVEL

AMARA
an imprint of Entangled Publishing LLC